Praise for
ULYSSES D

A bold and deeply personal novel about real life drama that few really think about. To many of us life cannot help but seem humdrum and boring but the reality is that life in the real world can be deadly, dramatic, and full of fiery adventure. And yet this same life can be impossibly romantic. Through Penelope's eyes we understand the experience of thousands of girls who are kidnapped and become statistics of human trafficking. Through the courageous intervention of a young girl, she escapes and ends up living with other children in the Teguciligapa city dump. Her hero is Ulysses a Nez Perce boy raised in the rugged Wallowa mountains in Eastern Oregon. Where he and his six brothers and their Beauceron dog have many adventures even being hunted by a monstrous bear. Ulysses and Penelope fall into sweet romance as teenagers. Both are marginalized people who are torn apart when Ulysees must go to Vietnam in 1968. His quest to win his true love back takes him through the worst of Vietnam and a struggle of professional football and the Olympics. Penelope and her son Telemachus are left alone to work towards the miracle of US citizenships all the while avoiding the retribution of the international gang to whom she once was a slave. The ending will both surprise and inspire you as you will experience a powerful paradigm shift giving you new insights into human trafficking, and immigration. You will see American Latino's and native Americans and their patriotism in a new light through this timeless story of indomitable love.

Excerpt -
"I (Penelope) was his worst nightmare-a former victim who had strength that he never imagined. I followed their trail as a Nez Perce. I was not going to let these men continue to impose their evil ways on little children any longer. I could hear war drums. I took mud and put the stripes of war paint on my face."

Tim White is well known as an intense crusader for the marginalized. He is the author of two other books To Dreamers Long Forgotten published in 1997 and Astoundingly Joyful amazingly Simple published in 2012. He is the senior pastor of Washington Cathedral in Redmond, Washington. He is an adjunct professor at Northwest University. Tim White was raised in the Wallowa Mountains he has a B.A. in research psychology with a minor in history from Eastern Washington University. A Masters of Divinity from George Fox University in Portland, Oregon. A doctorate of ministry from

Fuller Theological Seminary in Pasadena and has studied Archeology at Jerusalem University in Jerusalem Israel.

"I appreciate how this fictional story addresses the realities of brokenness in our world. Orphans and vulnerable children are those who pay the highest price for our social problems despite not causing them or without any ability to solve them. This books offers us hope of a better world. "

—Dr. Rey Diaz Executive Director of Orphan Outreach

"*Ulysses Dream* is a fictional novel intertwining true historical military events with romance, sports, social issues, and adventure. Although the story told is fictional, it incorporates many, many factual elements. I have been to the Honduras dump six times and personally witnessed the conditions described in the book. As a retired police officer and someone actively involved in the ongoing fight against Human Trafficking, this story tells of events that no one really wants to hear about but everyone needs to know of because it is happening everywhere."

—Retired Seattle Police Detective Karen Haverkate

"I hope this novel helps people understand the drama that many of us lived through in Vietnam. We were there because we cared for the people and honored our country. I hope that the next generation will catch a sense of heart felt American patriotism that our soldiers feel when called upon to live an adventure they did not choose."

—Marine Colonel (ret) Erskine Austin, two tours in Vietnam. Received 21 medals while in Vietnam

"'Truth,' we are often told, 'is stranger than fiction.' But sometimes fiction tells strange truths more deeply than a mere recitation of facts could ever do. As pastor of one of America's most ethnically diverse churches, Tim White has deeply listened to the truths of thousands, told in every accent and in living color. Out of those stories, he has woven a mystical fiction that will awaken truths that readers have never dared to confront."

—Joseph Castleberry, Ed.D. | President of Northwest University

"A compelling story with the blending of two people from two different Native American people groups. Tim White nailed it describing the native heart, mind and family culture. "

—Cherokee Chief Chet McVey

"After more than two decades of listening to Dr. Tim White's stories, I found reading his novel was a pleasure. One of the greatest storytellers and visionaries that I ever met has produced a novel with characters that are fallible and yet most strive to not only improve themselves but also the world they live in. As told through the eyes of a successful elderly Honduran woman, of her husband's (Ulee) life from a patriotic Vietnam veteran, football athlete, and passionate minister. This novel covers some difficult subjects and in a very difficult time in America's history, the book is loaded with entertaining accounts of events that is committed to providing its readers with a glimpse of the way our world could be and probably should be."

—Lieutenant Colonel (ret) Bill Zappone, U.S Army Reserve

"You are going to love this book! It's original, it's heartwarming and it feels 'personal'. Truly, I wish you all could know Tim White personally. This is a man with a truly creative mind and a deeply committed heart. You will perceive both as you read this book. Don't just breeze through it, let its principles sink into you. Internalize them. If you do, you will join a huge group of people, myself included, who have been made a better human because of Tim White."

—Dr. Dean Curry, Pastor, Life Center, Tacoma, Washington

"The book follows a modern day warrior of Nez Perce descent and the heartbreaking childhood of the girl he loves. A contemporary tale based on the Ulysses saga, "Ulysses Dream" delves into the plight of those trapped in the darker side of life. The book takes you into the world of child prostitution and slavery, illegal immigration, the lives of children working in the dumps of Honduras and the horrors of the Vietnam war. Then you witness, even with people whose lives are broken and wracked with guilt, the redemptive power of Love and Forgiveness. An engaging and thought provoking tale."

—Judy Willman, Key-contributor of the *New York Times* best selling *Boys in the Boat*

"As a Vietnam veteran, that loves his country and has a realistic view of our need to continue becoming a more perfect union, I appreciate that I have a church I can attend, without having to choose between my patriotism and my faith. For me, they go hand-in-hand. Pastor Tim has a very unique ability to talk for something, rather than against.

His meek and gracious approach has allowed my love for my country and my faith to continue growing, as I try to become part of the solution for the greater good! Tim White saved my life so I can't recommend this book enough."

—Sergeant David Gerzsenyne, May of '69 to March of '70 first infantry division US Army stationed Lay Khe Vietnam

"As an Olympian who was inspired by my own pastor to chase the Olympic dream as an 11-year old, Pastor Tim White's novel struck a raw nerve with me from the first word. But Ulysses Dream reaches for much more than the athletic ideal, and makes it just as apparent as the stark contrast in the recent Rio Olympics between what happens in the venues of the world's biggest sports stage, and the ravaged sections of the city surrounding them —along with the souls whose tragic lives unfold there. No one's attention is focused in that direction, but his book engages you to deal with it."

—David Currier, '72 Sapporo, Japan Winter Olympian

"This book is definitely a bestseller! Once you start reading it, it's hard to put down. I pray that the reader will be motivated to come aboard and champion this cause."

—Leon Patillo, lead singer for Santana 1974-75 top individual recording artist until present

Ulysses Dream:
A Timeless Romance

by Tim White

© Copyright 2016 Tim White

ISBN 978-1-63393-294-4

Published by

◣ köehlerbooks™

210 60th Street
Virginia Beach, VA 23451
800-435-4811
www.koehlerbooks.com

ULYSSES DREAM

a timeless romance

Tim White

VIRGINIA BEACH
CAPE CHARLES

The book is dedicated to my granddaughters,
Isabela Diaz and Evangelin McCary
To my daughters, Elise Diaz and Becca McCary
To my wife Jackie Ann White
And to my mom Elizabeth Jane White

These strong women have taught me the importance
of heroic women if injustice in this world is
ever going to be challenged.

Special thanks to my younger brother James Floyd
White who told me to write this book, and to my
friends Rod and Randy Halvorson the two longest
surviving patients battling Duchenne muscular
dystrophy. The courage that they have brought to
bear on their challenge inspires so many and tells me
that if not for this dreaded disease they could have
been world-class athletes. Both of them have been
world-class coaches. Through the power of fiction we
get to play with this fantasy.

Author's note

Is there nothing new under the sun? Since the dawn of time broken people, families, racial groups, language, and ethnic groups have been migrating around this planet. These massive immigrations have been met with unfathomable conflict. Cataclysmic collisions of people and ideas have resulted in horrible injustice and heroic moments for humanity. Each opposing side has some legitimate motivation searching for safety and prosperity for their families. And of course there have always been apex predators taking advantage of the weak in such perilous seasons of human history.

This work of fiction is about such times. It is about those who would dare to stand up to others who would prey on the vulnerable. These heroes are the stuff of legends. Civilizations and cultures melt away under the pressure of this momentous struggle. And yes, there are love stories in the midst of such unfathomable complexities. These stories have been, for the most part, passed down through storytelling around campfires. Through these campfire myths we often find our identity, our morality, and our way into the promising future. This dramatic folklore is where new generations find a fresh sense of authentic faith, patriotism, and inspiration to confront the overwhelming challenges in today's world.

This book is based upon real legends and real people. Some of the characters are real in name and deed; others are imagined or composites of several personalities. Some feats in these stories really happened and others are exaggerations or imagined. The places where these characters dwelled are real, as is their historical significance. This is storytelling as it was in the days of the Greeks—mystical.

Prologue

The Cabin

IN AN ARCHAIC timber lodge, I sit through arthritic pain as the native children beg for a story. Everyone grows silent with anticipation, lulled by the popping fire. The older kids listen from the lodge loft. Adult family members gather closer, and everyone grows silent. They have all heard my stories before, some about the most ancient times, others of nearer generations of our people. I am always tempted to start from the beginning, the earliest days where mythology and fact mingle.

Each time, my audience listens intently, culling little facts they may have missed at earlier tellings. The smell of ponderosa pine smoke fills the lodge, its heat sizzling venison steaks, and warming sweet corn, fry bread, and huckleberry dessert. The roar of the mighty Wallowa River fills the background like a soundtrack. This trappers' lodge is the oldest structure on the river, sitting at the head waters of picturesque blue-green Lake Wallowa in Eastern Oregon. A festive, feathered headdress, shield, and lance hang in one corner of the lodge. An old 45-70 government Winchester 1886 rifle is mounted over the fireplace with a feather at one end of the leather sling. It was Ephraim

Sundown's hunting rifle, the patriarch of our family. Next to it are his spurs and the silver bridle he had won at the Elgin Rodeo when he was young. These walls are lined with history and tradition: skins of cougar, wolf, bear, and the antlers of bison, elk, and deer. Crossing Marine sabers bring us forward. Next to them are medals and pictures of three generations of Nez Perce who had fought in the US Marine Corps.

The boulder shores of the roaring Wallowa River outside our lodge door are covered by the shadow of towering granite Mount Joseph, Mt. Howard, and Mt. Bonneville. Mt. Joseph is named after Chief Joseph, Mt. Howard after the general that pursued him, and Mt. Bonneville after the French-born officer who was an early leader of the US into Nez Perce country. The mountains symbolize the enemies of the noble Chief Joseph respected by his enemies and called the Red Napoleon. Mt. Joseph is surrounded by his opponents Howard and Bonneville. For generations, the family has bathed and taken its drinking water from this river; we have caught trout from this roaring source of life.

There is no running water in the log lodge. The cold box was a screened-in area outside, kept cold by the weather. The outhouse is down the path; it's well built and doesn't smell too bad. The fireplace is made from river rocks. A ladder leads to the loft where the youngest children slept in warmth. A chest is at the back of the loft, and it was full of medals, dress blues, and pictures of generations of the Nez Perce Sundown family.

On the wall of the cabin hang Uncle Grant's track shoes. He was the fastest kid at LaGrande High School when he was a boy, and he won a scholarship to SMU to compete on their track team. Also there is the basketball of Caleb, which he was awarded for scoring one thousand points at State College Eastern Oregon; the naval hat of Howard for his service in WWII; and Roy's badge when he worked for the FBI. There are bows, rugby equipment, and canoe paddles.

This log cabin was given to the Sundown family by the Methodist church for our grandfather Rev. Ephraim's work in pioneering its church camp there. It is now our gathering place, our retreat where we reconnect with each other, ourselves, and spirits past. Our band of Nez Perce is made up of in-laws, cousins, and nephews, not to mention adopted family members.

I am an elder in this family and a beloved storyteller. The family history lives in me and it is my responsibility to keep it alive. My voice is deep, resonant, and my Spanish accent from my early days in Honduras still lives. My name is Penelope.

Our lineage has spawned many warriors. I look at the anxious faces and see my ancestors staring at me. I see our roots in their eyes, the shapes of their jaws, the color of their skin. These are my people, the descendants of ancient nomadic African tribes, Mayans, and Native American warriors who long ago settled in the Americas.

I begin my storytelling with the Greeks. Our family enjoys classic literature. "Odysseus in Latin means *Ulysses*," I remind them. "He was a great warrior who left their home for ten years to do battle. Ulysses was bewitched in the arms of a sorceress. His fellow warriors were killed; he was tortured. His wife and family thought Ulysses was dead." I go on. "He was a hero, and his adventure is a path that guides all cultures and civilizations through similar hopeless paths to fight for love, home, and country when nothing seems to make sense," I say.

I'm interrupted, just as I thought I would be.

"Not *that* ancient story," shout the children. "Tell us one about our people and your life."

I react coyly, trying to look serious and mysterious. My looks suggest both. I am an old woman with long grey hair, dark skin, and dancing brown eyes. I try not to smile. I knew Ulysses was not the story they wanted to hear. It's too distant; too abstract. I tell it anyway to stress our common roots with all civilizations.

"Oh, you want the story of *my* life and our people," I say slyly.

My father-in-law Caleb takes his queue and begins to pound the drum softly to the beat of a human heart. He is setting the cadence that will lull the group into the journey as if their hearts were beating as mine had. My mother-in-law Elizabeth begins to play the plains flute, made of maple, and this skilled artisan warbles back and forth between harmonic pitches, casting a vision of ancient times. The mood is set; this storytelling craftsmanship is as old as time. My eyes widen with excitement and glisten with tears as memories surface. I begin, again.

"Some say Ulysses Looking Glass Sundown was a great warrior." The drum beats softly.

"Men of honor called him a hero—men of dishonor branded him a traitor."

"Christians say he was a mighty man of faith." The drumbeat continues but becomes unnoticed. "But he was always on the edge of quitting formal religion."

"Even his enemies reported that he fought with chivalry and indomitable persistence." The atmosphere works its magic.

"All Natives claim him as a hero: A light—a path to follow into the next century."

The drumbeat grows bolder, the smoke smells sweeter, the shadows in the lodge become more enthralling, and pine logs pop and sparkle, making the lights dance over the memories in the lodge.

"People scour his life, looking for answers, explanations, for dirt, for hope, for the way out of the quagmire that lies before our whole nation." The kids begin to smile and the adults nod their heads with twinkling eyes.

"But I just say he was simply the love of my life."

My voice soothes almost to a whisper as the story unfolds. My still-lingering Spanish accent emerges more pronounced. Each telling brings me back; and each telling is the same, but different, depending on the listener.

Chapter One

Seven Brothers

THE CHILDREN ARE settled, now. The adults relax and focus silently, as if watching a movie in a theater. If a young one begins to speak she receives a hush.

I continue, speaking of the lands, of places, our ancestors and their traditions. I speak of the boys, some grandchildren of Ephraim:

Δ Δ Δ

Silence in the woods is always terrifying. The mighty ponderosa pine and hundreds of majestic old ferns scented the forest with an ancient smell dating back to Mesozoic existence. Silence at dawn in this mountain meadow meant something—feelings and facts noted by the native boy.

No chattering of chipmunks, no cawing of blue jays, and no busy noise of insects in the early morning light. This silence led to a conclusion the oldest boy feared, but knew all too well: they were likely in the territory of an apex predator. The oldest brother deduced that it could be a man—the most dangerous of all predators. But it most likely was a cougar. They often shared the Wallowa Valley with the mountain lion. It could also be a pack of wolves or a black bear. Dealing with these predators required caution, and the training that their dads and uncles had given them growing up in this wild land. The native boys were covered in light beads of sweat even though they only wore the Nez Perce loincloth when making their daily run in the woods. The boys also wore their Native American bone chokers made from turquoise and bones. An eagle's feather was woven into their long hair. Each wore a gift from their grandfather strapped around their waists: a handmade, bone-handled bowie knife for protection from backcountry threats. They wore Converse sneakers, essential for the long runs. Little packs of deer-skinned pants and jackets were tied around their waists. The older boys had scarring on their pectoral muscles from their sun dance, which proved their manhood. They had danced in the sun until they tore their flesh with an elk bone. This tradition was borrowed from the Lakota and was part of the Sundown family. It was how a boy proved he would be a warrior pledged to protect his tribe. The older boys carried homemade recurve bows with a quiver of arrows. The younger boys ran with light bows that seemed like practice toys for being a warrior. Ten miles every morning was the assignment by their grandfather Ephraim. While in the high mountains, the boys were accompanied by the family dog, given to them by Ephraim. He was a Methodist minister and shepherd. The dog protected his flock of offspring.

Our neighbors were sheepherding refugees from the Basque region of Spain, and in this new land they grazed their herds in the high Wallowa Mountains of Eastern Oregon. These shepherds brought a collection of prize herding dogs from the mountains of Spain and France. They had many Great Pyrenees, which were skilled at protecting the herds. But it was another shepherding dog that interested WWI veteran Ephraim Sundown: The Beauceron, a mighty dog used extensively in the great war, almost to the point of wiping out the breed. This war dog, which he received from Basque friends, was one hundred thirty-five pounds of solid muscle, thirty inches tall with coloring similar to that of a Rottweiler. They have double coats that keep them warm in ice water or winter storms. They are affectionate to their owner's family and shy with others, but love small animals; it is not uncommon to see a kitten sleeping on top of one on a cold night. They play with squirrels as if they are small dogs. And they think they are the sheriffs at all times. Parents cannot spank their kids in their presence. Other dogs cannot fight without the mighty Beauceron breaking up the scrape. They have a head that looks more like a Lab than a Rottweiler. Their cute floppy ears and Great Dane-sized, puppy-like appearance is irresistibly cute until they are ready for war; then they are a fearsome black dog. They are incredibly athletic and can outrun a bear or jump a six-foot fence without thinking about it. Their agility is renowned and the reasons they have been a favorite war dog for centuries. Some say they descended from Roman war dogs. Their lineage dates back as a breed in France to the emperor Charlemagne, who was buried with two of these fiercely brave and loyal dogs.

The Basque refugees from the Spanish Civil War who settled in Eastern Oregon brought the war dogs with them. Ephraim named this dog guarding his grandsons and the other boys 'Argos.' He was the alpha puppy of the pack. This fierce protection dog slept on the bed with one of the boys each night, cuddling as if the boys were fellow puppies. Now Argos growled a low growl to sound the alert and let the boys become aware. The boys trusted Argos; they knew what he was bred for and that he was ready to die to protect them.

The parents of the seven boys trusted the dog for the protection they would need in the high mountains. This had been the way of primitives since the dawn of time in their symbiotic relationship of humanity and these wolf offspring. Moments of testing were not new to these native boys. The boys froze motionless when they sensed danger, prey or predators, just as their father, uncles, and grandfather had taught them.

Fifteen-year-old Achilles Joseph Sundown was the eldest of the boys. He had dark brown skin and was very muscular for fifteen. He was as handsome as any native warrior had ever been. He was athletic and an agile leader in every way. His brothers called him Joey. His parents Caleb and Elizabeth both loved Greek mythology since they had met in tiny State College at LaGrande Oregon and fallen in love, so they named their boys after Homeric heroes and Nez Perce chiefs from the time of Chief Joseph.

Joey gave the command for his brothers to move silently and quickly upwind through the swamp toward the river. He stopped and smelled for the predator while his brothers looked for signs. As they moved through the swamp that they called city water, they avoided the quicksand, as they knew this section so well; it was near their favorite deep blue-green fishing holes lined with monstrous slabs of granite, looking like a concrete swimming pool. Huckleberries and mushrooms covered the ground in the timbered swamp. The ferns and old growth cedar gave the landscape a feel of the Mesozoic era. No other human knew of this secret fishing hole protected by quicksand, swamp, mosquitoes, ticks, and an impenetrable wall of poison ivy and oak. They did not even bushwhack their trail because they did not want to leave a trail for any competitors to find this hidden dream of every fisherman.

The little brothers kept eating berries instead of staying focused. After no more than five minutes, Joey figured out the mystery: they were being stalked. The squirrels told him. If you listened to their sounds they would shout a warning to you when a dangerous predator arrived.

The boys followed Joey without reservation. It seems it was always that way. His Nez Perce father, Caleb Joseph, and his Irish/Scottish mom, Elizabeth Cundiff Saunders, had noticed the heroism in their firstborn the day they brought him home. He had a mind of his own. Now Joey was six feet, taller than his dad. His brothers felt safe with him, as they could see why Joey was named after the ancient warrior Chief Joseph and the Homeric hero Achilles. Achilles Joseph Sundown–their big brother Joey. All of Caleb's biological sons were named after Greek heroes and Nez Perce chiefs from the days of Chief Joseph.

As they stood on the west side of the river with their band of brothers, Joey and his thirteen-year-old brother Ulysses "Looking Glass" Sundown whispered their plans. "Ulee," as he was called, was always competing with Joey, and being smaller and younger, he never quite measured up.

Joey had dark skin, which contrasted with the light-skinned Nez Perce tribe. He was Ulee's hero, his nemesis, his friend. Ulee was thirteen and had the skin and hair of his mother's Scottish Irish ancestors. Without the braids or the deerskin loincloth, no one would guess he was native. Ulee's claim to fame among the brothers was that he was fast. As he and Joey whispered, they presumed that whatever it was that was stalking them was moving against the wind. It had their scent, and it knew how to hunt, as it was moving silently towards its prey . . . the boys.

Joey gave the orders: Ulee would stay behind and climb one of the ponderosa pines to see what they were up against. Joey was confident because Ulee was fast—the fastest boy the brothers had ever seen. The whole family would bet on Ulee's speed. His uncles would set up matches in the state campground with full-grown men so they could bet money on him. His brothers would arrange races against older kids all to brag on the freakish speed of their white-skinned brother.

Their brother, Patty, twelve-year-old Petrocolas "Crazy Horse" Sundown, walked up to hear Joey's plan. His middle name "Crazy Horse" was not wasted on him. Petrocolas was nicknamed Patty, and he had beautiful brown skin like Achilles and black hair and eyes that every native boy wished for. He was stocky—strong, even as a boy. The girls always loved his looks. He was not particularly tall, but what he lost in height he made up in strength and fierce courage. Patty could relate to anybody and was fiercely loyal to his brothers. Joey's plan was for Patty to stay with Ulee to find out what was following them.

One of the rules of the mountains for them was the buddy system. "Always stay with a buddy," their grandfather Ephraim would stress. It was a law of survival. Jackson John Sundown, age eleven, was disappointed that he could not join his two older cousins. Jackson was the son of Joey and Patty's Uncle John who had died saving the life of his brother Caleb in the Korean War. Jacky was being raised by his African mother in Florida. He was named after their great grandfather, nephew of Chief Joseph and the Nez Perce Rodeo hero Jackson Sundown.

Their uncle John had met a devout Pentecostal African-American woman whose home was Florida, and that was where she raised her son, their cousin. But Jacky was always in trouble and spent a lot of his time being raised by the Sundown family in the Pacific Northwest. Their grandfather, Ephraim, and their grandmother, Quanah, had raised six biological boys in addition to two adopted African-American boys and an adopted Navajo boy. You can imagine what a party it was when all their grandchildren got together.

Joey's parents, Caleb and Elizabeth, were devout Christ followers. Like Ephraim, they adopted extra boys. They adopted Donnie Pielstick, whose parents died in a car crash. The boy's father was German and his mom was mostly African-American.

Their youngest biological son, Whitey, named Hector "Whitebird" Sundown, brought home his best friend, Heath Duncan Sundown, also aged five, who was being raised by his aunt, but they called him brother, and his unknown heritage didn't stop him from fitting in with the native boys as a member of the family. He was nicknamed Dunk. This pack of boys was a gaggle of blood brothers, adoptive brothers, and cousins once removed. Regardless of lineage, they were a tribe, practicing ancient traditions in a modern world.

They were seven boys running together, confronting danger. The oldest was fifteen, the two youngest were five. At dawn each day they ran ten miles, a regimen that they were growing acquainted with to prepare them to be the warriors they were meant to be.

The oldest four boys all had eagle feathers in their hair. It was the sign of a man who had completed the vision quest. They had spent several nights in these mountains alone waiting for their life vision. They had also danced the sun dance and had their pectorals pierced with elk bone and tethered until they could dance and pull out, leaving the scarring that would show their tribe that they were warriors who would protect their people with their lives. These four boys all carried self-made recurve bows with forty-pound tension on the string, and their big brothers, Joey, Ulee and Patty, had recurves that carried sixty pounds of tension. All the boys carried bone-handled bowie knives around their waist that were made by their grandfather, and they had carried them since the age of five. It wasn't safe in the mountains without something like this. Predators could smell fear on a man, so the protection helped the young boys in their daily treks in the wilderness.

△ △ △

As Ulee waited in the branches of the red ponderosa pine, he had an intuition of what was hunting the brothers. This was not the first time they had been stalked. They had been stalked by cougars more than once. They had been stalked by a bad man, a felon who was working as a sheepherder, watching a herd grazing in the high mountains. Man was by far the most dangerous predator to be feared in the high mountains. The predator that stalked them now was not a man; it moved through the thick forest in a different way. In fact, this predator moved like something he remembered: the last of the Wallowa Mountain grizzlies. He was a man killer, but no hunter had been able to corner him. Many a hunter had left to finish the last of the grizzly in these parts but had ended up being the prey. All the other grizzlies had been hunted down by ranchers to protect their herds. The rumors were that this bear was descended from the ice-age bear that no longer existed. His nickname was Big Foot. And the native rumor was that he was as much spirit as animal. The boys had encountered this man-eater before on the Grand Ronde River where it flows into the Snake River by Troy, Oregon, in Hells Canyon.

That was a memory, but now as Ulee waited in the ponderosa for the apex predator, he had a feeling that the same grizzly was their present stalker. He believed this was that bear and it had come for Joey, his beloved older brother. Bears are smart. If you are not used to them, their intelligence is often more than a match for a man. Ulee was terrified, as he saw and heard the crunch of birch trees breaking as a giant was moving fast his way. He jumped down from the tree and called to his younger brother, Patty.

"Let's run!" Ulee spoke with fear. Patty whispered, "Did you see it?" Ulee said, "No, but I know what it is." They ran, leaping over fallen trees and moving with a speed that would surprise you unless you knew these boys. It did not take them long to catch their brothers, who were moving downriver towards the rapids and, eventually, the ninety-foot falls before their cabin.

"Joey, I think it is Big Foot," said Ulee.

"How do you know?" Joey asked.

"You know me brother. I know—I can sense it in my bones."

They both knew without saying that he had come for Joey. Joey looked afraid in front of his younger brothers. It didn't matter—all the brothers still looked up to him. Joey stopped and said, "We need a new plan; he will catch us before we get to the falls as the canyon narrows." They paused, waiting for their older brother to give them a plan. Argos looked like a war dog and began a low growl with the hair on the back of his neck standing up. Normally if you are trying to outrun a bear, your chances of going downhill are better than uphill. They have short legs but are so strong that running up hill doesn't seem to bother them. On a steep incline, boys can jump and slide under control down a mountain. But he was going to catch them if they continued running for home, so Joey made a leadership decision.

"Come on," said Joey. "We're going to make it to the ridge, to the Matterhorn. Bigfoot can't climb the granite mountain like we can."

So, they ran uphill towards Ice Lake. The trail was steep. A mountain goat would have had trouble. Ulee and Patty acted as a rear guard, and when they needed to, they tracked the boys as they changed course. Finally, they reached Joey.

"What is wrong?" asked Ulee. Joey was slow and weak. He was sweating too hard.

"I am feeling sick," Joey said.

The older boys knew that Joey had leukemia. It was a poorly-kept family secret that no one talked about but they all knew. All the boys knew wild predators would instinctively pursue the sick and the weak. It was a law of nature.

"I think it is a white man's disease," said Joey. "They say I am going to die from it someday. Mom and Dad won't say it, but I can see it in the doctor's eyes. Maybe the spirit of the bear has come to give me the death of a warrior."

"We are a pack of wolves," Ulee said. "No grizzly can take us if we fight together. This is just a test by the Great Spirit."

Joey formed a plan.

"The war dog Argos, Jacky, and Ulee will slow down Big Foot," Joey said.

"This is what Chief Joseph did when he led the Wallowa band on their retreat, remember?" Jacky said.

"I'm staying too." Patty said. "You are too slow."

"Yeah but I can fight," said Jacky.

Ulee looked at his older brother, out of breath, and then turned to Jacky to whisper. "Okay, but you will learn to run today."

Joey, Stick, Heath, and Hector all took off as fast as they could. Hector and Heath could really run for five year olds. Off and on, their big brother would carry one or the other.

Ulee stood on a huge granite bolder, maybe forty tons, with Patty and Jacky at his side. This rock was a fortress in itself. Argos stood next to Ulee and leaned over on him to calm his nerves. This was a common trait of Beauceron. The pause was terrifying. And then there it was. It was more than nine feet tall.

The grizzly stood to its full height and roared. The entire forest was filled with sickening hopelessness. The behemoth huffed as he pounded the ground with his front paws, threatening a charge. The three boys let out war cries just as they had been taught, burying their fear. The second growl of the grizzly was even louder, making the hair on the back of their necks stand up and petrifying them with primordial panic learned by humans over thousands of years. Even their running brothers stopped when they heard the roar of the bear echo throughout the mountainside. Then they smiled and started to run again when they heard their brother's brave war cries.

"Just like Chief Joseph's retreat," said Hector, speaking in Nez Perce. He was referring to the retreat of Chief Joseph with the Wallowa Band made up of 750 Nez Perce and only 200 warriors who retreated 1170 miles trying to find freedom in Canada while defeating three armies of US troops time and time again until they surrendered forty miles from Canada on October 5, 1877.

When the bear was thirty feet below them, they began to fire their arrows. They did not miss. They had grown up shooting these bows—hunting with them and practicing with them. But the arrows didn't seem to slow the grizzly. The boys' arrows barely pierced its hide. The predator pursued the three boys who climbed the side of the hill, as the bear closed in, it was met by Argos, their canine protector.

The dog surprised the bear and turned its attention from the boys. Argos bit and tore at the bear and then spun to get out of his way. This was the fighting technique of the Beauceron. They were bred to fight bear, wolves, and wild boar. This intrepid battle stalled the mighty bear, giving the boys time to rejoin their brothers.

"We are a band of brothers," Jacky yelled.

"That bear doesn't know what he is messing with." Patty said.

Argos battled the bear until the boys were clear. His bites tore at the bear's flesh. And the 135-pound dog spun around and dodged to avoid the bear's reprisals.

The boys could hear the bellow of the grizzly, the growl of their dog, and finally the death howl of their family pet.

Dunk yelled out, "Argos!" This was the dog who slept at his feet every night; he was family within the family. When five-year-old Heath had a terrifying dream, feeling all alone from the death of his parents, Argos would wake him with a lick and some snuggling.

"Quiet," Joey commanded. "Argos gave his life to buy us time. Don't give away our position."

Meanwhile, Ulee, Patty, and Jacky made it to Ice Lake, where their brothers were standing out on an iceberg in the middle of the lake. They swam to meet them. Joey was shivering more than the rest, but he had picked some huckleberries, mushrooms, pine nuts, grubs, and wild onions when he was on the shoreline. They huddled together on the iceberg to warm their older brother. This blissful picture didn't last long before the bear appeared.

Of the nine arrows the boys had left in the bear, only a few were still sticking. There wasn't much blood that they could see. The bear roared while he looked at Joey. It started to swim for the iceberg, and the boys all swam hard for the shore, running up Matterhorn Ridge.

Ulee and Patty waited and shot more arrows into the bear. Patty put an arrow deep in one eye, but the bear knocked it off with a massive paw as the eye bled. They were hoping and praying that he would give up. It looked like a fight to the death—an instinct as old as time.

They dove off the floating iceberg at the last minute and swam rapidly for the shore. Jacky and Stick shot at the bear as he followed their brothers in the lake. This was the retreating method of the Nez Perce. Jacky and Stick stayed and threw big rocks at the swimming bear when he got within twenty feet. The two boys shooting from the lake edge ran to be covered by two of their brothers firing arrows about sixty yards away. This was Ulee and Patty, and when they had given Stick and Jacky enough of a head start they ran with incredible speed to join their brothers.

△ △ △

By the time the four boys began to reach the granite walls of the Matterhorn, the bear was right behind them. It was long enough for the boys to get to the sheer granite side of the Matterhorn. A mountain climber would use all their equipment to climb this cliff, but the boys had perfected the ability to run up the granite. It is hard to imagine unless you have ever done it, but they would climb using the techniques that they had been taught. They used feet and hands and always had a safety grip at each advance. The bear's size made it difficult to pursue the agile boys. But the one trick they knew that is hard to imagine is that when the cliff reached a seventy-degree angle, they would stand up and run on the nearly vertical cliff with the rubber from their sneakers holding on to the smooth granite like a basketball court. They could only do this in twenty-yard bursts, but they lost the bear, and by nightfall, they were at the summit of the Matterhorn.

"We are safe, for now," sighed Joey.

Heath and Whitey started to cry.

"We lost Argos." Joey replied as a grown warrior. "He gave his life for us. He was bred to do that, just as we were bred to fight with fierce courage."

Joey then commanded the boys like he was their father.

"Ulee, you stay here. No fire, no sound. Rub off the scent of your sweat with the feces of the mountain goats. Two brothers on guard with bows to the ready. When anyone sleeps, keep your hand on your knives. Remember what dad says, 'To fight like wolves.' All of us together—we are invincible."

"Where are you going?" Ulee asked.

"I am going out to scout for weapons, the enemy, food, and sign," said Joey.

There was a storm coming in, and it was starting to rain.

"This rain will make you cold, so huddle together, but in the dark it will make me invisible," Joey said.

The boys gathered the water in the granite niches and drank. Joey disappeared into the darkness.

Ulee could smell the bear. Patty said it was his imagination. Stick said he heard it. Ulee led his brothers to the tunnels that had been mined on the surface of the granite. It was about a half a mile from where they left Joey on the ridge to Sacajawea Point. They squeezed in and scavenged some of the small evergreens on top of the mountain and prepared to start a fire at the entrance. They waited and rested; truth be told, they were all still terrified.

They heard a sound. This time they all heard it. Ulee let out the sound of a ground squirrel. It was answered. All the boys smiled; it was Joey. He had been gone for two hours. He came back with more firewood, some wild onions, and some worms to eat. The onions made them a little sick, and the earthworms just tasted like dirt. He even had a six-inch trout he had caught with his hand in one of the high streams between Matterhorn and Sacajawea Point. That meant they each got a bite. This was delicious even raw.

Joey sent Ulee out while the boys were eating. "Find a hiding place and make sure to disguise your scent. Roll in some of the evergreens so you smell like a tree, not a man. And stay alert, smelling, hearing, or seeing him before he sees you."

Ulee was scared and his heart was pounding. He wished Patty could have come with him, but he could see how much more invisible he was in the dark by himself. Mud camouflaged his light skin. He listened and breathed as quietly as he could, one hand on his knife, the other on his bow.

The boys heard the sounds of squirrels sounding their warning in the distance. Ulee was all alone out there. Patty woke up and told Joey, "You should not have sent him out alone. Remember the buddy system." Patty said.

"Yes, but this is war, and he needs to be invisible," Joey said. "I am going out to get him; you are war chief here, Patty. Light the fire at the entrance if you know the bear is nearby. Remember, everybody fights together."

Ulee was hiding in a crevice in the granite on the west face of the mountain. He watched in the darkness set against the small light from the summit view. In his bones he knew the bear was nearby. He wanted to panic and run. He began to tremble from the cold thin air. He was at nearly 10,000 feet. But just as Ulee's father had taught him while hunting, he took control of his breathing. He willed his muscles not to shiver. He told himself the wilderness was his home. He felt at home. Then the bear appeared on the horizon but it did not see him. Ulee was invisible to the half-blind bear. The native boy slowly sat up—he was in a shadow.

Ulee pulled back his sixty-pound bowstring just like he had a thousand times. He didn't even need to think about it. He slowed his breath and let the arrow fly, as calm as he had ever been in his life. He saw it strike just behind the shoulder of the grizzly and pierce all the way through both lungs. Big Foot had no idea what had happened; it was all so silent. The grizzly just felt the pain and ran off with a burst of adrenaline, looking for his attacker.

Just as Joey was getting ready to leave, they heard a painful growl. Patty said, "Ulee got him!"

Then in ran Ulee. "Light the fire!" he said with enthusiastic urgency. "Big Foot is out there."

Joey asked, "Did you get him?"

"Yes," Ulee said. "The rain storm made me invisible just like when we hunt. I heard him coming and I lay in a crevice. His silhouette gave me a perfect target from ten yards away. I put one right behind his shoulder. It should have hit the heart and pierced both the lungs, just the way we would take a black bear."

"Did he go down?" Joey asked.

"No," said Ulee. "He ran off, so I can't be sure. But he is bleeding out now."

They heard a sound and saw a huge dark figure with bright eyes following Ulee's trail. Finally, the intruder galloped toward them, knocking Heath over with his final leap. Ulee started to stab when he realized it was Argos, who was licking him like nobody's business. Argos broke the silent code and cried as he licked Heath and Whitey. Ulee told him to be quiet. Beauceron are smart, and Argos quieted right down, still bleeding where the bear had slapped him. Joey quieted them all.

"I think we should not have lit the fire," he said. "And we

should not have made so much noise when Argos came back.

Immediately, a low growl came out of Argos. Big Foot was near. Argos could smell him. Joey stoked the fire at the entrance of the tunnel and said, "Big Foot knows where we are now." Joey had brought back some sticks, which they each sharpened and hardened with the fire, finally peeing on them, which made them somewhat poisonous. The bear lunged in and grabbed Stick, dragging him out of the tunnel. Argos, though wounded, attacked and tore at the groin of the bear. This was the technique of the Beauceron in hunting bear or boar. The spear sticks in the hands of the boys just snapped as they formed their flanks at the entrance of the cave. Ulee grabbed Stick's legs and was trying to hold on, but the strength of the bear was unpredictable and he escaped carrying their brother in his mouth. He was gone in the darkness on the peak of the Matterhorn. Immediately, Joey told Ulee to give him his knife. Ulee said, "No, I go with you—we will die together." Joseph Achilles Sundown commanded, "Get my brothers down safely. Live a long life. This is my moment."

Ulee handed Joey his knife. There was no time for a goodbye. Ulee dove into the darkness. The bear towered over Stick, whose collarbone had been broken with the first bite of the bear. Argos, still holding on to the bear's groin and tearing with his jaws, was batted to the side by the bear, breaking a leg. Joey ran headlong into the grizzly, shouting war cries, stabbing him twice with the two knives. The bear swatted at Joey, but Joey blocked him with the razor-sharp bowie knife that was given to him by his grandfather. The cut nearly took off the bear's paw.

Ulee came out of the cave with his bow and could not get a shot. He finally let another strong shot go into the leg of the bear that his brother was gripped with in a death struggle. The other brothers all came out with knives in hand. The bear looked up and was distracted, knowing this was his end. Joey shoved the blade of his other knife under the bear's chin and through its brain and then twisted the knife, just as he had been taught. Now Joey tackled the bear on the sheer cliff that they were standing on precariously, and together they fell over 1,000 feet to their deaths.

It all happened in what seemed like a moment. Ulee gathered the boys back in the cave and started another fire. No one said anything. Than Stick began to yell.

"Joey, Joey, Joey!"

Patty carried Argos back to the cave, where the dog was whimpering. Heath joined in: "Joey!" Hector wouldn't stop, "Joey!" Jackson yelled, "Joey, you are a great warrior."

Patty cried, "Joey, you are worthy of Chief Joseph's name. You too are a chief. The spirit of the bear is with you." Ulee said nothing.

Chapter Two

My Odyssey

THE CHILDREN CLAP and the adults smile as the story of the seven brothers ends. They have had heard it so many times before, but always react with the same surprise and enthusiasm. They glance at the huge brown bear rug on the wall still looking fearsome. They see themselves in those boys. And, I suppose they see themselves in me.

Just as they have done so many times before, they ask for me to share my story. I pretend to be reluctant, but I know my roots are theirs. To know themselves, they must know me. I relent. Mine is a dark story, sad. It conveys darkness and then light.

Δ Δ Δ

I was born in 1954 in a small village in the cloud rainforest of Honduras. This was the same year that Ulysses Looking Glass Sundown was born in the Wallowa Mountains of northeastern Oregon.

My first memories are romanticized with time and the fog of childhood. Growing up in the paradise of Comayagua, a little village in the cloud rainforest of Honduras was idyllic. My mother was beautiful. Her name was Isabela Maria Morales. My father was a good man named Jesus Benito Morales. He worked for an equivalent of fifty cents a day in the coffee fields or banana plantations. He rented his machete for twenty-five cents a day from the plantation owners, who owned much of our nation; in fact, they had once owned what is now Southern California.

We lived in a grass hut with a mud floor as most of our people did. I was the oldest of six surviving kids. Two of my brothers had died as babies. I did not know it, but the mud floors were terrible for passing parasites, which killed many of our people. The lack of safe water and sewage problems caused lots of death and illness, too. And hornets used to hide in the thatched grass. If they bit you, they made you very sick, much like the bite of the scorpion. So many died when they were children in our village.

Our grief was hard, but it was not a trail that we walked alone. Our family and our village were very close, which made us collectively rich. We grew our own corn and we had our own chickens—even a goat.

None of us had been born in a hospital, and so we did not have birth certificates. Technically, we were not citizens of Honduras, or any country, although our people had lived here for thousands of years. In fact, in legal eyes, we were non-persons.

My father had been educated by missionaries at a Wesleyan Christian orphanage called Manuelito. Papa loved history and would tell me imaginary stories of the history of my people, the Mayans. In fact, on cool nights, our village neighbors would gather around a fire and listen to the romance and idealism in my father's stories.

First there was dancing and then the big fire. My father would tell his stories in response to the pleas of the children of the village. They would grow silent; we could hear the sounds of the jungle and the crackle of the fire. I studied him, sitting proudly among the villagers, feeling special.

My father would become very animated. "In this cloud forest there are poisonous snakes, jaguars who weigh up to 300 pounds, and crocodiles that villagers say measure up to thirty feet. But it is in this very jungle that our grandfathers and grandmothers built a proud civilization. They were ruled by no man from the outside. They knew more than anyone in the world about mathematics and the stars. There were kings and queens and princesses. Noble warriors fought for our safety and came home to be rewarded with the love of princesses. I think my beautiful wife Isabela Maria is descended from the blood from such princesses. And some of you are, too. Others here who look like you are descended from the crocodile or wild boar."

Everyone laughed because they knew he was teasing us. When you are poor and you don't own your home, your tools, or your land, it feels like you are a slave. Many of the children died with bloated stomachs from infections that could be cured with a clean water source or modern septic systems. All of this pain caused our joy to be simple and sweet. The next morning, after the fire story, I heard my father ordering my eldest brother, Jose, to get ready for work. At a young age, the boys became laborers. They were part of our income and our family protection. Jose did not look like himself. My younger brother Homer teased that he looked like he was descended from the crocodile. He looked a little green. Jose did not want Mamma's handmade corn tortillas for breakfast. He would not even drink water.

After they left for work, I walked around the village with my brother, Homer, looking for kids to play with. The mosquitoes were terrible this time of year. A few of our friends told us they were sick, and the rest told us their parents were afraid of the mosquitoes and they needed to stay by the fire. About an hour after Jose and Daddy left for work, my father came home carrying Jose in his arms like a baby.

"Isabela—Isabela—Jose is burning up from fever."

Some other women came to our home to try and feed Jose a soup made from roots that might help. He was so sick from both ends. He hallucinated and cried out and then shivered.

About that time, my younger brother, Homer, came down with the dreaded illness. I took my turn caring for them, and when I brushed Homer's hair back from his face, he cried and said, "Penelope, stop hurting me." Mamma said it was all right; that is what dengue fever does. We were all circled around Jose, who was more ill than Homer.

Our family priest said the last rites when Jose took his last breath. I walked out of our hut crying; my mama tried to comfort me, but grief overcame her. My dad, Jesus, walked up to try and say something that made sense of this senseless theodicy, this tragic act of God. He broke down and cried like a baby when he tried to speak. I went to Homer, my little brother, and hugged him. At least he was still alive. We didn't know that the second time you get dengue fever is the most lethal time. This was Jose's second time and Homer's first. We held on to each other in the craziness of this horrible moment. Homer began to recover, knowing how close he had come to death. We were scared because we could hear our mother and father crying as the priest tried to comfort them.

The priest told my family, "Death is expected; life is the surprise."

While the village mourned Jose, I slipped away with Homer, who was feeling better but still weak. We played in the rainforest. There is so much life there. There are eighteen species of lizards and more kinds of snakes than we could count. Flowers, plants, waterfalls, and a variety of insects more numerous than a peasant family could keep track of. Amazing insects would buzz out a warning, telling us ahead of time when there would be an equatorial downpour just by how they sensed the humidity increasing. The flowers were a world of faith unto themselves.

My early memories are surprisingly clear, but most of all, I remember the lovely simplicity of our lives and the beauty of the land of our forefathers in which we worked and played. Papa Jesus Morales told us we were no better than slaves; I did not know what he meant. I remember missionaries coming to visit us. They would give the children candy and then take pictures of us sitting on their laps. All I knew of this was that my father resented it.

ΔΔΔ

When I was five years old, my papa took us to the Copan ruins. We rode the bus; one of the guests of the missionaries had slipped my father some lempira—this was the money that allowed our family to travel for the first time. We saw the Mayan ruins and learned more about our heritage being Mayan, or native, as well as Spanish.

In Copan, the Mayan culture was one of the most important in America. This ancient culture flourished in the western part of Honduras, leaving many different costumes and traditions that can be traced to days long past. In some of the mountain villages, the people still wear the colors of their ancestors as the Mayans continued to revolt against the Spanish and aristocracy for almost five hundred years for their independence. And they were forced to wear only the colors of their village so that they could not travel and organize revolution. As a child, I remember that we wore these colors with pride, and I wondered which village band our family was descended from. Papa's enthusiasm for our noble heritage was contagious.

I didn't want an uneventful and safe life, I preferred an adventurous one.

My mother, Isabela Maria Morales, looked beautiful and almost always seemed to glow, seeing that my father, her husband, loved their six children. The second oldest brother near my age was Homer, who was eleven months younger. He too was so proud that we were Mayan, but he agreed with his big sister on most things.

The greatest danger to our lives was my mom's beauty. When men would come through the village, she always hid herself, along with me and my three younger sisters.

My brothers acted as men starting at six years of age. We all worked. But a special burden was put on them that was part of the machismo of our race. On a typical day when my father was at work, someone in the village raced into the center of the line of huts and yelled, *"La policia esta llegando!"* I still wake up at nights sometimes covered in sweat, my heart pounding remembering one of those moments.

There was something about the way that the police pickup trucks were driving to my village that sent panic through our community. My mother hid me and my brother Homer behind a tree a short distance from the village. She covered us with a bush. The babies in our hut were crying. As she rushed back to her babies, she was grabbed by two men, and I covered Homer's eyes so he could not see. They abused our mother and then killed her while they were laughing, and I was watching.

I cried out, *"Papá, alguien, vienen ayuda Mamá.*

Necesitamos un héroe, si Dios quiere!" It was a stupid thing to do, but I was only six years old. A big man with a big head and large hands whose uniform hardly fit him came over and found us. He grabbed me and Homer, pulling us from under the bush.

"I am the only hero you will see—and now I am your papa," he said.

That was the last time I saw my home or my family. Homer was only five; he bravely hit the man with all his force. The man who called himself our new papa grabbed Homer by the neck with one hand and me by the other and lifted us off the ground, cutting off our oxygen. The men just laughed.

I remember hearing gun shots and riding in the back of a truck with a dozen other children. We had no idea where we were going or what they had done to our families. I thought my dad would come and rescue us. I remember whispering to my brother that when my dad came home from work he would take his machete and make these *"hombres malos paguen por lo que han hecho!"*

No hero came to save us. We cried, we prayed, and no hero came. My prayers changed to hoping my dad would *not* come; all these men had guns. I did not want Papa killed, too. I prayed for him and the rest of my family. I prayed for the soul of my sweet mother. And I prayed for Homer and asked for strength and wisdom to protect him.

We were moved to a big house in Tegucigalpa where I was told that I was a slave. I learned later it was abuse—modern human slavery but—then it was just a nightmare that no little girl should ever have to call real.

I will never forget Hernando Cortez. He was a large man who radiated evil in every way. He was the first to abuse me. And then he made me watch as he abused my brother. Cortez was a horrible, evil man: a monster. And there were evil tattoos all over his body. He was always sweating. I saw him shoot one girl right before my eyes. I try to forget watching my brother Homer being abused by him. They locked Homer and I in a room with other kids who had lost hope. Homer cried, "Papa . . . Mama!" I reached out my hand in the dark. It took a moment and I felt Homer's tiny hand fill mine.

"I promise you, little brother, I will protect you and never let you go. I love you. Brother, I am your big sister. I will be your hero."

When Cortez came to abuse me, I asked him, "Why do you do such terrible things? Are you really a follower of the devil?" He had a picture of Satan on his chest with 666 tattooed on his forehead. He was trying to sweet-talk me.

"You are a smart girl, I am not going to lie to you, we use the satanic theme just to put fear in our enemies. Actually, I am a born-again, Bible-believing, spirit-filled Christian." He went on speaking in all sincerity. "I was saved from the streets and gangs by courageous Christian missionaries. When I rose to lead MS-13, it was my destiny. I knew it was God's will because of all the good I could do. I take care of poor families with my money; if the whores work with me I treat them like royalty. And with my wealth, I keep far worse people from taking over our country and our people."

The next day, Hernando Cortez, the born-again, Bible-believing, spirit-filled Christian sold my brother Homer, and he was gone. As they took him away, I was tied to a bed. I was broken; they had abused me repeatedly, but I no longer cried. They had drugged us both. But I still fought and scratched and bit when they took my brother away. I left some scars on Cortez, and he left a small scar on my face when he slapped me with his big gold ring on. My brother called my name: *"Penelope por el amor de Dios me salve! Hermana mayor Pleše por el amor de Dios me salve."* (Penelope for the love of God save me! Please older sister for the love of God, save me.) I can hear his cries now. This was the last time I saw my little brother.

△ △ △

My roommates were other girls my age. They gave us drugs that took our memory away and made everything seem like a dream. One day we were standing in front of one the large international hotels dressed as prostitutes waiting for some old Americans to come and pay to use us. As we stood there, with men gawking at us and telling us how beautiful we were I began to cry. My friend, who was an older beautiful girl named Gabriela, tried to get me to stop because our Pimp Hernando Cortez was watching from inside the hotel lobby. Finally, he came out and started to yell at me to be friendly to the Gentlemen and that he owned me. Just then, from across the street came a Christian girl from Honduras who was there with her youth group. She was beautiful. Her name was Maria Jose Santos and her little sister Belen Santos followed right behind her. Nine or ten other Christian girls from lower middle-class families followed. The men in their group waited in a van watching. They were from the Wesleyan Church in Tegus. Maria and Belen are some of the most courageous people I have ever met. Little Maria stood up to Hernando and told him her testimony of how she had given her life to Christ and everything was forgiven and she was a new person. She quoted him John 3:16 *For God so loved the world that he gave his only begotten son that whosoever believes in him will not perish but receive life eternal life.* She spoke with otherworldly authority.

Hernando was a threatening, evil-looking man and he ordered them to get out of there before he killed someone. These girls belonged to him. Maria protested, No, these girls belong to Jesus. All the girls circled around those of us who were slaves and began to sing a Spanish praise song.

Oh alma cansada y turbada
¿Sin luz en tu senda andarás?
Al Salvador mira y vive
Del mundo la luz es su faz
Pon tus ojos en Cristo,
Tan lleno de gracia y amor,
Y lo terrenal sin valor será
A la luz del glorioso Señor
De muerte a vida eterna
Te llama el Salvador fiel
En ti no domine el pecado;
Hay siempre victoria en Él
Jamás faltará su promesa;
Él dijo "Contigo estoy"
Al mundo perdido ve pronto
Y anuncia la salvación hoy

As they sang about Jesus, it was as if Hernando Cortez was running up against an invisible spiritual wall. This little girls' choir of determined, pure-hearted Christians sang this old song without musical accompany so sweet and touching. The evil Hernando could not penetrate this forceful display of Godly power. He turned and left.

The real story behind MS-13 and other gangs is that even though they do very evil things and are confused many times they have been known to let a person out of a gang if they know they are really converted to following Christ. But if they stop following Christ then they will kill them for leaving the gang. It is a world bogged down in desperation—a world in search of a real faith. These stories are few and far between and I did not know it until I was in my sixties.

We all cried as we watched this courageous drama unfold. The Christian boys in the van were all too afraid to enter this conflict. They watched with tears running down their cheeks as God worked through these pure-hearted girls. Out of all the slaves only Gabriela and I chose to go with the Christian girls to find a new life. But the first chance we could find we ditched these courageous girls and headed back to the streets. The tattoos on our chests portrayed us as Mayan gangsters, communicating that we had become prostitutes and that we were owned by this terrible gang. We did not wish any harm on these courageous Christians.

MS-13 was a Salvadoran gang started in the US for protection against other criminals, and now this gang was becoming strong in Honduras. MS-13 stood for *Marva Salvatrucha*. Marva was the name for gangs, coming from a fierce ant. Salvatrucha may be a combination of *Salvadorian* and *trucha*, or alert. They formed for protection of Central Americans in the US from Mexican and African gangs in Los Angeles. Today, it is reported, MS-13 openly has satanic rituals, marking their children with 666 as they give them to the devil. They are international, having more than 70,000 members. They specialize in drug trafficking, illegal immigration, prostitution, kidnapping, human trafficking, gun running, theft, and extortion.

Both Gabriela and I wore scarves covering our faces, as many of the children on the streets of the city do. We dared not beg, so we stole food from the markets. Finally, we were caught by a police officer named Zeylaya who told us that he owned us now and that we would work for him. He took us to a corner, where an older police officer named Micheletti fought him for us. I hope you will never know what it is to be six years old and see two full grown men fight for you—to witness firsthand how brutal men can be when they fight—and knowing they are fighting for ownership of you—and yet not knowing who it would be better to win. Micheletti left the other police officer bloody and gasping for air as he put us in the back of his pickup.

Officer Micheletti drove us across the river into the hills to the city dump. He told us that there was no safe place for us and that we were now people of the dump. We had no birth certificates—no place to run too.

"I have a father named Jesus Benito Morales and a little brother named Homer Salvador Morales; he is only five years old!"

The old policeman said, "Your family is gone. Forget about them. There is only one possibly safe place for you, and that is the city dump. The only reason that I am risking my life against MS-13 is because I am a good Catholic and I have daughters your age. Even the police are often ruled by the gangs. I am risking my life and family to take you to the dump."

He dropped us off at night, and we saw his taillights disappear. We looked around in the dark to see things that were made of a human being's worst nightmares. The first thing you notice is the smell of the dump. Think of the most putrid garbage that you have ever smelled and make it a thousand times worse with continual fire burning it like incense. Mix in the smell of dead and rotting cattle, hogs, vultures, and human beings. We both vomited our guts out. We were having dry heaves when we could see people and animals moving through the dump. I had heard of hell, and this was what had been described to me. We ran holding hands, not knowing where we were going except away from those that were moving towards us, stalking us as prey. We tripped over something rotten. We both screamed.

The smell of the burning fires shed a little light, reflecting off the haunting forms of human beings scavenging around as they sized us up. Some cardboard boxes had little flames in them. We hid in the dark beneath a sheet of plastic and tried not to breathe all night long. We held each other's hands tightly and could feel roaches run across us, trying to make their way into our noses. Rats were aggressive, and we were woken up by rats gnawing on our shoes. We held our cries and squeezed one another's hand; this was our only form of communication.

By daylight, a little boy named Rolando had found us. He pulled back the plastic and asked us to give him our shoes. We said no, but even though Rolando was half our size, he looked scary with the mask covering his face. He also held a knife and a stick. When he reached out his hand, he had growing folds of wounds that looked more like something alien. I didn't know it then, but it was scabies left unchecked. All the people of the dump had horrific health problems. In fact, it was the rampant venereal disease and community health problems and the stink of the dump that kept us safe from the gangs. We were considered garbage.

We stepped back from Rolando, but if you saw us from a wide-angled lens you would see that we were now in a place worse than Dante ever imagined his inferno to be. Children were eating rotten garbage; a little baby from a girl not much older than Gabriela was stored in a box to protect it from the vultures flying low over our heads. Gabriela screamed as we watched two vultures dive on the box and begin to peck the baby being stored there. Its mama was too high to notice. I tried to chase the vultures away. Now there were five, and they were almost as big as I. They pecked and squawked at me. One bit me in the small of my hand. Gabriela swung a board, hitting the bird with the nail at the end. The birds retreated. The baby cried; its eye was gone. It bled on me as I picked it up to carry it to its mother. A wild dog scampered towards us to claim the baby; this was a feast for such scavengers.

I ran and tripped, staring face to face with a wild boar, mean, snorting, and squealing as it bit Gabriela on the ankle, causing her to fall. She slapped the baby out of my hands and lifted me up as we ran to the body of a car to see the wild dog and boar fight over the right to eat a baby in front of all the subhuman inhabitants of the dump. The baby's mom was too high to know anything was happening. We were too afraid to help. A garbage truck backed over the baby and killed it, putting it out of its misery. I can still remember the crunch of the baby being crushed. The mother did not even cry. No one showed grief. Gabriela and I vomited dry heaves from the smell and the sight. Flies covered us and mosquitoes bit us.

All of the dump people would eventually die of disease—it was only a matter of when. This is the life of the poorest of the poor in the emerging world—the people without birth certificates or identity. They have no nation, no protector that does not want to use us. Here, God does not hear our prayers. Or if he hears our prayers then his people do not hear his direction or purposes. This is hell—real hell on earth, as garbage burns and our hearts turn subhuman. At least in Tegus the high altitude kept us safe from the mosquitoes that carry malaria. Rolando handed us a couple of lids from peanut butter jars to hold over our mouths and noses to block the smell. Inside the lids were glue so we could get high and numb the pain of living in Dante's inferno. This glue or paint thinner also killed brain cells, and many of the kids acted like they had brain damage. The men came over to claim us. We both tried to fight.

A crazy lady named Lucy hit the men with a baseball bat and claimed us. The men backed off as if we weren't worth the trouble. Crazy Lucy looked like someone who would kill another in his sleep. She took us to her home: a wooden box with plastic over the top with a little fire and some garbage that we would eat. Today it was rotten avocados. Lucy was crazy and talked to herself all the time. But evidently she wanted to save us from the sexual abuse she had suffered for years, so she gave us a safe place to stay.

At night the gangs would come and drop off dead bodies. Gabriela and I would hide in Lucy's box. They would take the recycling that had been found and pay for what they were given. A spoon was worth a lot. Jars, clothing, rubber tires, old wallets—it was amazing the stuff we would find. All of it was sold for almost nothing. If we could earn twenty cents a day we were doing great. We had to pay protection money to a gang to protect us from the police. Kids would mate at the age of eight to ten—if they were not being used by another old man. No one ever mentioned it, but HIV ran rampant in the dump and hunger was our constant companion. Gabriela began to sell herself for food to take care of me, and Lucy didn't seem to mind. It was a horrible thing she had to do, but she said it wasn't as bad as the abuse or slavery from before because now she got to keep the pay. The pay would often be a few pieces of stale food or costume jewelry scavenged from bodies. Each day someone was killed or injured.

Explosives would go off or infected needles would poke someone. A hog or cow living in the dump would get a kid or the vultures would get a baby. There were only a couple thousand of us living there, but as many died, there were always fresh-faced new kids the next day. They had been driven to experience their own hell by not being able to survive on the streets.

We liked the fact that once in a blue moon we would get a meal out of the relief workers and the chance to rob Americans. Their cameras, watches, or wedding rings could be sold for a week's pay when we sold them to the middle-men. We enjoyed touching the relief workers with scabies-covered hands. Or giving them lice with a hug.

Finally, it was bound to happen. Someone saw Gabriela's MS-13 tattoo, and our owners came to get us. They reminded us that we belonged to them and that we must stay in their gang or die. We told them that we would rather die, so they took Lucy and threw her off a bridge to demonstrate to everyone that they were not to be resisted. I ran down to Lucy's body out of breath from the smoke and inhalants that I had lived on. And when I reached her old, decrepit body she had a few breaths left.

She said, "Daughter, I pray to Jesus for you," and then she died.

Gabriela told me to run and crawl while she distracted the men. When MS-13 came to get us she told them she would make up for them not finding me. She was a very pretty girl and persuaded them to leave me for another day.

Δ Δ Δ

That evening, I was alone—a victim without hope. Most people never know really what it is like to have absolutely no home except hell on earth. It is a cold feeling at the core of your being swallowing your sanity, and I will never forget.

As I sat there, too sad to cry, a family returned to unload their garbage. They were poor; I had seen them before. Their youngest daughter, Belén had smiled at me another time. I was six and Belén was five. Belén was with her dad, Cruz Santos, who had grown up on the streets, robbing to stay alive. He had been taken in by an orphanage named *Manolito*. He was raised there by kindly Christians, and when he became a teenager, he left for his home country of El Salvador. There he began to run with the gangs until he met a saintly wife, Elicia. She too had been raised on the streets and had turned to Christ, becoming involved in a good church. The two fell in love and were married. Cruz began a new life to work for the church. Now his youngest daughter, Belén, kept asking him who was going to help the kids of the dump. That night, when Belén saw me, she spoke to me as a person. *"¿Cuál es su nombre, chica guapa?"* (What is your name pretty girl.)

I replied, *"Mi nombre es Penny y yo no soy una chica o incluso un ser humano."* (My name is Penny and I'm not a girl or even a human being.)

Belén turned and ran to her dad and started to cry. "If you love Jesus, Daddy, we need to adopt Penny."

So I rode home with the Santos family that night, and that was the beginning of my faith. I became a member of the Santos family, headed by a former thug named Cruz who married a beautiful Christian lady named Elicia. They had three children: Maria Jose, Pedro, and Belén. I became a member of the Santos family and they were a godsend.

The Santos family lived within a mile of the dump in a little village of squatters living on land they did not own. They did not have running water, but they did have electricity sometimes. It was like heaven to me.

The next year of my life living with the Santoses was a dream. I can't say I became a Christian, but I definitely had a big place in my heart for Christians. The first time mama Elicia called me *daughter*, I cried. My addition made three daughters, and Elicia treated us all as strong-minded, intelligent women. She was way ahead of her time in the way she wanted to be treated as a woman and the potential that she believed was in each of her daughters.

In response, I gave them all kinds of trouble. One time I asked Papa Cruz how he could believe in God when we lived so close to hell. Cruz explained that only God understood everything. He explained that he was follower of Jesus Christ because he represents more than religion. For Jesus it was all right to question. He had affirmed the questions of doubting Thomas. And you cannot have faith without doubts or answers without questions. Papa Cruz didn't know why God allowed kids to be abused in a dump, but as a follower of Jesus Christ, he was going to do everything he could to help.

The Santos family sent me to school, and I learned to read and write very quickly. English seemed to come easy for me. Maria Jose was a child prodigy at playing the violin.

I will always remember the little village one mile from the dump where everyone had a simple home made from blocks and corrugated steel roofs. The kids played football (soccer), and as the sun set, my sister played Sergei Rachmaninoff's *Rhapsody on a Theme of Paganini,* which was composed in 1934. Her violin brought humanity to our suffering and a soundtrack to our mythological crucible. Even to the most ignorant, this genius of a violin sounded like it belonged. And the sad part that was no one that heard it—the police, the gang leaders or the missionaries—ever suspected that Maria was a genius. It was so common we got used to the fact that she was a genius child prodigy. She played with the Youth Symphony of Tegus until some men broke into our home and stole her violin. Maria Jose Morales never really recovered from that atrocity—the day the music was stolen from her soul.

MS-13 eventually found out about my location, and word came that they were going to punish the whole family because Cruz had once been a member of MS-13 before becoming a pastor. We expected a death squad to come any night. A noted pastor named Jorge in our area came to our rescue, and we packed everything we could. He was sending us to the US on a temporary visa so Maria Jose could play violin with the San Francisco Youth Symphony.

When we arrived in San Francisco, we could see the men from MS-13 checking us out. They were American looking, but the colors and gang signs were easy to spot, so we simply did not show up for Maria Jose's concert. We used all our money and bought bus tickets to go to the Pacific Northwest, where we were told that Latin people could work for fair-minded farmers who needed our labor to make their farms work.

Every illegal has his own story, and ours seemed much easier than those who traveled here with untrustworthy criminals called *coyotes*. We were not the only illegals living in Finley, Washington, fifteen miles outside of Kennewick. We lived in the orchards at first with all the other illegals that this country counted on to harvest their crops. Our whole family worked during the summer. And we all worked after school. But because our dad, Cruz, was a man of leadership, integrity, and strong Christian faith, the farmers soon found that he could be trusted to run these large fruit farms. We were given a trailer house for our home. Our days of living under a bridge and never knowing plumbing were over.

There was Ku Klux Klan in Kennewick, and they expected people of color to be out of town by sundown. The African-Americans lived in East Pasco, and the railroad was the dividing line. We Latinos lived on the reservation in the Yakima Valley, north of Richland. People didn't know the difference between a Mexican, a Guatemalan, a Columbian, or a Honduran. We were all Mexicans to them. But we knew the difference, and so gangs kept us divided. I kept my tattoo on my neck and chest covered. I detested my tattoo.

We moved around with the crops and, yes, we endured the police constantly threatening us with deportation. The farmers helped to hide us. They could not afford to harvest their crops and use white labor.

△ △ △

The first time I saw Ulysses Looking Glass Sundown, we were both very young. He and his brother Patty were working alongside some of their friends—Lalo Rivas and Adolph Perez. I had not seen an Indian before.

The Latinos treated Ulee and Joey like family. Their families took them in and fed them a hot breakfast and lunch. Whole families worked together in those days. Ulee stood out like no one I had ever seen. His hair was blond and his skin was fair but freckled from the sun; he was the most muscular kid I had ever seen. His eyes always seemed to twinkle with courage and humor. I always thought dark hair and dark skin was more attractive, but there was something about this kid who spoke Spanish like Tarzan. His Spanish was so bad that it was laughable. I asked about him and they said he was an Indian. I had never heard of an Indian except in school and did not think they existed anymore.

"Isn't their hair black and their skin brown?" My brother, Pedro, told me that Ulee's brothers were mostly dark haired and dark skinned. But their mom was Scottish/Irish and that was where Ulee's looks came from. But he was more Indian than the rest.

Caleb and Elizabeth Sundown had moved to the Tri Cities—Pasco, Kennewick, and Richland, Washington—to take a small church after Caleb graduated from college and seminary. He took this church and changed its name to the Cathedral of Joy and then made it a church for all nations. The church was small; Elizabeth worked as a nurse. She worked the night shift at Kennewick General Hospital. And the seven boys worked the fields and split their time in the Wallowa Mountains about four hours away. Their grandparents helped to raise them; they were a handful. They all hunted and fished with their spare time like they were Huck Finn.

Ulee got in a lot of trouble, so his dad had a Marine friend and vet of Korea start him on Jiu Jitsu when he was in the second grade. Ulee had his black belt by the time he was in the sixth grade. He then started with a friend into Taekwondo and had his brown belt by the time he was fifteen. All the Sundown boys were outstanding basketball players, spending their time playing street ball in East Pasco with the blacks. Ulee also won the conference wrestling championship when he was in junior high after he was kicked off the basketball team. Ulee was a star wide receiver on the grade-school football team. Before he died, his older brother, Joey, was the star quarterback, who was inspired by Sunny Sixkiller, a Cherokee quarterback and basketball star from Ashland, Oregon, who dreamed of going to Oregon State but was recruited by the University of Washington. Joey and Ulee had the chance to meet Sunny Sixkiller and play basketball with him. He had a major impact on both their lives.

When Joey died at 15, Ulee, who was 13, became the quarterback and practiced passing through a tire 200 times a day all year long—even during basketball season. He threw with the same release that his hero Sunny Sixkiller had taught him. Every day, Ulee was obsessive about his workouts. He would wake up and run ten miles.

△ △ △

He and his brothers lived in the desert farmland of the Tri-Cities and spent the summers in the Wallowa Mountains of Eastern Oregon with their grandparents at their family lodge. They slept down by the river whenever they wanted. They seemed to not be afraid of anyone; the seven boys were like a young pack of wolves.

One day, as we were picking cherries, the INS showed up in force. The farmer, Mr. Allen Truman, yelled, "Run, the INS is here." But by the time we got down to the swamp bordering the cherry orchard, my sister Maria Jose and my mother Elicia were gone. Everyone was crying at the swamp. Ulee stood there as if he wanted to do something or say something. His friends were laughing. What were you running for? Your skin is white." You will never imagine how broken and lost we were to lose our family like this.

Cruz set about applying for US citizenship. Citizenship was possible because Papa Cruz was so favored by church leaders in the area and the farming community. Pedro was sixteen, but looked older, so he joined the Army and asked to go to Vietnam. His reward was citizenship. Belén and I were allowed to go to Finley Elementary School; no one asked about our citizenship. Our whole community depended on Spanish labor—and the disappearance of our family members was an unexplained horror. When Cruz became a citizen, he borrowed money from the Truman farms to go back to Honduras to look for our family.

Elicia and Maria Jose had made it on their own after being dropped off in Honduras by the INS. Finally they met a very friendly Christian wearing a hat and clothes to cover his gang tattoos. They thought this Hernando was a Godsend. Both of them were drugged and abused. They were separated and forced into prostitution; Elicia fought her way out until she got help from a kindly priest. Thankfully, the day came, and with the help of some of the churches in town, Cruz was able to travel to Honduras, where he found Elicia in sanctuary at the Catholic cathedral. They both searched for Maria Jose, but they never found her. When Cruz got there, he knew his way around the streets and the rival gangs. He had lost his daughter, the tenderhearted one who was a virtuoso violinist. She had the brains to become a doctor but would spend her life as a slave prostitute someplace in the world. No one would listen to him, and he could not get a visa to get to the nation where she remained enslaved. But he did find his beloved Elicia, and they returned with broken hearts that would never heal. Miraculously, they returned to Los Angeles where the Truman family came to get them. While Cruz had earned his citizenship, Elicia was still an illegal. Belén and I lived with the Truman family.

Cruz threw himself into his work and became very trusted by the farmers in our community, and he earned more than any Latino had ever earned—at least in this area. All the money he earned went to his attempts to find Maria Jose. He never quit trying. We never heard violin music without one of us breaking out in tears. We never had a family prayer in which she was not remembered, but we were so thankful to have our strong-willed mom back with our loving dad. Everywhere we went, we realized that boys and men stared at Belen and I. It seemed like such a dangerous world out there. After my past, to be considered attractive always felt like a curse. We both grew our hair long though, which was the style of the times, and we were both cheerleaders starting early in junior high. We both wanted to be accepted by our foster nation, and being non-citizens, we tried to hide in plain sight.

One night, a pick-up truck pulled up to our trailer. My dad, Cruz, met the four men at the door. They looked like trouble to me. I was afraid they were MS-13. He told me and Belén to go hide under the bed and asked Elicia to go get the shotgun. The men opened the door before we were ready and in Spanish told Cruz that they had run out of gas. He asked in his street-savvy way, "You ran out at my doorstep?" One of them pulled a gun and ordered him to go outside with them.

We watched from behind the drapes as he got into their car and they drove away. We never called the police, but we did contact the Truman family who ran the farms we worked for. They called the police, and within twenty-four hours, we received a ransom demand for $50,000 or our dad would be killed. We did not have close to that kind of money, but the Truman family put the money together and gave it to the FBI.

Papa Cruz disappeared; somehow the men got the money and we were all certain that they killed our dad. We don't know which gang it was—they all specialized in kidnapping and home invasions. And they targeted illegals like us. After a year they found Papa Cruz's body.

Pedro returned from his tour in Vietnam; he was now the man of our family. Later, we held a funeral service for Papa Cruz at the Salvation Army in Pasco. After, several people spoke about Cruz and what he had meant to them. I walked up to let Mama Elicia, Belen, and Pedro Santos know what Papa Cruz meant to me. As I stood there, I never liked to be in front of a crowd, I was overwhelmed by all the grief of my life: the end of my first family in a village in Honduras; becoming a slave to the MS-13 gang, living in the dump with Gabriela, the INS taking Maria Jose away. Life was not fair. I heard someone whisper – *"ella es una belleza incred*íble" or "wow, she is an amazing beauty."

I thought of all the entitled white kids who lived in our community and knew nothing of our lives—faces of the children I had met in the dump that did not even have a birth certificate let alone a nation with citizenship. I remember the children in the dump riding bicycles that had no tires with big smiles on their faces. I just began to cry—no sounds, just tears running down my face openly showing my shame and self-pity. People started to whisper. I thought, *where is Homer? Where is Maria Jose?* And then I began to sob. Not a soft sob. No one knew the injustice I had experienced. How could there be a God? How could there not be one? The sob grew louder than anyone had heard someone sob. No brave words of tribute, just a moan coming out of the heart of a girl who knew what it was to be a slave, standing at the funeral of a man who had rescued me and become more than a father figure to me; he was a genuine Christ follower.

Chapter Three

Ithaca

WE TOOK A break for the evening as the children started to become sleepy. Some wanted to stay up and listen some more. Others cried, hearing my story. I tell all not to feel sad about my story, but to be grateful that their lives are without such pain. I tell them that I am grateful, as well, to have survived. "Every day of my life is a gift," I say. "I have never taken one day for granted."

The next evening we gather again in the lodge, food sizzling and its aroma filling the air. The river again woos us and the drumbeat sounds to get our souls in rhythm with our hearts. The children want me to continue with the story of my life because they know my story belongs to their heritage.

Δ Δ Δ

My side ached, my muscles were exhausted as I struggled for oxygen and endured this pain. The desert sunshine of eastern Washington burned down on me as I forced my stride up the hill with sheer willpower, passing boys with far less tolerance for pain. As I rounded the flag, one of the women teachers in the school yelled, "You are in first Penny! You are beating all the boys! Keep it up!" My stride turned into a gallop, running down the hill as I imagined I was a horse. I was drenched in sweat. The breeze felt refreshing as I accelerated. The smell of sagebrush in the spring smelled like freedom to me: freedom from slavery, freedom to dream, and freedom to discover who I was in this great nation of opportunity. A boy at least a foot taller yelled at me as we ran. "I am not going to let a girl win, you tomboy." I smiled and picked up the pace.

No boy could keep up with me when I ran. I ran the Finley Grade School cross-country run with all the other kids in the sixth grade. I was fifty yards ahead of the fastest boys in the school when I finished. It felt to me like the male teachers stared at me. One thing I had learned in my unfortunate pilgrimage was that most men were driven by lust and a need to control. I knew I was humiliating the boys, and I enjoyed it. I had set a new school record. The male teachers berated the boys of the school for losing to me. This race was a part of our Presidential Fitness Test. It was about a mile-long run, but I made them pay; there were no girls' sports in those days. I knew that my teachers would let Mama Elicia know at the teacher-parent conference. We were all given physical fitness at Finley Elementary School. Everyone wanted the Presidential Fitness Award. I also worked hard in the classroom. All the pain of my life turned into a work ethic—like many of us who were immigrants. Rednecks used to tell me to go back to my homeland. I had no homeland. I would never be able to go back to Honduras. If I tried I would disappear, like my birth family or Papa Cruz or Maria Jose. And yet this wonderful land in the Pacific Northwest was not mine either. I was an outsider. It was a contradiction. My brown skin and accent made me invisible to many. When we spoke in Spanish, it brought too much attention to us, so we only spoke our native tongue with our immigrant friends when we worked.

The farmers we worked for were friendly; their economy depended on us, since most immigrants were not paid fairly. The Truman family was the exception—they were real Christians who had heard God's instructions and followed his purposes. They were some of the best people in the world. We were happy to be there. The teachers knew we were not citizens, but they just loved kids. Every spring, as part of the president's physical fitness program, we had an all-school race. The winner would qualify for the all Tri-City race in one of the high school stadiums. We were allowed to run the border of the school property in the spring. I, Penelope Isabela Morales Santos, held the school record. I think we were all surprised when I was invited to go to the all-city elementary track meet at Kennewick Stadium. I was the first girl ever invited to this track meet. Finley was a small school only fifteen miles from Kennewick, so we were considered part of their school district. But we were the outcasts; they called us goat ropers. But in this kids' meet at Kennewick Stadium, only the best kids in each event were invited.

There was a long jump, standing broad jump, high jump, softball throw, 50-yard dash, 100-yard dash, 440, and the 880. Yes, they called us goat ropers because we lived and worked on farms. We had a large Hispanic population who lived there and worked on the vineyards, orchards, beer hops, cornfields, etc. I had a boyfriend who was three years older than me. My teacher seemed to get a kick out of making sure I always had a boyfriend. My boyfriend was white, and his dad was a rich farmer, so Mama Elicia seemed happy that even though I was in the sixth grade, I was already going steady. His name was Kevin, and his friend, Brad, was going steady with my best friend, Julie. She was also from Central America, but she was from El Salvador. Kevin constantly gave me flowers; he had me over to his house for dinner with his family. The four of us, Julie and her boyfriend, Brad, and Kevin and I would go hang out at the pool hall. We also went to a Willie Nelson concert at the fair and rodeo. He was always really polite to me, but I did not feel good about the expensive presents that he kept getting for me. One day he bought me a diamond necklace, and when Mama Elicia saw it, she was really angry.

"In Finley, the girls get pregnant and sometimes married before they are fifteen," she warned.

Kevin did not want me to go to the all-boy city track meet. But I had no trouble telling him we were not married and that I was only in the sixth grade. We had sixteen kids on our team from Finley, each with our red Finley T-shirt. No one really believed that we had a chance against the big schools from Kennewick. We brought alternates in case our first team track person could not perform. Kevin was an alternate, so he rode on the bus with us. I was the only girl at the meet, and my one event was the half-mile. A lot of people were staring at me. I guess I was getting used to it. But just as I could see people pointing and whispering, I noticed the attention shifted as the team for Washington Grade School, one of the biggest elementary schools in Kennewick, showed up in their bus.

Washington Grade School only had one kid on the bus. It was Ulysses Looking Glass Sundown. He was such a dominant athlete that he won every event at his school and the other kids did not want to come even as an alternate. Everyone said he would be a professional athlete. At school he was actually banned from playing football on the playground because he was just too good. And in dodgeball he hit a teacher in the head who was participating, and so he was banned from that sport. He was the talk of his grade school. He stood there with his pupils dilated as if all these white people were his enemies. At the same time, he looked white. His Caucasian hair often was dressed with a feather, but in his eyes there was the wild, the native, the untamed soul that he had become famous for even in the sixth grade. His skin was light, and his eyes were brown. "Ulee," as he was called, wore an Indian choke collar. His parents were not there. His brothers, who were mostly brown with long, black, braided hair, yelled his name as they sat in the stands.

Ulee's mom was a nurse and seemed to always work to support her family. His dad was a pastor and was always on an emergency. So when it came to family, it was usually just his brothers. His coach, Mr. Snyder, was also the high school sophomore basketball coach. He acted like he had a secret weapon. Other coaches and teachers came over to talk to him about why he only had one kid on his track team. They kept mentioning Jim Thorpe, a famous Indian boy who had been good at all events; he was the whole track team, and he went on to play pro football and pro baseball. He won medals at the Olympics, but they were taken back because he was deemed a professional.

△ △ △

The track meet began with the 50-yard dash. Everyone was nervous for this first event. One boy threw up before getting into his starting stance. Each runner was given a trowel to dig starting blocks in the cinder track. Ulee just stuck his trowel in the ground like he was throwing a knife. Each of the boys running this event knew each other. They all knew they were fast, but no one knew who was the fastest. On one side was a big black kid named Marquis Lincoln; he was amazing in his speed in the 100-yard dash. People were already talking about how he was going to be a world-class runner. Next to Ulee was the city record holder in the 50. His name was Sean Dunn. This Irishman was the smallest of the boys but was quick. On the other side was another boy from East Pasco, Ulee's friend, Tyler Sherman. Again, he was the only one who could challenge Marquis Lincoln in the 100-yard dash. Everyone was Tyler's friend, and he laughed when he ran. He and his family were just plain fast. His younger sister would become a world-class sprinter in the Olympics. Most of the city turned out for the race, including judges, coaches, business leaders, and the mayor; the grandstands were full. All the boys seemed nervous, except Ulee, who was whistling a Christian hymn. Ulee had athleticism in his blood as his great grandfather was the legendary Jackson Sundown. Jackson was the nephew of Chief Joseph who as a boy was put in charge of the horses during the Nez Perce retreat from Wallowa to Canada. He had been one of the few who had escaped and made it to join Sitting Bull in Canada and later he came back to the states and became the world rodeo champion after the age of fifty. He was a legend for his athleticism.

Ulee kept whistling as the boys took their starting stances. The fifty-yard dash is all about the start, and Ulee had ten yards on everyone. He didn't need to dig his starting blocks in the cinder. His whistling and cocky confidence had distracted the others. Some of the other boys' dads were yelling at the starter that the Indian boy was cheating. Some of the other boys wanted to fight, but Ulee's six brothers were all around him at the finish line. They walked to the middle of the field, where he was given a blue ribbon.

The rest of the track meet was an amazing performance. Ulee won the 50, 100, 440, high jump, standing broad jump, running broad jump, and softball throw: seven blue ribbons in all. People just shook their heads and said, "We have another Jim Thorpe here."

The final event was the half-mile. I dreaded that I had agreed to go to the all-city meet. We walked over to start, and Ulee looked me in the eyes and said, "Hi, Penny." I didn't know that he knew my name, and he spoke to me in Spanish. "*Hola Penelope. ¿Cómo estás? Es bueno verte en esta carrera de atletismo. Que Dios los bendiga ya que se corre el major.*" (Hello Penelope . How are you? It's good to see you in this track meet. May God bless you as have your best run.)

I didn't speak back; he seemed so proud. I wanted to beat him so bad.

I came out running as fast as I could. I needed to be in the lead, even if just for a while. Every girl depended on me. All my anger, all my fear, all my insecurities made me run. And after 100 yards I was in first with Ulee running right behind me. As another boy tried to pass me, Ulee blocked his route and moved to my side. I looked to the side, and his stride was so natural that it seemed like he wasn't trying. He spoke again to me in Spanish.

"You are doing good Penny. I think you can win this one. "Keep it up."

I ran faster; he was making me mad. It looked like he was going to let me win. That really did it. I pushed even harder out in front of him. That created a space that three boys used to push by both of us. He said in Spanish, "I am sorry, I should not have let them through."

And then he took off like we had been standing still. He caught the boys, who had a pretty good lead, and then beat them all to the finish line. I followed him on his sprint and had never ran so fast in all my life. As he approached the finish line, he turned around surprised to see me come up on his side.

I smiled at him and said, "I think you have a crush on me, Ulee." He blushed and I passed him to win first place; the only race he lost. I was sure he had not let me win—I had outsmarted him. It was such a victory for my family, my school, and for girls. But the first one to congratulate me was Ulee. "*Usted es un ganador Penny."* (You are the winner, Penny.)

Ulee had won every event at the all-city track meet except the 880, which I won. An AAU (Amateur Athletic Union) coach was talking to him, as was the high school football coach. Afterwards, his brothers ran over and tackled him and had a dogpile on him. They looked like such a fun family. Belén, my sister, gave me a hug and said, "You really were amazing, Penny." All the females at the track meet waited to congratulate me. I can't tell you how proud I was when I was the only one other than Ulee to win a first place. Mama Elicia cried as she hugged me and whispered in my ear, "You are a very special girl; God has a wonderful, wonderful plan for your life."

△ △ △

I lived with my mother, Elicia, my brother, Pedro, his wife, Rosi, and my sister, Belén. We lived in the trailer my dad had earned, and Pedro worked at my dad's job for the Truman family, running their orchards. Mama Elicia had always been extremely bright. While in Honduras, she had gotten a bachelor of arts in political science from the top-rated university in Honduras, Central American Technology University, in Tegus. While in the US, she continued to read everything she could get her hands on. She went on to get her master's degree in history through Washington State University. Her intellect helped her become a citizen of the US. She had friends on both sides of the border.

Elicia became a leader in the Hispanic community and was a person the white society knew they could trust. She kept her radical ideas and admiration for Caesar Chavez to herself. She realized that most of the white community were not ready to hear her ideas. She had an amazing sense of history, of how things stood and where they were going. As you can tell, I am very proud of Mama Elicia. She taught me to make up for being objectified by being the top student in my class. She wanted me to be a doctor, just as she had her missing daughter, Maria Jose, and I didn't want to disappoint her. At physical education, I could beat the boys in running. Even though I always worked several jobs, life still seemed like a game in those days. Our lives were still painted with sadness and grief: the loss of our sister, Maria Jose, and then the kidnapping of our dad, Cruz.

Pedro never talked about it, but he did his best to be the man of our family, and the farmers trusted his work smarts, his people skills, and his faithful integrity.

△ △ △

The Sundown family found a home when their parents moved from the reservation to the Tri-Cities. They were there to be pastors at a little independent evangelical church called the Cathedral of Joy, an all-nation's church. Caleb and Elizabeth were poor enough that they qualified to live in the government projects. It was government housing for the poor called Sunny Slope Homes.

In reality, it was hard for the Sundown family to live in the Tri-Cities. Ulee had to fight from the beginning. The first day of school as he walked to kindergarten, a big boy punched him in the face, bloodying his nose and saying, "Welcome to the neighborhood, mother." Fights were arranged by neighbor kids. Ulee lost more fights than he won and usually had to fight more than one kid. He worked in the fields with the Latinos, and most of his friends came after a fistfight to get to know each other. Because his skin was light and his hair was blondish brown, he had to prove himself more than his brothers. And he had to fight for his younger brothers. Sometimes they all fought together. Fighting was their main preoccupation—that and a family love of reading.

One day, Ulee came home from school in the third grade, and several older boys in high school had beaten him up. They had picked him up and thrown him against a wall, which broke his nose. He deserved it because he used to mouth-off to the big kids and then he would dodge them, running circles so that a half a dozen could not catch him.

His mom had become a licensed practical nurse, and after taking him to the hospital, his dad talked to a fellow Korean vet who taught Jiu Jitsu. Ulee had his black belt by the time he was in the fifth grade and enrolled with a friend in Taekwondo (Korean kicking and striking fighting), and he had his black belt by the time he was in the ninth grade. If any of his four brothers got into trouble—Ulee was there in a furious way to protect them. It was the spirit of the bear. After age thirteen he would never forget watching his brother Joey give his life fighting a grizzly to save the lives of his brothers.

The rule was, that if you picked a fight with one of the Sundown brothers, you picked a fight with all of them. And even when they were in grade school, more than one high school kid learned that seven tough little Nez Perce warriors all fighting together were a foe they did not want to mess with. People referred to them as a pack of wolves. And with their dog, Argos, the meanest sort of man would steer clear. Another time, the Sundown boys snuck out as they liked to do during the summer, and they caught about twenty teenage boys breaking into their dad's church and stealing the sound system. The seven of them, Joey, Ulee, Patty, Jacky, Stick, Heath, and Whitey, all stood in the doorway and the twenty big boys had to retreat. (This was before Joey was 15 and lost his life fighting the grizzly.) The neighborhood gang made a dash at them, and the Sundown boys let out war cries as they took down big boy after big boy. When the police finally arrived, they were holding down ten boys. Ulee had one in a scissor lock with his legs and two with neck locks with his arms. The police had a good laugh as they arrested the big boys who were taken down by a pack of Nez Perce little boys.

Δ Δ Δ

When we were in the ninth grade. I was at Kennewick High School for cheerleading tryouts. Like all girls, I was wearing a miniskirt, which was quite fashionable at that time. My senior boyfriend was walking me to his car across the field. Ulee was at a track trying the pole vault for the first time. "If you make the qualifying height, you can get our team a third," the track coach told Ulee.

Ulee was uncharacteristically nervous. He knew rivals wanted him to fail, even some kids on his own team. He got at the back of the runway with butterflies going in his stomach. He then sang a song out loud, as if he was a knight getting ready to charge. He then turned and looked at me, calling out "You are a beautiful princess, and I dedicate my every victory to you." I blushed; my boyfriend got mad. And Ulee charged down the runway. It was amazing for his first pole vault. He gave his full weight to the fiberglass pole as he planted it. He kicked his legs high in the air and vaulted way above the qualifying height. But he overshot the foam pit and landed outside on the hard ground. Everyone looked away. I could hear people say, "That has got to hurt," and they were laughing at this ninth-grade boy and the declaration of his love like a fool from Cervantes' novel. It may have been one of the most romantic moments of my life. I can't say I fell in love with Ulee that day, but I was blushing while everyone—except my boyfriend—laughed.

Chapter Four

Sundowns

AS I TELL my story I try to be mindful of young ears. It's important they understand hardship, but that they not be frightened or intimidated. I don't want them to fear romance, or sex or love. Yet, I also refrain from being too graphic. I don't want to make ugly what can be beautiful. It is through truth that my family will become strong. I continue.

Δ Δ Δ

The Sundowns were the only family I felt entirely comfortable around—except for my own. There were so many warriors with such virtue in that family. Grandfather Ephraim and Grandmother Quanah seemed so in love even in their frail age. The whole community loved them. Pastor Caleb was one of a kind and was considered to be a pillar of the community. His wife, Elizabeth, was a favorite nurse in the Tri-Cities and was so popular with just about everyone in Kennewick. And then there were the boys.

Every spare second, Ulee's family would either work the fields together for money to get by or glean fields to can for the winter. They would hunt, fish, and gather mushrooms and asparagus. There were plenty of ducks, pheasants, quail, wild turkey, and even a wild hog now and then. The big mule deer were winter meat for their family and friends. All the boys had recurve bows. They shared an Ithaca twelve-gauge shotgun and they had a British 303, their grandfather's gun; a Winchester 45-70, which was a bear gun; and a Remington 700 that was loaned to their dad by a rich person in their church. The boys made money from bounty for the pelts of coyotes, ground squirrels, and mountain lions. They stayed summers at the cabin in the Wallowas with their grandparents and also made the four-hour trip to Lake Wallowa every chance they could get. When the boys were not hunting, fishing, or backpacking, they were playing sports. They used to walk around the Tri-Cities looking for a sandlot game of football or to get into a community center to play basketball. They each would do an intense workout because they all wanted to be pro athletes. They did thousands of pushups and pull-ups. Their dad bought them some free weights, and they loved to work out.

Ulee threw a football through an old tire 200 times a day because that is was what Sunny Sixkiller said to do. When Ulee was in the ninth grade, he was kicked off the basketball team for fighting, and he switched to wrestling, where he won the conference championship for his weight class. When he entered junior high, he was discovered at a boxing match after school by Spankee (a Cuban boxer who attended Ulee's dad's church) who enrolled him in his gym, which was a part of the Golden Glove boxing program. Ulee never went to any tournaments because of all his other commitments to work and sports, but he knocked a few champions out while he was sparring. Their dad, Caleb, wanted all his boys to be pro basketball players

There were other large families in Eastern Washington. Some African-American, some Hispanic, but all were viewed as gangs. They fought one another as teams, almost like it was the thing to do—no hard feelings intended. Most got involved in crime, and all of them were involved in sports. The neighborhood the Sundown boys grew up in was tough. Lots of kids ended up in prison eventually.

As we got ready to go into high school, Mama Elicia decided that I should go to the big Kennewick High School. It was one of the biggest high schools in the state of Washington. I was getting far too much attention from the boys for my looks at Finley School where many of the girls would get pregnant while in high school. In my sophomore year at Kennewick I was selected as a varsity cheerleader, and one of the cute senior boys, who was a state wrestling star, asked me to go steady with him. I think the thing that saved me was that I had three jobs. I cleaned houses, I worked for the Bon Marche on their fashion board as a model, and I worked as a cashier for Tri-City Pools. I also babysat with my extra time. My nose was always in a book because I was determined to become a doctor, not a teenaged pregnant bride.

I can't say I didn't enjoy the attention from all the boys. But Mama Elicia watched after Belén and me like the protective mother she was. It was the wild 1960s, and I tried drinking alcohol, smoking grass, even mescaline at parties, but each time, Mama Elicia would show up and pull Belén and me out of the party.

Of course, I admired Ulee. Almost everyone did. But I was not attracted to him. As I said, there was warpath in his eyes—he was not a ladies' man and could hardly talk to girls. He was as full of machismo as a young man could ever be. And he was not the type of person anyone felt close to, except maybe his sports friends and coaches.

Ulee had been kicked out of school for a very serious fight. The principal asked him not to return. The coaches protested, saving Ulee from expulsion. But Ulee's temper could turn violent, especially when a family member was threatened. One time a Pasco football player was picking a fight with Hector Whitebird (Whitey) at Zips hamburger stand on a Friday night. When Ulee looked up and saw the senior kicking his little brother while he was on the ground, he lost control and flew into the fight, which was so intense that the police were called. Ulee was sent to the juvenile delinquent jail.

After Ulee's release, the principal tried to kick him out of school. He called Ulee's dad in and told them that Ulee was going to end up spending his life in prison. Ulee's dad stood up and got in the principal's face, telling him that Ulee was a good kid, that God had a plan for his life and he would not allow anyone to prophesize differently about him.

He said, "You should be ashamed of yourself. I passed kids doing drugs in their cars in your parking lot. Ulee has paid his debt to society and learned the consequences of fighting." Pastor Sundown gave that principal a sermon he would never forget. Ulee was allowed back in school just in time for football season.

During this growing up time in the Tri-Cities, there were protests and race riots. Many of the football games ended up with whites fighting blacks, and the police would come and haul blacks to jail. If you were a teen or an adult and you had dark skin, after the tear gas cleared, you were going to get arrested. The Tri-Cities was not Detroit, but at times racial tensions were just as intense, and there was amazing conflict over the Vietnam War. Many of the cowboys and farmers, which made up the Cathedral of Joy, Reverend Caleb Sundown's church, never thought anything but duty, honor, and country during the war. At the same time, the baby boom generation that didn't trust anyone over thirty had a majority protesting a war that nobody fully understood.

Oddly, the turmoil of the 1960s also pushed a lot of young people toward religion. Many people started to envision Christianity as lived by Jesus Christ. Their slogan was "Christ is the answer." It was called the Jesus People movement.

Δ Δ Δ

There was an older man named Ken Johnson who contracted cancer and was being treated at Kennewick General Hospital where Elizabeth Saunders Sundown worked on the night shift. This group of nurses had so much fun working together that race or economics didn't bother them at all. They were all best friends for years. Liz, as her friends called her, quickly called her husband to come down and visit this nice, hard-working man who wanted to have a certainty that he was going to go to heaven. Caleb traveled down to the hospital to meet Mr. Johnson and begin a conversation about how this man from a holiness background could have a certainty of salvation. After many conversations, Mr. Johnson prayed with Caleb and had a new sense of faith in Christ in his life. Mr. Johnson called his son Joshua in to talk to him in the hospital.

He said, "Son, I am going to die, and I want you to promise me that you will give your life to Christ so I can see you in heaven someday."

Joshua couldn't make that promise to his dad, but he said, "I'll try, Dad." Six months after his dad died, Joshua visited Pastor Caleb regularly in his office to ask questions about God and what it would be like to follow Christ. Finally, one morning, as he was shaving, he looked in the mirror and said, "I can think this thing to death. Am I going to live for God or not?" And right there he gave his life to Jesus Christ.

The next day, he came into Caleb's office to tell him. He was shy about it. He fumbled with his baseball hat and finally blurted out that he had given his life to Christ and that he would have Caleb's back for the rest of his life as they tried to spread the gospel.

Joshua was a hard-working carpenter—a handsome man who was a part of the fire department underwater rescue team. He was put in the position of being the youth pastor at the Cathedral of Joy. He would preach with his Bible rolled up in his hands like a hammer and share the good news with kids in such a way that they knew that he would be there for them. The group began to grow exponentially until one of my friends invited me to come. I sat there and listened every week. I would feel guilty about everything that had taken place in the past.

During this time, I had been modeling and a cheerleader. My grades were good and I wanted to be a physician, but being a beauty queen felt superficial. Every word that Joshua preached struck me in the heart: about forgiveness, living guilt free, healthy relationships, and Jesus. One night, as I lay in my bed, something woke me. It was someone's voice whispering my name. It sounded like my birth mother and father. I wasn't scared—I got up and saw the moonlight streaming into my room. Then I heard Maria Jose's voice in my dreams. I remembered so clearly her singing *Turn Your Eyes Upon Jesus* in Spanish, so sweetly and courageously, as she faced Hernando Cortez.

"Penny, go to your Bible."

Then I heard what I believe was the voice of Jesus. He said, "Read it." His voice was so kind. I opened my Bible, and it fell open to the gospel of *John 3:16*, and I fell on my knees and gave my heart to Jesus Christ. The moonlight streamed in the window, and I knew I was a Christ follower. The next morning, I told Mama Elisa and Belén. They both went to church with me the next week.

I told Joshua that I had become a Christian and Pastor Caleb baptized me in the worship service. When Ulee saw me sitting with my boyfriend and getting up to be baptized, he could not believe it.

When I tried to go to Bible study, so many of the girls were such gossips that they and their moms began to tear me apart behind my back about my past. They called me Mexican, greaser, and I even heard myself referred to as a spic and a slut. The Jesus who Joshua Johnson talked about just didn't seem to be at church. I did get to see Ulee walk the aisle to commit his life to Christ during one of his dad's messages. I was very proud of him. Maybe this would help him to find peace.

I am not going to lie; beyond my misgivings, going to high school as a sophomore in my cheerleading outfit was fun. Football in these parts was so festive. Kennewick was rated the top team in the state in the highest division. The stands were full during our games, almost as many spectators as small colleges. High school varsity football was the focus of the entire town. Many people said the culture in the cowboy communities of Eastern Washington reminded them of football in Texas. There were all-city pep rallies and dances after each game. It was all a very big deal. Being a star on the team meant status and recognition. Ulee craved both.

Ulee was only a sophomore and named the second team varsity quarterback. He was still a bit small compared to a lot of the seniors who had lived in the weight room and used steroids. The starting quarterback was a tough guy with a full beard and already balding as a senior in high school. The team ran the ball most plays, which was the style of the Vince Lombardi days.

For the opening season inter-squad scrimmage, the stadium was full. It was a benefit for the Shriners, and it brought a lot of attention and local news coverage. Kennewick football was divided in two for the game. The black jersey team was the varsity first string. The orange jersey team was the second team. When Ulee walked on the field, the coach of the second team told him to run the ball and not to pass. Ulee had other ideas.

"Go deep," he told his pass receivers. "Everyone else block." The wide out was a crazy senior named Frank Wolf that had never gotten to play because he was suspended half the time for drugs and alcohol. Ulee barked out the signals, and his voice was so high that all the men on the opposing team started to laugh. These senior players were not only taking testosterone shots but they used speed just before games to play at a level that was just brutal. My brother Pedro called them Neanderthals.

Ulee dropped back, gliding as if he had done this a thousand times. He pumped the ball to the left side of the field. Then he snapped back and hit crazy Frank Wolf on a deep banana shaped pattern. He was covered by two defenders but the tight spiral came in where only Crazy Frank Wolf could catch it. The defenders bounced off, almost in disbelief. Crazy Frank waltzed into the end zone. The coach of the second team was irate despite the touchdown. He called the plays, not Ulee.

"You're out Indian," he screamed at Ulee.

Ulee was the official punt returner, so once they had stopped the first team the coach put him back in to take the punt return. The punter really got a hold of it, and it flew over Ulee's head as Ulee ran full speed into the end zone to retrieve it.

The coach yelled at Ulee to let the ball roll into the end zone.

"No Ulee—no let it go."

Ulee caught it over his shoulder and, with his blazing speed, ran the ball to mid-field. He broke several tackles on the way back, looking like an athlete that outclassed his competition. At half time, the coaches tore into Ulee, telling him that this was not sandlot football; they were trying to learn the wishbone running offense. This was not a passing team. Ulee acted contrite, winning back his coach's confidence.

In the second half, Ulee got to start. And again, he ignored the coach's game plan to run the ball. Four passes later, Ulee's team scored. The crowd was impressed—the student body was amazed, and half the coaching staff was wondering why they weren't going to work with this young quarterback. They put Ulee back in. This time he ran the wishbone triple option as directed, but he came out so fast he missed the hand-off to the fullback and scrambled, carrying the ball himself. Ulee raced eighty yards and scored. After the scrimmage, the coaches wanted to talk to him. The kid had talent, but he was hardheaded and a wildcard. They couldn't trust him on the field as quarterback.

"You can stay on varsity and return kicks, punts, play special teams and sub in as a receiver and a defensive back. But you're no longer going to play quarterback."

When Ulee walked into the locker room after the game he was met with taunts from some of the older kids on the team, most notably the starting quarterback whom he had just shown up.

"We don't need any savages on our team," The senior quarterback said.

Ulee tried to step around him, and a defensive end, who was the friend of the quarterback, kneeled behind him while the senior quarterback pushed him over. Ulee fell hard, hitting his head on the concrete. Before he could get up, the quarterback was on top of him, punching him repeatedly in the face. Ulee was half unconscious before he knew what was happening. There was no one on the varsity team that was going to step up for him. None of his brothers or friends were on varsity at this point. The coaches closed their door and acted like they didn't hear anything. It was all over in a couple of minutes, and then everyone went back to their former business, acting like nothing had taken place. Ulee got up, walked to his locker, and dressed without showering.

△ △ △

As he walked home, I drove by with my senior boyfriend in his brand new red Dodge Charger. When I saw Ulee's face, I told my boyfriend, who was a senior wrestling star, to drop me off. I ran over to Ulee and asked if I could walk him home.

Ulee laughed. "Isn't the man supposed to walk the lady home?"

I coyly replied, "Not when a girl is as tough as I am."

Ulee thought that the last thing he needed now was a romantic relationship. I was not really interested in boys that way either— not after my nightmare childhood. But there was a friendship between the two of us that had been slowly developing for some time. Maybe it was that his brother had died and I had lost my sister and stepdad. We both felt close even though we did not know each other very well, and it was based on deep respect that was more profound than either of us realized in our crazy lives.

"Why do you get in so many fights?" I asked. "I think you lose more than you win."

Ulee tried to laugh, but it made his face hurt. He said, "No one understands me, including myself."

I said, "I thought you played magnificently today."

"What part?" asked Ulee.

"I don't understand football; it bores me. I heard your name on the loudspeaker quite a bit. You made a home run didn't you?"

Ulee pushed me playfully. "There are no home runs in football!"

We both laughed.

When we got to his house, since he didn't have his driver's license, it was a fifteen-mile ride home on the basket of an old bicycle. I started out pedaling as all his brothers laughed, with Ulee in the basket. We were both worn out about half the way there, and then Ulee pulled over at a pasture of a friend of his and grabbed an Appaloosa there. Bareback, the Nez Perce boy gave me, a peasant Honduran girl, a ride home on the beautiful Appaloosa.

When he helped me off the horse he said, "Thanks for being a friend."

The next day, our family started to get phone calls, and then when Mama Elicia would answer the phone the caller would hang up. There must have been at least seven. Finally, I answered the phone; it was Ulee asking me if I would go out with him on a date and go swimming to the Kennewick Lagoon. I said I was busy and had to babysit, so sadly he hung up. The next week he tried again, and once again I had to work. He called me a couple of days later and I told him I had to babysit.

He said, "I will pay you fifty cents an hour to go on a date with me."

I was insulted. "I am not for sale."

He said, "I am sorry, I just want to go swimming with you."

So I said, "Okay, tomorrow after school."

After school, he came up and asked me if I was ready to go.

I said, "No—I wasn't feeling well."

He was crushed. I did not want to be seen in a bikini—I could not stand the way men looked at me—so I made up the story of being sick. We both knew I was lying. My friends scolded me as he walked away. They all had a crush on him. I told them I had a boyfriend and I had no business going out with him.

They advised me to break up with my boyfriend. I told them I wasn't that kind of girl. That night, my boyfriend and I decided that he was leaving for college next spring and that he wanted to date college girls, so we broke up. Ulee called me again soon after. He was a man who did not give up. This time he asked me out to a movie and dinner. We were both so shy the whole evening we didn't talk except to say hi and goodbye. He did hold my hand on the way out of the theatre. I thought we would never go out again. He was sweating he was so nervous. And during the movie he did not watch the movie, he just watched me. The next time, he asked me out to go bowling and play miniature golf. I asked him why he stared at me the whole time during the movie.

"I'm sorry," he said. "I can't hardly breathe when you are in the room—you are more beautiful than Helen of Troy or Roxanne, whom Alexander the Great had to conquer the world to meet. You are Guinevere of Camelot or Dulcinea of Don Quixote Del La Mancha. You are Penelope, and I am Odysseus, and I would slay an ogre to win your favor."

I giggled; he was so over the top. Then I looked at him sternly and said, "Don't objectify me!"

"What does that mean?" he asked.

I told him to look it up.

On our second date, he gave me a Bible and asked if we could pray to start the date. His prayer was so sincere it was obvious that he did not objectify me—he really cared for me.

When we bowled, I was so bad I dropped the ball backwards, and we both laughed so hard. When we played miniature golf, I kicked off my shoes to play—moccasins were in style then. He said he loved my feet—we both laughed the whole time. He was so funny—I never relaxed that much with anyone in all my life. When he walked me home, I asked him if he was going to be a pro athlete.

"I would like to, but I gave my life to Jesus, and I want most of all to be a pastor and serve people like Jesus." That was when

I loved him. His words were so inspiring. He was John Kennedy and Martin Luther King Jr. all rolled up into this silly native boy who had hero written all over him.

When we got home, I knew he was going to kiss me. I just didn't know he had never had a girlfriend or kissed before. He closed his eyes and puckered up—way up. Then he kissed and missed me by about four inches. I turned and giggled and ran into the house to tell Mama Elicia and Belén. We laughed so hard we could not breathe, especially because Pedro heard him walking home singing. *"Zipadee do dah zipadee day, my oh my what a wonderful day."*

Δ Δ Δ

We were young and in love. I made him a blueberry pie in the shape of a heart. His brothers were always spying on us. We both had part-time jobs, in addition to trying hard at school, so our dates were once a week, and we sat next to each other in church. He gave his testimony at church, and I was inspired to hear him speak; he was such an idealistic Christian. I really didn't care for his sporting events. He played summer basketball, and everyone said he was amazing, but I didn't know. He was genuinely a nice guy. He would see a game going with little kids, and we would pull over and I would watch him out there playing with the kids in his undersized church suit. He was a horrible dresser with no sense of style.

Ulee taught Sunday school and visited the elderly at the old folk's home, holding a worship service for them. He visited the insane asylum and played football with a boy named Danny who was blind and would play like he was a sports announcer while they played. We had Greek mythology together, and the teacher always started class by telling the class of the weekly athletic exploits of Ulee, who he called "golden arm."

Old people would stop and tell him how to play better—little kids would follow us and throw something at him to get his attention. Every young hoodlum who didn't have a dad—he watched out for them. The little thugs of the town made up his Sunday school class. He taught nearly fifty boys in that class. Mama Elicia, Belén, and Pedro loved him—he always did the dishes and mowed our lawn. Pedro liked him because he spoke fluent Spanish and always helped on projects around the house. I ate dinner at his house and met his grandparents and all his brothers. His brothers tripped all over themselves to make me feel a part of the family. I made him picnic lunches of fried chicken and we played tennis, went fishing. We laid down on the Columbia River bank near where the archeologist would someday find the 9,000-year-old Kennewick man" (a forefather of the Nez Perce and the Mayans). We lay on his Indian blanket and just looked at the clouds for hours.

Sometimes Ulee and I talked for hours. I soon learned about the one thing that troubled him most. The story of Joey, his closest friend and older brother's death.

As Ulee told me the story of Joey's death fighting the bear, he shared so many things he thought he could have done. I saw the tears in his eyes, and he cried from his heart in front of me confessing his sins to me, his sister in Christ. So I slowly, with no emotion, told him that I had not been living a virtuous life. He took my hand as a friend, not as jilted boyfriend. I went on and explained that I had been abused when I was six by MS-13.

"My brother was abused and sold into slavery. I was turned out as a prostitute. I never thought I could really believe in God after this life in hell," I said.

Ulee told me that sometimes he struggled to believe in God, but even if there wasn't a God he wanted to be like his father and grandfather. The stars were out in full panoramic display as we sat in Columbia Park. Under those stars, he promised me that he would protect me and that hell could not keep him away from building a loving family with me.

I told Ulee as I cried, "This is a promise you cannot keep. It is a fanciful myth in the mind of a native boy who has never seen the horrible evil that I have experienced firsthand. When I was stolen away and terribly abused, I prayed with all my heart to a loving God to send me a hero to save me. I was thinking of my daddy. He must have been killed trying to be a hero. This world destroys heroes, and I know in my heart that evil is stronger than kindness and heroism." Ulee cried as hard as I did. We just held each other lost in the pain of our broken hearts.

Δ Δ Δ

Ulee and I picnicked a lot. I made lunches with Honduran food and fruit pies, and Ulee tried to ride his bike while carrying this huge picnic basket. He tried to be macho, but he could not keep up with me. I was fast on my bike. We spread out the Nez Perce blanket that his grandparents had given to me. And we ate lunch and laughed. He told me how beautiful my eyes were. I don't remember the words, but he always said I was more beautiful every time he saw me. He said he could get lost in my eyes for eternity. He was so corny, so romantic, that every time he said something, it made me laugh. Ulee never knew anything about popular culture, and every time he used a romantic line it was from a song on the radio and he didn't know it.

He would say something like, "I'm a believer I couldn't leave her if I tried," or "something in the way you move," or "Ain't no mountain high enough to keep me from you."

In my mind I would think of the artist that wrote those words and just start giggling. I would tell him, "That is a song," and he would get mad and say all the rock and rollers were taking all the great lines from him.

Finally, one Friday night, Ulee got his chance to play varsity football as quarterback. It was a home game, so everyone was there. There was one person I didn't want to see.

Hernando Cortez heard that I was in the Tri-Cities, and he appointed Raul Roberto Diablo as the head of the local chapter of MS-13 to find me. A new level of evil began to cast its shadow over our cities.

The starting senior quarterback had his hand broken as sophomore Norwegian Randy Halvorson accidently stepped on it when he was down. At the time Kennewick was behind 0 to 8. Ulee came in and it was his dream game. Ulee had thrown five touchdown passes, four to Rod Halvorson whose athleticism seemed unstoppable. Rod was six-foot five, fast, strong and could catch anything. His twin brother Randy caught the other touchdown and looked so much like Rod that the opposing team thought they were seeing double. Randy was also the punter and kicker and at a muscular six-foot five he was a formidable tackler after the kick. Randy was also a basketball star who was already being scouted by the University of Washington. Ulee had run for three touchdowns and seemed like he could score at will as

Kennewick walloped Bora of Boise, Idaho, fifty-six to eight.

After the game, I ran out to kiss my boyfriend, but Raul emerged in the frenzy, grabbed me and kissed me in all the confusion. Then he showed me a handgun. Raul was strong— and maybe twenty-seven years old. He was covered in satanic tattoos from head to toe. He had that look of someone who had served hard time in prison and was a complete psychopath. A policeman at the game saw him force himself on me but he was afraid to do anything. Raul exuded hate and power. He grabbed me by my long dark hair.

"You belong to me or your boyfriend is going to die on this field."

We walked to Raul's car surrounded by his goons, and there stood the senior quarterback, with some of his Neanderthal senior football players.

"What the hell is going on over here?" he said with a splint on his hand and chewing tobacco in his mouth. He was trying to be a tough guy—a hero. Raul took out his gun and pointed right into the nose of the senior athlete.

"Being a hero here is a lot different than on the football field. Are you sure you want to play the tough guy?"

The senior quarterback just looked at the ground, and each of the hoodlums spit on him. MS-13 had Belén with them also. I was terrified; they had given her some kind of drug and she didn't know where she was. Raul kissed me again, smelling of alcohol, tobacco, and just plain bad breath. I punched him in the nose—making it bleed.

"My boyfriend is going to find out," I said, "and he does not like bullies."

"Si little sister," Raul said. "You mean football players are tough?" The MS-13 gang pointed their guns at the senior quarterback and his Neanderthal friends and they ran like scared rabbits.

As the tough guy senior football players ran one way, my brother Pedro ran up to the gang with his farm-working Latino friends. Raul grabbed me by the neck, and his henchmen just beat down Pedro to the point where I was afraid he would die. Remember, Pedro had served in Vietnam, and he was a tough vet, but no match for the MS-13 guys. While they were beating up

Pedro, Ulee's littlest brothers tried to help. Whitey was knocked out cold, and Dunk had his arm broken by the vicious gang members.

Just then, out of nowhere, old Argos came flashing in from the dark with primitive viciousness. He knocked over one gang member, biting him in the neck and drawing a lot of blood. He spun around like he did when he was fighting the bear and grabbed Raul by the testicles, inflicting great pain. I grabbed Belén by the hand and ran to the alley behind the science building. Belén cuddled up with Argos as he licked both of us, showing us he would protect us with his life. He was such a cute dog with his soft floppy ears. Just when we thought we were safe, we heard a deafening shot. Raul killed Argos. The gang grabbed us, laughing as we walked by my big brother and Ulee's little brothers beaten half unconscious. We drove away. I was crying, and Belén was out of her mind, and I knew that life as I knew it was over. All my dreams, my faith and my loves were gone again. Why would God allow this to happen?

Raul took us to east Pasco to a place the police were afraid to go. I don't know how many people were there. Half were drunk or high. Men and women were acting like gangsters. Even the Hell's Angels were there to form an alliance over drug profits. They threw Belén around from man to man. I sat humiliated on Raul as he groped me. I was a poor example for Belen, but she was too high to notice. I sat compliantly a slave again. Once you have suffered helplessness and abuse it is easy to fall back into the same "deer in the headlights" syndrome.

Then the door smashed opened from the force of a Harley motorcycle. It was Ulee. He looked fierce and had the black smudge that football players wear under their eyes and smeared down his cheeks like war paint.

Raul pulled his gun and swore at Ulee, "Get out of here kid or we will kill you where you stand. Ulee spoke calmly but with pent up anger.

"You hurt my two little brothers, you killed my dog, and you treat this little girl like property.

He pointed at me, sitting on the lap of a thirty-five-year-old Hell's Angel, who was groping me. And you are molesting the most virtuous woman in the world, the love of my life, Penelope

Morales Santos.

Raul laughed, "Oh you noticed, kid!"

"I am a Nez Perce warrior and I have been preparing all my life for a moment such as this." Ulee walked up, while Raul stood up, throwing me to the side.

I cried out, "Ulee just leave. This man is evil and he will kill you. I don't love you—I am not worth it."

Raul pointed his gun at Ulee, pushing it into his face. Raul towered over Ulee as a muscular full-grown man and his tattoos were terrifying, covering his face. Ulee slapped Raul; Plains natives would consider it the bravest of acts to slap your enemy with an open hand. It is called counting coup.

"You offend me by treating women like this. And you offend God. Today you do not meet a victim but a warrior."

Everyone laughed; I sobbed, afraid my prayers were answered—a hero had come to rescue me. The back doors came open, and in walked Ulee's other brothers and cousin. In addition, were Pastor Joshua's two sons and daughter. They had heard about the confrontation and went home to retrieve their cache of weapons. The Sundown kids were outnumbered. Then, through the other doors came the African-American gangs with about twice as many black friends with some connection to sports all carrying handguns and knives; one even carried a javelin from track. My big brother Pedro had recovered enough to be there with a shotgun; he had returned with his Latino friends, now with guns. The muscular Rod and Randy Halvorson came in with their two brothers and a half dozen Norwegian 'Viking' friends ready for a fight. The tables were turned; the good guys had twice as many as MS-13 and their allies had on premise.

"Okay sophomore, it's between you and me for the Penny," Raul said.

Raul tackled Ulee, but Ulee fell back and kicked him over his shoulder in a perfect Jiu Jitsu move. Raul flew through the air and broke a table on his way down. But he was drunk with evil rage and he grabbed a knife and lunged at Ulee, cutting him across the face and leaving a scar. Ulee pulled out his grandfather's bowie knife and it was a bloody fight. They both slashed and punched and kicked each other, with Raul having the advantage by height and weight. Finally, Ulee took Raul's arm and almost broke it as he took the knife away from him. Ulee threw the knives on the ground.

Now they boxed, and Ulee dominated. Every punch by Raul missed, as Ulee bobbed and weaved and landed well-practiced combinations. Raul's face was all messed up, but there was an evil inside of him that gathered more and more strength. He grabbed Ulee, head-butted him, and then proceeded to choke the life out of him with his strong hands. Ulee did some sort of martial arts move, wrapping his legs around Raul's neck and slamming his head onto the ground and breaking his neck. It was a horrible sight. Police sirens sounded. Everyone started running. Ulee, his family, Belén, and I were left. All the boys were handcuffed. I tried to explain but they took Ulee away in a police cruiser.

△ △ △

A deal was made; the prosecuting attorney was not going to file second-degree murder charges. Ulee's grandpa Ephraim was the judge's retired Marine buddy. Ephraim appeased the prosecutor by saying that he was going to do something about Ulee's growing violent history. Ulee was going to join the Marines and go to Vietnam. This was something that everyone knew he would be good at, coming from a long line of Marines. It was something that the nation needed, more young men for the meat grinder that was Vietnam. And it was an out for everyone.

Ulee's parents signed for him to join the Marines on November 1, 1968. Ulee was still too young to serve, but his parents produced a fake birth certificate showing he was older. Ulee came to see me when he got out of jail and was getting ready to leave. I met him on the porch in the moonlight. We kissed. I started to cry and to say thank you.

"To me, this freedom that I now have from MS-13 proves there is a loving God," I said. He cried and said that he had never killed a man before, and now he had broken one of the Ten Commandments. Ulee spoke hesitantly. "To me this proved there was not a personal God who would allow something as terrible as this to take place."

He knew in his heart that he would not come back alive from Vietnam, so this was goodbye. I bawled and said, "Don't try and be a hero. I love you—I want to raise a family with you. I want to reach our dreams together. Remember, you are nonviolent—passive like Gandhi or Martin Luther King or Jesus Christ. Don't be a hero—just come home."

He took a hold of my shoulders and said, "I won't try and be a hero, but I have to follow the path of my destiny. I have to try to do what I know is right in my eyes."

I said, "If you no longer believe in God, then how could you have a personal destiny?"

"What about doing what is right by God not just your emotions?"

"Pray that I have a good death—like my brother Joey."

"No I won't pray that," and he walked away

Chapter Five

The Trojan Horse

THE FAMILY AUDIENCE in the old Sundown lodge had heard this story before, and they would hear it again. As tragic as it was, it was our tradition to retell these stories for the young and at the same time it always felt new for those who had heard each other tell this family tale. For Native peoples it is somewhat like the Jewish Passover where the eldest of the family tells the trials and tribulations of generations of their family as motivation to challenge the future. So I began again the next night continuing the legend.

△ △ △

It was November, 1968, when Ulysses Looking Glass Sundown enlisted to become a Marine. We were both age fifteen. It was the same year as the Tet Offensive, when the war in Vietnam changed. The Tet Offensive turned the war from the enemy being primarily Viet Cong to North Vietnamese power. While we look back and see that the US won the Tet Offensive from a military perspective, from a public relations perspective, the American public began to turn against the war and think of it as unwinnable. As Ulee entered the blue bus for MCRD (Marine Corps Recruiting Depot) in San Diego, he seemed like such a boy. From now on he would be called *bullet sponge, dead meat,* and *bullet catcher* among other derogatory names aimed at Marines. Ulee had no comprehension of what he was headed for in Vietnam. More than 53,000 US soldiers were killed in action and 2,600 listed as missing in action. Another 800 were prisoners of war.

Some of the recruits laughed when they saw Ulee get on the bus for boot camp. He looked like a kid, and in fact was just about to turn sixteen at the end of the month. He was just over six feet tall, but a mere 155 pounds. His boyish face showed no beginnings of a beard. He wore a cross around his neck. When he arrived on the bus, an older guy from East LA named Paco tripped him, and he slammed his face on the back of a seat, giving him the beginnings of a black eye. A big guy named Bruce helped him up and invited him to sit by him. Bruce was way overweight, and though he had played offensive line in community college, he was not in football shape; he had packed on extra weight prior to joining the Marines by eating too much junk food. He introduced himself to Ulee.

"Everyone calls me Big Bruce." He pulled out a picture from his wallet and said, "This is my fiancé, Cindy. I am going to marry her before we go to Vietnam. By then I will be a lean, mean fighting machine."

"I am Ulysses Looking Glass Sundown."

The guy in front of them, a big Samoan Nicknamed Luau, asked, "Are you some kind of a hippie with that name?"

"No I am a Nez Perce warrior."

"What's a Nez Perce," Luau asked.

"It's an Indian, you big Samoan," Paco chided.

Ulee explained. "Native, from a tribe in Oregon and Idaho."

"Then why are you white?" Luau asked.

"Because my mother is Scottish/Irish and my father is Nez Perce, so I was cursed with this white skin."

They nicknamed Ulee "Fresh Meat" and "Baby Indian."

Ulee knew to keep his head down and mouth shut. Out of all the recruits, he stood out as the boy who had not shaved, but whose lean muscular body seemed in perfect shape already, and who had warpath in his eyes. There were big surfer dudes from San Diego, gang members from East LA, loggers from Oregon, cowboys from Montana, and construction workers from Arizona. Over half of the recruits were drafted, and the rest all had a story.

△ △ △

I myself felt lost, not hearing anything from Ulee during this period. I no longer had to worry about MS-13. I seemed relatively safe as an illegal alien, but there was a big hole in my heart. Ulee was the hero I had prayed for all my life. And every day I ached to see him again.

Ulee believed he was born for this; he was a warrior from a long line of warriors. Nez Perce had always helped the US— not because it was perfect; they knew better than most of its imperfections. Nez Perce had been betrayed by the treaties and had had to fight the US themselves when they were chased off their Holy Land—the Wallowa Mountains. Most Nez Perce were somewhat impoverished, except for their sustenance living in hunting and fishing. A job as a warrior was honorable work as long as the cause was right.

According to the 2010 US Census, 150,000 American Indian veterans were living in the United States. There are more Native Americans in the military proportionally than any other minority. This was true even before 1925 when Natives finally became citizens of the nation that had conquered them. This paradox of patriotism for the US by a conquered people reveals timely truths about real American exceptionalism.

There was a nobility and a crucible ahead for every Marine. During this period, Ulee felt that he discovered the background to the Sundown philosophy.

△ △ △

They had eight weeks for boot camp and then four weeks for infantry training school. Ulee lost his hair, as did each of the other recruits. It was a rite of passage when they went through the humiliation of the Marine haircut. Ulee couldn't wait to see what that M-16 could do. It was like Christmas from Uncle Sam.

He may have been the only one who dreamed of war in his sleep. But when they had to get naked to shower as a group, the other men saw the scarring on his chest from his vision quest.

The first time they stood for inspection, they were berated by the hats (drill instructors). Sergeant Daugherty swore at him, but Ulee didn't move his eyes, just as his family had trained him. Every answer was in the third person. "Yes, Drill Sergeant—No, Drill Sergeant. This recruit is happy to be here, Drill Sergeant."

Sergeant Daugherty was a big-boned, muscular man of over six-feet two and 220 pounds.

"Do you come from Marine stock?"

Ulee reported, "Yes, Drill Sergeant."

"How did you lie your way in here; you must be just a baby," growled the DI.

"Yes, Drill Sergeant," Ulee said in a manly voice.

"I hear you think you are an Indian."

"Yes, Drill Sergeant."

"You look like a white boy to me. Your daddy better check to see who your momma has been sleeping with."

"Yes, Drill Sergeant."

"So you are not an Indian?"

Ulee replied as if his family had prepared him. "No, Drill Sergeant. I am a Nez Perce."

"You think you are a Nez Perce, but you look more of a white than redskin to me."

"I am all Nez Perce.

"Well, if you are all Nez Perce, then how are you going to be a Marine?"

"I will be a fine Marine, Drill Sergeant. Just like my dad, my uncles, and grandfather were all Nez Perce and all Marine."

Sergeant Daugherty kind of liked this kid. He definitely stood out in his squad as a leader. But the sergeant wondered how he was going to break him. He had to be broken to be built up as a Marine and to be a team player.

Δ Δ Δ

There were few letters from Ulee; while in boot camp they were cut off from home so that they could be remade as Marines. Stupidly, I still hoped I would hear from him. When

I did get a letter from him, it felt like Christmas. I got the mail every day, fumbling through the letters looking for one with his handwriting. His first letter made me cry. I read it at the mailbox at our house in Finley. I trembled as I read his words:

> Beautiful, I love you and miss you. My time here is pretty much like I thought it would be. A lot like football. I am so sorry I got myself into this. You deserve the very best. I feel like God has abandoned me sometimes. But it is nothing different from what my people have faced through the centuries. I still love Jesus and am trying to figure out how to serve him in my present predicament. I pray for you daily, you are so smart and the best person I know. I know you will be a doctor someday. Keep studying. I love you. Your friend for the rest of my life, Ulysses Looking Glass Sundown.

I kneeled each night by my bed and prayed for him, shedding a few tears as I looked at his sophomore football picture. During this period, I was saying no to other guys asking me out. I spent a lot of time on my studies and no time for social life.

∆ ∆ ∆

On Firing Week at boot camp, recruits were awakened early in the morning to prepare for the rifle range. They spent all day running through a distance course of fire in order to practice their marksmanship with live rounds. Recruits had to qualify with a minimum score in order to earn a marksmanship badge and continue training. Ulee helped his squad to qualify as Marine marksmen. The first time they put the rifle in his hands the gunnery sergeant knew this boy was a prodigy. When Ulee shot, the DI (Drill Instructor) said, "I have never seen a recruit fire so fast and accurately in my whole life." Everything the Marines did was instinctive to Ulee. Just as he was a record setter in sports growing up, everything he did at boot camp was a new record. And it did not go unnoticed. The boot camp DIs let the word out that they had a very special weapon in this Nez Perce warrior. Even in hand-to-hand combat training, he volunteered to take on the drill sergeant after he had hurt his friend Luau. Ulee broke the DI's leg. As the other DIs ran to help, Ulee took on five of them with his martial arts skill and ended up in the brig. The master sergeant had a long talk with Ulee and told him they had special plans for him but he had a lot to learn. He was third-generation Marine hero, and more than that, he was extremely gifted in the business of war.

△ △ △

On the ten-day leave, Ulee came to visit the Tri-Cities, and he came to Kennewick High School to see me. He spotted me as I walked from one building to another. And then Ulee decided not to see me; he couldn't bear to hold me in his arms, convinced that he would undoubtedly die in Vietnam.

Ulee turned with tears in his eyes to walk away and never speak to me, the love of his life. As he walked to his parents' Volkswagen bug, there I was waiting for him.

"You were not going to even say hi?"

"I love you," he said tearfully, "more than anything I have ever loved in this world."

"I know, you romantic sap."

And then we kissed. It was a kiss that if I lived a thousand years I would never forget. We walked hand in hand to the city park; I cut class. We sat down holding hands under an oak tree. The green grass mixed with clover smelled so good. Even in the winter in the desert Tri-Cities some days were springtime. I thanked him for what he did to save Belen and me from MS-13. I asked him about his faith in our Lord, and he told me that he knew Jesus was with him but that it was hard to be a Christian in a violent environment.

He told me that he still had a real problem with his temper. I prayed with him for forgiveness asking that he could stay close to Jesus, even in Vietnam. It was the longest eight days and the shortest of my life. I can't remember saying goodbye very well. We both did not know what to say. He told me to move on with my life—that he did not think he was going to come back alive. I yelled at him, swearing and calling him a SOB. It just came out and it didn't make any sense. Then we kissed. I don't remember much after that.

△ △ △

Ulee's squad was selected to receive training as a reconnaissance unit. Upon graduation, they each were awarded the MOS 0321. Ulee also spent time with the sniper school and the infantry squad leader's course. He was the only one who was receiving this kind of cross training.

By the time Ulee graduated from infantry training battalion (ITB), he was a corporal. Then these newly trained Marines were assigned to their first unit, a Marine fire squad.

Ulee landed at Da Nang on April Fool's Day: April 1, 1969. As they got off the transport, bodies were being shipped back and the living troops looked like death warmed over. No discipline—all attitude. They shouted out insults, referring to Ulee and his squad as fresh meat and bullet stoppers. Ulee's friends became a part of First Battalion, Fifth Marines. They were moved to Quang Nam province and met their new gunnery sergeant Hilton. His eyes looked tired; I guess they call it the thousand-yard stare. He treated his men like they were not real people. He didn't ask about them or their families. He left Ulee to be their nursemaid.

Ulee was commanded to lead them into battle and try and come home with as many as possible. It was fourteen days of search and clear operation. Sixteen Marines would die with 162 wounded. The first sign of conflict was no sign. They were walking through a rice patty. It was really quite beautiful—the land was so green. The peasants working the field seemed so enchanting to Ulee. A crack rang out, and Sergeant Hilton died from a sniper's shot. Six of the peasants rose up from their bent-over position of working in the rice and with AK-47s (supplied by the Russians) and opened up on the platoon. Eight of the sixteen killed in this action died in the first moments of this ambush. The experienced Marines soon put down the peasants in the ambush. That was when a mortar opened up on them with extreme accuracy. A Russian-made machine gun fired from about 150 yards pinned everyone down.

Ulee, seeing his friends die, jumped up and ran. One of the other sergeants got ready to shoot him for running, but before he could react, Ulee was out of sight in a ditch and running back to a tree line. It took him about five minutes to make the one-mile run to circle the enemy emplacement. He broke in on two Viet Cong on the machine gun and two on the mortar, and another three firing AK-47s at the pinned-down Marines. Ulee ran in the middle of them just as if he were breaking into a herd of deer to get his family meat for the winter. He fired single shots at all seven enemies—before any of them returned fire.

Ulee had a gift from hunting as a child. Everything would slow down for him. He and his brothers could shoot four ducks with three shots while a friend with a semi-automatic would miss everything. Sometimes he could reload and fire three more shells, dropping three more ducks before the friend knew what was happening. This is just how it felt as he shot in the middle of the Viet Cong. It was slow to him, but his actions were far too fast for them to react: one shot each, pause and access, then deliver the kill shots just as rapidly. Twenty shots all together from his twenty-round magazine. He walked over to one of the bodies and turned it over to see a young woman.

Ulee let out a cry that sounded Native American, "*Ahhhhyeeee!*" and fell to the ground crying. He kept saying, "I am sorry Jesus."

The pinned-down Marines did not know what had taken place, but they all moved toward Ulee's position. A sergeant from the platoon kicked him. "Swallow it, Marine. Get used to it, Marine. You kill them or they kill you and your fellow Marines." Luau picked up Ulee. "Come on brother, you just saved all our lives."

That was the first action that Ulee saw, and he killed seven people. All of them looked like neighbors—not warriors. Soon there was a helicopter coming in to take away the dead and wounded, and then they resumed formation and kept their search and patrol. This sort of routine continued from April 6 through April 20, 1969.

As Ulee saw his friends from boot camp die, it changed him. Ulee was like the little brother and big brother of every man in the squad. For example, Ulee had made sure that the overweight friend had made it through each phase of the training. Bruce had slimmed down and muscled up. Ulee loved Bruce's dark sense of humor. Big Bruce hated everything about the Marine experience, and the way he described it just made Ulee fall on the ground laughing. Bruce had married just before he left for Vietnam and they announced that they were expecting a baby.

He carried a picture of his wife in his wallet. Her name was Cindy, and she was cute. Bruce was twenty-four and acted like an offensive lineman who wanted to protect his quarterback—Ulee. Ulee was Bruce's best man at his wedding. Now he carried a picture of their baby in his pocket.

There was a lot more time spent bored than in action. Even for Ulee, who seemed to be picked for every mission that turned into a firefight. On one of their more boring moments in Nam, Big Bruce stepped on a land mine. The blast took off both of his legs and ripped open his intestines. Ulee held his hand as Big Bruce screamed and then grew quiet.

Big Bruce whimpered. "I don't want to die." Then he sighed his last breath. Ulee just got up, determined that he would do the fighting for his men from now on.

He asked to stay at point man. He was the best at it by far anyway. Ulee walked carefully, like a Native, and he used his tracking skills. It was not hard for him to spot the land mines that others might step on. The master sergeant was right; Ulee was a killer by heritage, and Ulee concluded he could save a lot of his friends if he just took out the enemy by himself. He continued on point but took it to a new level. Forget the teamwork; these good-hearted hippies were not ready for warfare. They were being sent to slaughter; they were bullet catchers. Ulee did not expect to come back alive, but his focus was not on dying but on killing the enemy to save his friends.

News of mission Operation Muskogee Meadows made it into the newspapers. Ulee had been awarded the bronze star for his heroics. The *Tri-City Herald* ran a big story on their hometown Kennewick boy, Ulysses Looking Glass Sundown, who killed seven and saved his fellow Marines.

△ △ △

I came home from school and Mama Elicia asked me, "Did you see the paper this morning?" There was a picture of lance corporal Ulysses Looking Glass Sundown in his dress blues and an article about how he was cited for heroism in Vietnam and saving his company as he took out a machine gun nest that had his squad all pinned down. I didn't want to see it, but mamma Elicia saved the article in a scrapbook for me. She believed this was all I might have left from my first love. I wrote a letter to him with my homecoming picture in it. I told him how much I loved him and was praying for him to come home safe from the terrible war he was involved in. I wrote the thirteenth chapter of Corinthians out for him in calligraphy style.

Just as in ancient times, Ulysses went away to a just war in Troy to retrieve Helen of Troy with the other allied Greek heroes, and the war grew to a stalemate, dragging on and on until the meaning of the war was lost to everyone concerned. Ulee was intermeshed in the quicksand of Vietnam, unable to pull himself out.

△ △ △

Most service during a war is filled with times of long boredom, but Ulee was reassigned to a new mission on April 22, 1969: Operation Putnam Tiger. This time he came in as a sniper to assist Second and Third Battalions. This conflict was in the Kon Tum and Pleiku Provinces. Lieutenant Colonel Gary Carter commanded the battalion , and they were attached to LZ (Landing Zone) Nicole with Charlie Company. They operated out of an attached firebase. Their mission was to patrol and set up listening posts (LPs). They were to call in fire on enemy activity. Most companies while out on patrol were attached a forward observer. Ulee was told that he was created by God to be a forward observer and that they needed an Indian brave to do this job. They didn't know that their attempts to play off his heritage were demeaning, and he didn't tell them. Ulee ate Vietnamese food so that his feces smelled like Viet Cong. He applied some of the swamp smells of the jungle to eliminate his scent. Unlike the patrols, he moved silently off the path through the jungle. This was uncommon, as the trails seemed the safest and the easiest.

Ulee had spent his life bushwhacking while he was hunting, and he was hunting again. He made sure they moved against the breeze, and he learned the local animals and bugs that would give away the position of the enemy. He applied camouflage and got rid of his helmet; it was a dead giveaway for the shape of a Marine. He had to be careful because he was equally afraid of being fragged (killed by his own troops) He taught his men his bird whistles so they knew it was him. This operation was bloody business; 563 Americans were killed and 435 wounded.

Ulee grew used to living out on his own. He traded his M-16 in for a Garand 30-6. He learned the bugs and small vermin that he could eat. He seemed to be immune to malaria and dysentery. Maybe it was all the mountain survival he had done as a child. Mosquitoes never did like his taste. He would sleep in the midst of monsoons by building his bed off the ground with three poles between trees that were wrapped in leaves so that he felt invisible and comfortable. Ulee got used to killing. He would spot a small sortie coming after his platoon and would set up booby traps that he copied from the VC or had learned from the Nez Perce. He then would take a position and ambush them with a bow he had made—just like at home. He instilled fear in the enemy, which dubbed him "*người giận dữ*" (The Savage). He would catch them grouped together and take out ten at a time as they crossed a river. His platoon would hear Ulee's fire and would set up a defensive position. Ulee would return with his whistles and tell them they were all safe and that he had gotten them.

△ △ △

One day, I was sitting in the Kennewick High School cafeteria, something I rarely did. Everyone started to yell, "Somebody do something!" I turned around, and one of the big senior football players, who was maybe 300 pounds, had fallen into his food face first. He was an African-American, and his skin had changed to an ashlike color. He wasn't breathing. I ran to the table and asked his friend what had happened. A teacher came in a complete panic.

The teacher yelled, "Go get the school nurse!"

As the teacher yelled at me to wait for the school nurse, I said, "I need to save this guy's life." I checked his mouth and saw it had food in it. I cleared what I could with my hand. I tried to reach around him and do the Heimlich maneuver, but he was too big. I was only five-two, 115 pounds. But I am a Honduran girl and very tough, so I formed a fist with one hand on his solar plexus and picked the guy slightly up and slammed him on the table. That put my back in a spasm. No one would help, so I just kept slamming this guy into the table with the corner aimed at his solar plexus. A few times and I was done for. I started breathing hard and feeling like I was about ready to pass out.

"Someone else take over!" I yelled. "Where is the dang school nurse?" No one stepped up to help, not even his friend. "Don't let Pete die!" someone yelled. So I jumped back up filled with adrenaline and started slamming him against the table.

A chip flew out and big Pete took a breath. The big man sat there in the chair while I took his pulse, and an ambulance team showed up. We were only two minutes from Kennewick General Hospital.

Pete turned to me and said, "You saved my life."

The teacher said, "You are going to be one fine doctor."

I walked back to my books and everyone in the cafeteria gave me a standing ovation. I was very embarrassed. The rest of the week, the boys in the school kept faking like they were passing out and telling me they needed mouth-to-mouth resuscitation.

I would tell them they needed a colonoscopy, and some of them were dumb enough to say, "That sounds good too."

In Homer's ancient ballad, he tells about the shocking incongruity of enemies following tradition and respect for one another in the midst of deadly violence. Homer's poetic contemplation of humanity at war covers an area every soldier knows to be true. What are the consequences when warriors disregard their humanity and the rules of war? Sometimes this ends up in disaster, as with Achilles' death, and other times it ends up with clever victory, as with Ulysses' plan to leave a wooden horse as a memorial. Of course the horse was hollow and filled with Greek heroes who would sack the great city of Troy.

Δ Δ Δ

Ulee came upon a Buddhist monastery and orphanage. Ulee greeted a beautiful young Hmong Vietnamese lady who met him at the gate. *"Chào buổi sáng Madam, tôi ahve đến để tìm hiểu về tôn giáo của bạn và xem những gì tôi có thể làm gì để giúp đỡ các trẻ em mồ côi"* (Good morning Madam, I have come to learn about your religion and to see what I can do to help with the orphans.)

She spoke back, *"Tôi không hiểu bạn - việt của bạn là rất nghèo. Bạn đang làm gì ở đây - chúng tôi không muốn có bất kỳ rắc rối."* (I don't understand you—your Vietnamese is so poor. What are you doing here? We do not want any trouble.)

She took Ulee's hand and led him into the convent. She pointed to herself and said, "Ahn" (a Vietnamese girl's name which means intellectual brightness). Ulee responded by repeating her name and then pointing to himself and saying, *"U . . . lee."* She pointed to him and repeated his phrase. She was beautiful and probably ten years older than Ulee. Ahn had large, beautiful, dark eyes, sparkling with intelligence. She had dark hair, full lips, and she was petite with small hands and feet and yet a shapely figure of a woman who was more than a girl Ulee's age. She had an innocence and yet a worldliness to her as a woman who knew that she was attractive. When I saw her picture I felt like she was the antithesis of me. I knew that God had blessed me with beauty; as I said before, it was sometimes a curse. But let's face it; most men are attracted to women, and the variety of beauty has tempted mankind since the dawn of time. Her long black hair was elegant and added serenity to her whole being as it interweaved with her complexion and features to create a rare woman. I suppose every person is that way if you can see it. And Ulee, in all of his loneliness, saw that beauty in Ahn.

A Buddhist priest came up to translate for them. He was old, maybe fifty years old. His head was hairless, his eyes twinkled, and he kind of glowed with love and peace. The priest had a radiant beauty about him that was missing from Ahn, despite her tranquility. Something about Ahn seemed deeply troubled— like many of the beautiful faces of the noble Vietnamese people who were experiencing the hell of war in their homeland.

The Buddhist monk spoke excellent English and said, *"My samana (name) is Rhapseda Dawa.* You can call me Dawa. I hear you are trying to learn our language."

Ulee replied that he was a follower of Jesus Christ and needed a rest from the war and that he was a man who wanted peace and would like to help the orphans in the name of Jesus. Dawa asked, "Are you Catholic?"

Ulee said, "Yes, Catholics are my brothers and sisters in Christ. But I am a Native American and my father is a Protestant pastor." Dawa invited Ulee to have some tea as Ahn brought it to them.

"You have an honest face, and you are a boy. What are you doing in the Marines?"

Ulee said, "It is a long story." Dawa said, "We all have long stories. I do not say that Christians are evil, but let me tell you our story here in Vietnam.

"In May 1963, in the central city of Huế, where President Diem's elder brother Ngo Dinh Thuc was the archbishop, Buddhists were prohibited from displaying Buddhist flags during Vesak celebrations, yet a few days earlier, Catholics were allowed to fly religious flags at a celebration in honor of the newly seated archbishop. This led to widespread protest against the government; troops were sent in and nine civilians were killed in the confrontations. This led to mass rallies against Diem's government, termed as the Buddhist crisis. The conflicts culminated in a Buddhist monk, Thich Quang Duc's, suicide protest by lighting himself on fire. President Diem's younger brother, Ngo Dinh Nhu, favored strong-armed tactics, and Special Forces were sent to raid Buddhist centers, killing hundreds. Discouraged by the public outrage, the US government withdrew support for the regime. President Diem was deposed and killed in the 1963 coup.

"Political strength of the Buddhists grew in the 1960s as the different schools and orders convened to form the Unified Buddhist Church of Vietnam. Today, leaders of the Buddhists, like Thich Tri Quang, hold considerable sway in national politics."

Ulee asked many questions from this learned monk. "What are your thoughts about this war?"

Dawa replied. "I am a communist and yet I don't like many of the things that my side is doing in the war. I see their atrocities forcing our people to join the Viet Cong—punishing those who do not. But I believe you are here to fight for colonialism—the last failing attempt at the western powers to control as much of the world as you can."

Ulee replied, "I have heard that opinion, but one idea does not rule a democracy. I am sure that there are economic and political interests that have those interests whether they would describe them that way or not. But many of us are not so much against communism as we are against the totalitarian governments from the Soviets and Chinese who want to control the world, and someone has to draw a line somewhere against a bully."

"Are you a communist? Many Christians have practiced communism, even in the book of acts." Dawa asked.

"But it didn't work and the church of Jerusalem was so poor that Paul was raising money to help them," Ulee said.

"I did not know that."

"I think that if someone wants to be a communist it is all right by me as a failing economic system," Ulee said. "I think it provides no incentive to work and no freedom to rise from the bottom to the top. I don't think the capitalist system is perfect, but I hope it is on its way to become more honest and fair because it is governed by ever-growing democracy."

"You are a worthy opponent in an argument," Dawa said.

"I am not your opponent; we both have a love for orphans in common. Can I give you a hand around here?"

Dawa, said, "Yes, I think it is Karma."

The rest of the day was spent trying to fix the roof of the orphanage and playing with the kids. Two young orphans were just enamored with Ulee. They, like many, may have been descended from unions between soldiers and village people. The bigger one Ulee called Plato and the little one, who seemed the opposite of the big one on every issue, he called Aristotle. They loved to play catch with the American football. Ulee treated them like brothers and the kids began to teach him Vietnamese. Since he already spoke English, Spanish, and Nez Perce, Vietnamese came to him without too much trouble. But he had a long way to go—and learning was a joy to him.

∆ ∆ ∆

Ulee reported to his commanding officer, who told him that he was viewed as a special asset to the Marine Corps. He was going on loan to the ARVN 32nd Regiment operation in the An Xuyen province in Operation Quyet. It would begin at predawn on September 29. Five thousand South Vietnamese plus US advisors would be dropped behind Viet Cong forces and with grenade launchers and flame throwers, disperse Viet Cong strongholds. After this dispersion, sniper teams would pursue and eliminate the Viet Cong. Ulee said if he was going to be a sniper team that he wanted to choose his spotter and weapons.

Ulee chose Luau, the Samoan warrior who had become a close friend. Ulee asked for a new Remington 700 30-6 with a floating barrel and a state of the art scope for his weapon. He was also given a 44-magnum 626. Luau was issued the 44-magnum revolver and also carried a BAR, which was a 30-6 submachine gun that had become a mainstay of World War II and the Korean War. This way they could share ammunition. Ulee also took his self-made recurve bow.

When he showed up to the commanding Vietnamese officer, Do Cao Tri, Ulee saw one of the K-9 squads, and he could not believe his eyes; there was a Beauceron. It must have been left over from when the French inhabited Vietnam. It was descended from the French-Vietnamese war dogs. Still to this day, Beauceron are a loved breed in Vietnam as police dogs. It looked exactly like his dog Argos. Only this dog was just three years old. Ulee asked for the dog and was given it, even though snipers never used dogs. It was well trained and some people say that Beauceron are the most intelligent of dogs. They bond so deeply with their masters that they can practically read their minds. They can open almost any door. Or if it is locked, they will chew a hole through it or just break it down. They are gentle with those who they should be gentle with but can sniff a criminal or VC out of a crowd. Ulee trained this one not to bark under any conditions. He slept with his new friend, Cerberus, ate with Cerberus, and spent all his spare time training Cerberus.

Cerberus terrified Ulee's spotter, Luau. The big island kid wasn't raised around dogs, but he trusted his friend, and Cerberus warmed up to him. And the children at the orphanage loved Cerberus.

The concept of American advisors for South Vietnamese forces was at this time just a cover. A dozen extremely effective sniper teams from the US were sent in to set up ambushes for the fleeing Viet Cong. It was dirty work; Ulee hated it. And Luau was wrestling with the mission also. But they felt that each life that they took from a Viet Cong saved at least one life of their buddies. That was the code of the sniper. They were dropped in before the South Vietnamese attack on the Viet Cong, and they took the time to acclimate themselves to the environment.

They were placed in the high country, setting up ambush as
the South Vietnamese and American advisors swept this area
to eradicate the Viet Cong. This area happened to be the same
location of the My Lai massacre in March 16, 1968, where 345
villagers were killed under the command of Lieutenant William
Calley, who was tried and convicted and later pardoned by
President Nixon to two years of house arrest. It was an area
known since the French and Japanese rule as a center of the
resistance movement. It was a Viet Cong stronghold.

In central Vietnam near the coast, disease and mosquitoes
were rampant. Ulee and his team found cover in the high ground,
about a thousand feet above sea level. Ulee used the mosquito
ideas he had used in the Wallowa Mountains. In the high
mountains, millions of mosquitoes hatch at the same time when
the high meadows melt during a brief summer month. They used
mosquito net hats and gloves. With a tight silk weave for long
underwear, they only used repellant when necessary. Ulee did
not want bug spray aroma to give away his position. Mud made
from termite nests would have to do as their repellant (this has
been used by jungle natives since the dawn of time). At night, he
and Luau would stare at the night stars. They would talk about
how small the planet was and how big God was.

Luau was a fundamentalist believer, and he told Ulee that
he had promised God that he would go and fight for the Israeli
army if he was ever needed because he still believed that the Jews
were the chosen people of God. He asked Ulee to promise him to
go fight in one war for the Israelis if Luau died in Vietnam. Luau
was married to a Jew whom he had met on a spiritual pilgrimage
to Israel with his church.

"No I am not going to promise another war. I hate war,"
Ulee said. "But I love you, Luau. I am not going to let you die."

As the Viet Cong retreated, Ulee and Luau ambushed a dozen.
They both felt sick when they policed the bodies for information
that could be used. Some were old men, some were kids, and
one was a young woman. Luau vomited after they saw the
results of their ambush. He had never seen anyone fire as fast or
effectively as Ulee when he unleashed his Remington 700. Every
shot dropped an enemy, and he reloaded his four-round rifle so
fast that it was unbelievable. Luau served as a diversion with

high-powered spray of 30-6 bullets from a BAR light machine gun. When they took cover, Ulee picked them off with his scope. They were at 300 yards, which was a guaranteed shot, and Ulee moved after each four shots. Luau moved after each magazine was emptied. It was all a nightmare as Luau thought back about it, seeing the number of heads shot on the Viet Cong.

Under the cover of darkness, Ulee hunted with his bow. It seemed that Ulee had a gift for going a couple weeks at a time with only catnaps when in the field. After the initial ambushes, they switched tactics to stalking, just as if he were hunting. This was where Cerberus and Ulee's tracking skills were used with an amazing degree of efficiency. When they identified an old person, a woman, or a child, they let them pass. They knew that this was not up to the mission protocol and their brothers in arms would tell them that many troops had been killed by the elderly, women, and children. But they limited their targets to male combatants of fighting age.

They were pulled out in the midst of a firefight. It started as an ambush, but they were being stalked by Viet Cong who seemed to know every move that Ulee would make. Ulee and Luau called themselves Butch Cassidy and the Sundance Kid, but their Vietnamese allies couldn't even pronounce it. And the fellow American advisors just called them *kids*. But they carried out their nicknaming game by calling their smart VC enemy Pinkerton from the movie *Butch Cassidy and the Sundance Kid*. This guy seemed unavoidable as they kept saying who is this guy. He had been trained in Russia and was the most formidable foe they had met. "Pinkerton" also organized his forces in an invincible way until a mortar wounded Ulee and Luau, as well as Cerberus during an ambush. Luau picked up Ulee, who had taken a frag in his butt, and ran firing his BAR with incredible effectiveness. Luau saved Ulee's life and took both his friend and Cerberus to the LZ. Ulee put Luau in for commendation, and he received a medal from the South Vietnamese government (as did Ulee), a bronze star, and they both received a purple heart.

When Ulee was on the offshore hospital ship, he and Luau couldn't shake the shame that they felt for all the close-quarters killing. It especially bothered Ulee, and Luau could not comfort him. Ulee felt better once he returned to the Buddhist orphanage, trying to make a positive mark for this country torn by war.

Δ Δ Δ

As he worked on a playground for the kids, Ahn brought him water. Cerberus played with the children, licking them and herding them. Ahn was a beautiful woman, but Ulee's heart was given to me—and he still considered me the most beautiful woman in the history of the world. Or at least that is what he told me. He sang to me and wrote poetry to me attesting to my beauty and nobility. But Ulee needed a friend, and Ahn had a beautiful heart.

Dawa was always nearby and one day brought Ulee and Ahn lunch.

"We know what you did the last month. You killed many of our people," Dawa said to Ulee.

"So you are VC, Dawa?"

"No, but I am connected, as are many Buddhist monks. How does that make you feel as a follower of Jesus Christ to break one of the Ten Commandments over and over again?"

Ulee told him the truth. "It makes me feel horrible, guilty, shameful, and still alive."

"I think you are on the wrong side," Dawa said.

"I think you are on the wrong side," Ulee countered.

"And how would a Nez Perce from Oregon know what is best for our country here in Vietnam?"

"I have read Mao Zedong's little red book—have you?"

"Yes," replied Dawa.

"Do you think the dictatorship of the proletariat is the best for your people? Do you think totalitarian rule under a dictator is ever safe? I also have read the entire works of Karl Marx. Leninist Marxism and Mao's Marxism believe in a world revolution that would take away the rights of all individual freedoms in hopes that someday some communist society can work its way through the dictatorship of the proletariat. What about Mao's Cultural Revolution, where it was My Lai times a thousand? Don't you think that if Marxism takes over Cambodia that the same kind of massacre could happen there? Do you know that Trotsky helped lead the communist revolt and yet was killed in Mexico when he became disgusted with the way it was going? I think the domino principle is a theory, but once Vietnam falls, Cambodia falls, South Korea falls, the Philippines fall, and Japan will be invaded. Stalin killed more in his concentration camps than Hitler ever dreamed," Ulee preached.

The Buddhist monk yelled back, "And you are in the region where the My Lai massacre took place."

"Yes," said Ulee, "and my people have been massacred also. There is evil on every side. But that does not absolve those of us who can to do what we can to fight for the right with the justice that transcends war. Aristotle said that all war is inherently evil because the government becomes the parent and the warriors lose their human freedom. I believe war is too important to leave to evil men. That good men must do what is right and stand up for what is right."

"Well," said Dawa, "we disagree again."

"Yes," said Ulee, "but we are friends."

"How do you know I am not just using you?" asked Dawa. "Maybe I have lured you here with the beauty of Ahn."

"If you know what I have done on the battlefield than you know that I am not afraid of you or your connections. And as for Ahn, I love a girl named Penelope and I have given my heart to her just as I have given my heart to Jesus."

"What if I am VC?"

"Then I pray that you represent the moral warrior on your side that I do on my side and that we may respect one another during the insanity of war."

Ulee knew this was a dangerous relationship, but he trusted his heart and his skills. It was not a new idea for the Nez Perce to respect their enemies and to converse with them. His involvement with the children gave him a chance for sanity and an opportunity to hold on to his faith in this crucible that he had been placed in. And his understanding of his enemy's culture, philosophy, and wilderness skills were invaluable for him to keep his friends alive. He felt like the jungles of Vietnam were his home, and that made him a very dangerous warrior.

∆ ∆ ∆

Ulee woke nearly every evening with a nightmare. He would turn over the body of a Viet Cong that he had shot and see the face of Ahn or Dawa and sometimes even myself or one of his younger brothers. One night, under the stars, he and Luau were talking when Luau started to cry.

"I can't handle this anymore. I think we are fighting for the right causes—yet I am not sure any nation can solve another nation's problem. I don't think we should be here. But I won't go home and leave you here; you need me to save your skinny ass. Who is going to take care of your pup if something happens to you?"

"I know what you are talking about brother," Ulee said. "I feel the same way. The American people don't want us over here, and the Vietnamese don't really want us here. But there will surely be a massacre when some politician decides to leave. Think of all these people who have bought into the protection of the United States. I think we as a Christian nation have a duty to help defeat bullies, but hopefully we learn from Vietnam that we cannot build a nation against the will of their people. The people of that nation are the only ones that find their freedom. I pray that it does not take us a century to learn this lesson. I am growing more evil every year. I don't know how many people I have killed and I'm starting to not feel anything. I have so many things screwed up with the woman I love. I left her without my name, so she is not even a citizen of any country and she has been through hell. She is the most virtuous woman in all the world."

Luau tried to minister to him, but nothing seemed to help. Cerberus crawled onto Ulee's lap with him, and he fell back asleep thinking he was home.

Ulee finally wrote me a letter apologizing for not writing and telling me that this war was a lot harder than anything that he ever dreamed of. He felt like he was losing his faith and his sanity. He told me about the orphanage, the kids, Dawa and Ahn, Plato and Aristotle, Luau, and Cerberus. And then he told me that he could not keep writing or he would die. He had to be present in country to survive—he had to think that he was already dead or he would surely die.

I didn't understand—I still don't. But I felt like I was losing my faith and my sanity when I read his letter. I despised Ahn and had nightmares of Ulee being with her. Maybe it was best if we both moved on with our lives. At the same time, I had come so close to being deported back to Honduras, which would be certain death for me. I was rounded up working on the Trumans' farm, along with hundreds of illegal immigrants. The Trumans were forced to pay a million-dollar fine. And they paid it to protest how working immigrants were treated. It meant they made nothing as a family that year and were years behind now in staying flush on their farm. They hired a lawyer who advised me to marry an American citizen.

"No, I would never marry for citizenship."

"Honey, it is the world's oldest profession," the lawyer said.

I lit into him. "Don't tell me about prostitution. I was a child slave, and it is not the world's oldest profession; murder is—just read about Cain and Abel. That is a saying spoken by desensitized men who don't want to think that children are tortured into selling their bodies and they are not selling their bodies; someone else is, who is very evil."

The lawyer looked ashamed. "I am sorry Penelope. I have three daughters. I will never say that again."

He represented me in immigration court, and I was given a leave (a green card) for being an excellent student. I was now on foreign student status. I had worked hard to earn this. It came because I refused to sink into the dark abyss of thinking I was a victim. My faith in Jesus Christ and my friendship with my church gave me a whole community fighting to give me a chance to be proactive and not just reactive to all the hell in my life. I prayed for every marginalized person in the world to have the same kind of support.

Chapter Six

Ulee's Stand

I CRIED AS I completed that night's story. Legend telling was real for our people. It was a heritage laid open so our family could find our soul, our identity. The whole family could not wait for the next legend-telling time.

△ △ △

Ulee knew it, and I knew it, but I pretended not to know it. It was only a matter of time until Ulee would meet his death in some heroic way. Everyone who goes into the hell of war is a hero. But the real heroes are those that do not come back because their sacrifice has saved the lives of those who can come home and receive the medals and honors. The survivors only accept these rewards because they do not want to demean the sacrifice of the heroes who gave their lives so that they could make it home. Those in war have come to grips with the fact that they are going to die. This allows them the freedom to do the foolish acts that make war so dangerous. Ulee was a hero and there was no other way for him. That is the irony of this myth and my desire to have a hero who would save me. I knew that sometime, some place, he would die a horrible violent death. Do you know what it is like to love someone like that? Many have, but I loved a hero that I needed to come home—I still needed to be rescued, to feel safe in his arms.

In January 1970, the four CAGs (combined action groups) were formed as part of the plan to turn the war over to the South Vietnamese and to protect villages from Viet Cong influence. A combined action group consisted of a total of forty-two Marine officers and about 2,000 enlisted men, with two naval officers and hospital corpsmen.

Ulee and Luau joined a Marine fire squad that was patrolling to protect Montagnard villages. The Montagnard were mountain people who had always felt mistreated by the Vietnamese; they were fierce US allies, and as combatants, they are some of the best in the world. Ulee was promoted to sergeant and led the fire team. The fire team was made up of Luau as corporal; Paco, the short, stocky Mexican who was always making wise cracks from East LA and who had been through basic with them; Donel, a tall African-American who was always cracking them all up from Compton, California; and Red, a redheaded African-American who was tougher than nails and never said much to anyone except Donel.

Red had a temper that everyone feared, even Ulee. Red carried a Thompson machine gun with a twenty round box clip. Red wasn't afraid of anyone; if he couldn't take you in a fight, he would get you later. Donel carried the M-79 grenade launcher, and he also carried an M-16. Sammy was an African-American from Portland, Oregon. His parents were schoolteachers, and he had strong middle-class values and a Baptist faith. He was the radio operator, and he had the intelligence and mechanical aptitude to make his fire squad believe they had the best radio operator in the Corp. Bull was from Arizona; he was a big construction worker who was the first one to man the M-60 machine gun, and he was assisted by Benjamin, a Jewish boy who wanted to be a rabbi from San Francisco. Benjamin carried an M-16 over his back, which is incredibly light. But his primary function in a firefight was to assist Bull on the M-60. All of these guys had been through basic together, even though they had

split up over the months. Now they were the fire team trained
to be in specialized operations. They worked along with four
Montagnard. These South Vietnamese were all old enough to
be their fathers, and Ulee's well-trained team had a hard time
keeping up with them. The Montagnard had everything to teach
about the jungle and the Viet Cong.

They spent so much time together they all became like
a family. They would go on ambush, they would search and
destroy, and they stayed in the villages they were assigned to
protect. All of them were learning Vietnamese, and all of them
except Ulee took wives from the villages. They became not
only protective of the Montagnard villages, but they became a
little more Vietnamese as the Montagnard became a little more
American. The squad learned the Vietnam custom of leaving a
little food on their plates so that their hosts did not think they
were still hungry. It was as if the Combined Action Group was a
civilization caught between two ways of life.

It was during this time that two boys were sent to fight for
the Vietnamese—Plato and Aristotle. They had enlisted with
the Montagnard, not even official ARVIN forces. Ulee tore into
them, scolding them for their stupid actions.

"We are just the same age as your great grandfather Jackson
Sundown when he helped his tribe under Chief Joseph," Plato
said.

Ulee had told many stories to the orphanage, and his family
history was a big part of it. Ulee insisted that they stay in one of
the villages on guard duty. He assigned his dog Cerberus to stay
with the boys and guard them. Cerberus obeyed with joy—this
dog loved these boys. Ulee loved the people they were protecting
and fighting alongside. They reminded him of his ancestors.
They revered the land and lived in collaboration as a tribe. The
bloodshed now seemed more purposeful than ever, and Ulee felt
less shame.

Ulee went on a little scout trip by himself and spotted a
North Vietnamese regiment moving in.

All the Marines defending the village knew they were going
to die. The issue for them was that they were not going to let their
trusted allies be abandoned and overrun. At night, Ulee was able
to take out five men a night with his bow from about forty yards

away from each target. Ulee was out there for a week when he ran into a lost ranger recon squad. They were surrounded at night—Ulee took out seven NVA to clear a path for retreat.

Ulee snuck up on the group and made the sound of the meadowlark hoping that someone would remember it from the States.

He heard a reply and snuck in, and they asked who won the World Series this year. He didn't know; he said, "I play football."

They let him in, and he met a Lakota Sioux, named Ralph Timid Fox. He was the point man for the Army Ranger squad that had recognized his birdcall. Immediately, the two Natives were best friends. Natives are often from mixed blood, and Ulee probably had some Lakota in him as Ralph had some Comanche in him. They were really often related in some way. There was such a joyful reunion because every one of this eleven-man recon team was from Kennewick, Washington. They had all attended the other high school in Kennewick called Kamiakin. It was named after Chief Kamiakin, the great chief of the Yakima tribe. They were all Ulee's age and had grown up together. After their senior year in high school, they had lost the first four games of the season in football, and then the coaches tried to rebuild for the future. They ended up losing every game that season, going 0-10. That was the ultimate humiliation in Eastern Washington. This was football country. The starting senior eleven football players decided to join the Army as long as they could serve together and go and kick butt in Vietnam. The more they read about Ulee, the more persuaded they were that this was the right course of action. Their head coach tried to talk them out of it. Several of them had the talent to play Division I football, and others were excellent scholars. All of them were good kids.

While this was their first year in country, they heard that Ulee was in trouble in a last stand at a Montagnard village. They decided to get lost and join him at this Alamo. These were all big strong men who knew how to shoot and to fight. The center, Jack Groan, was the biggest and strongest man on the team. He was a 4.0 student, but came from an Army family and always addressed everyone as "sir." He was also a state champion in wrestling. Everyone on the team stood over six feet tall, with three of them over six-five. The fullback they called "Mack Truck" was a leader in the community and planned on becoming a police officer. The halfback, Slick, was from a rich family. He had his black belt in Taekwondo and was also a state champion wrestler. The reunion was full of quiet tears and silent joy. These big farm boys had brought with them some toys: two 50-caliber machine guns and two mortars. They were loaded down like mules carrying all the ammo.

They began to sneak out when it became clear that they would be discovered. Ulee moved off about 300 yards and at sunrise, he began to fire from his camouflaged position with his Remington 700. He quickly took out four NVA who never knew what hit them. He took a new position, this took him about fifteen minutes while the Rangers crawled at breakneck speed toward the village wire. Timid Fox sounded the meadowlark, and Ulee's men knew it was a friendly. Four more NVA met their end by Ulee's sniper fire. The VC began to move in on him. Ulee let four grenades fly, one right after another as if he were throwing touchdown passes. He pulled out his shotgun and ran—bullets snapped at his feet and near his head. He dove to the grass and fired five shots of double-aught buckshot from his Ithaca shotgun. Each shot carried the equivalent of fifteen 9-millimeter shots. It was enough to have those within fifty yards duck their heads.

Ulee ran. An NVA sniper stood and drew a bead on him, only to be knocked down by Luau's BAR. Then there was covering fire from multiple machine guns and M-16s as first the Rangers made it to the wire and turned to watch Ulee set a record for the 100-yard dash. He knew right where all the booby traps were and had never ran so fast. He accelerated the entire way—jumping over the barbed wire like a high hurdle before catching his leg and doing a belly flop on the village side of the wire. Montagnard were there to help him up and get him to the trenches.

The NVA had learned a lot about how to fight the Americans. Their mortar rounds were more accurate than ours, and it became impossible to get helicopters in or out. They would crush the village quickly because they were afraid of American air power. US air power cleared an escape path for some of the Montagnard families. Ulee scouted their way out and then returned, intending to die with his men and the men of the village.

The NVA doubled their forces, sending in another regiment and bringing in Viet Cong from distance to overrun this village. The enemy drove back the snipers and the rescuing platoon, and our boys suffered heavy losses. It was bloody business. Both sides inflicted death and casualties on each other. A reinforced armored Marine regiment was sent up Highway One to bring relief. It would be at least two days before they could get there—two days too long.

Ulee gathered together all the children and had the Kamiakin Ranger team lead them out to safety. He provided cover for them as a sniper in the jungles. The LT was there, but master sergeant Luau was really in command when Ulee was gone. The LT agreed with most of the decisions that Luau made and knew that this Marine had the experience.

"I will be back," Ulee told them.

It was two in the morning when Ulee slipped out of the camp armed only with his bow. The courageous Kamiakin Ranger team led the children through the jungle. Ulee insisted that Plato and Aristotle join them and they both carried M-16s to help with the escaped. Forty-seven kids and women crawled for over a mile. The Kennewick Rangers led the way, taking out the enemy in the starless night. Finally, they came into the group and the Ranger sergeant said, "Now we run." They ran three miles. They were being followed by Viet Cong, but a long-range Marine scout squad met them and drove back the VC. The kids were safe.

That night Ulee sat under the stars with several of his Ranger friends from Kennewick Washington having a smoke after all the drama. Ulee told them that they deserved a medal for saving all those children.

"It feels good to do something that really counts," Mack Truck replied. "Sometimes I wonder why we are over here. I know Communism is a threat but it seems like we want freedom for the Vietnamese people more than they do. They might be happy living under a communist state and just maybe it might become a democracy someday."

They all laughed. "Ya, and someday the Soviet Union is going to break up into separate nations and then throw out communism and become a democracy," another Marine said.

"There is going to be slaughter when this country falls, and these peasants are not that far from looking like my family," Luau said.

"We don't fight for politics we fight for the man next to us," Mack Truck said.

Luau laughed. "That is all well and good; I hear a lot of white men say that. Don't get me wrong it is true and I appreciate it. But have you ever thought if the man next to you would just go home then we wouldn't all be sweating our butts off and we could go home and get some good home cooking." Everyone laughed.

"We Natives fight for America and what it might be. We have a long way to go, racism, fair play in the economy, and education. But some day there is going to be a black president," Ulee said, "and a Latino President, and an Indian president, maybe even a Samoan president, a woman president or a Vietnamese-American president . . . and they'll have as much trouble as a white president." Everyone laughed.

"If we stick to our Judeo-Christian moral underpinning, I think God will bless America and we will get better," Ulee added. And part of those Christian values is to respect others who are not like us. That to me is what gives America the chance to be great.

"I used to go to your dad's church and he was always so encouraging and positive," a Marine named Slick said, "But it's hard to be positive. We are surrounded and outnumbered, and we all know we are going to die a painful death soon."

"We're not going to die," Ulee said. "We are going to win."

"Besides Heaven awaiting Christians, what else is good news about our situation?" Slick said. There was a long silence.

"The good news is we are alive right now," Ulee said. "We are sitting under these stars having a Kennewick party. We are laughing and we saved a bunch of kids. We are going to try and say no to a big bully and give him a bloody nose. The good news is we are alive today. Tomorrow, who knows? Everybody is going to die sometime."

A big Polish guy who played left tackle at Kamiakin changed the subject. He asked if Ulee would perform a marriage for him with one of the women from the village.

"I'm not a chaplain or pastor," Ulee said.

"Your dad and granddad are—that's close enough for me," the Marine said. "I know you were a staunch Christian before you killed that guy in Pasco."

"Who are you going to marry anyway?" Ulee asked. This muscular friend, who looked like he could have played professional football, was from a salt of the earth farming family. His name was Antonio and was drinking from a bottle of Jack Daniels.

"I don't care which woman I marry; I just don't want to die without ever getting married."

Ulee's friends roused up a widow looking for a husband from the camp and then, Ulee performed a marriage. After the wedding, the guys were sitting around asking Ulee questions—deep questions like, what it is like to be an Indian and still be white. They asked if Ulee died and they survived, if they could marry his girlfriend (me). Then the guys started to ask questions that every human being asks in situations like this.

"If I'm not a Christian, will I go to hell when I die? How could a loving God allow all the Jews, Muslims, Buddhists, atheists, and agnostics to burn in hell for eternity because they hadn't prayed the sinner's prayer?"

Ulee explained that he believed that God was the judge—not religious people.

"I don't like religious people. I don't know everything and I have a lot of questions. That is the Native part of my faith; we have room for mystery in our understanding of a God who is smarter than we are. I don't think you have to believe in hell to go to heaven. But I have seen a lot of hell in my lifetime. I don't think you are saved because of a doctrinal statement or a mode of baptism. Look at the thief on the cross; he never had a chance to get baptized or learn doctrine, and Jesus said, 'Today you will be with me in paradise.' I think a lot of Christians are going to be surprised when they get to heaven because they are going to find an atheist, Buddhist, or communist who was following Jesus better than the religious people. Those people just didn't know they were following Jesus. They were following their conscious and rejecting a false image of Jesus. I am all right with leaving it up to God to judge. I believe that we find God when we accept the love of Jesus and his lordship. And the important thing is we can know for certain that we have an eternal relationship with God through Jesus Christ."

"What does lordship mean?" asked one of the guys.

"I guess it means his absolute leadership. He is God and we are not. And we love him so much that we want to live his way the best we can. Always getting better at following him."

Jack Groan, the big center, pulled out his canteen. "Why don't you baptize us right now, Ulee? Is this enough water?"

The fullback nicknamed, Mack Truck said, "Make us Christians but don't make us Indians." They all laughed.

Ulee asked each one, "Do you ask God to forgive you of your sins because of what he has done for you on the cross and do you accept Jesus Christ as your Lord and Savior and trust him with all of your heart?"

Ulee used his canteen to pour a little water on each head and said, "I baptize you in the name of the Father and the Son and the Holy Spirit."

"You know what is really funny?" Antonio said as he held hands with his new wife who did not speak a word of English. "It's Christmas Eve."

Ulee walked outside under the stars and looked at the moon. He wondered if I was looking at the same stars. It was not even nighttime in Kennewick. But on Christmas Eve day I heard the song, *I'll Be Home for Christmas* and ran out under the moon and stars and cried my eyes out. Ulee hummed the same song to himself on Christmas Eve on the other side of the planet. This planet is not as big as we think, and love is real.

△ △ △

On Christmas morning, the NVA shelled the hell out of the village. Their accuracy was uncanny; they hit the Marine central bunker, taking out the lieutenant, and the villagers suffered terrible losses. That night they began to send teasers up and down the lines, looking for a weakness. They came from the south, east, and west and made it look like the north was the only way to escape. Then there was silence. Flares were set off, claymores were used, booby traps worked, and cries sounded out in the jungle. Then horns and whistles started to blow as a huge bombardment began on the village. The Marine firebase set away at a distance answered, but they were under severe attack also.

When Ulee peeked his head up, he could see the enemy advancing by the thousands on the north side. Ulee was scared because this was the stuff of nightmares. Ulee's hands were trembling until he took a deep breath and let it out slowly, killing one invader after another with his Remington. Ulee's friend dove and pushed him out of the bunker just before a huge explosion. Ulee was a brave man, but he literally wet his pants when a mortar hit right next to him, killing his friend Mack Truck.

The Ranger squad added so much to the defense. These guys were real heroes. The 50 calibers and their two mortars took out more advancing enemy than all the rest of the defenders together, and these Kennewick boys put themselves in harm's way—saving life after life. Ulee was knocked on his butt and wounded by an explosion. One of the big Kennewick boys picked up Ulee by the collar and stood him up so he could get back in the fight. Ulee took a position and used his Remington 700. He didn't remember missing—it was a target-rich environment. He was just too slow with that Remington. He had at least twenty kills—but it was nothing to the swarming enemy.

Ulee watched Luau stand up so his Marines could retreat from the wire to the center compound. The enemy must have shot Luau seven times with AK-47 rounds, as he just blew up. Ulee cried out, "Brother!" Their eyes met as Luau dropped to the ground dead. Ulee looked around at all the men who fought bravely; it was medieval: the cries, the yelling, the screams, the war sounds. He watched each of his men die heroic deaths. The fighting went on all day, and it was growing dark. The attacks still came, lasting through the night. It was down to just him and a few boys from Kennewick and a couple of Montagnard. The explosions were deafening.

The battle turned to brutal hand-to-hand combat when Ulee's Remington was out of ammo and too slow to load. The pump-action shotgun became his weapon of choice. Finally, in the darkest part of the night, Ulee drew his 44 magnum, and six men were blown away. There was a moment of safety for Ulee after his 44 had shot the immediate threats. As he reloaded, he watched as Paco was killed trying to get to Donel. Ulee sent

Cerberus to protect Donel. Just as Donel was shot and Cerberus wounded with a grenade frag—in jumped the formidable Sammy from Portland, Oregon. For a kid with middle-class upbringing, he was a warrior. He died a warrior's death. Ulee picked up an AK-47 and began to pick off men in the midst of his scuffle. Cerberus hit the ground for protection, digging a foxhole as the breed does when they are in trouble. Benjamin came out of nowhere to display surprising courage. There seemed to be nothing tough about Benjamin, but his last efforts were fierce, fighting for the protection of Ulee's dog—as courageous as any hero that died that day. Now Ulee could not see any of his Kennewick Rangers still alive.

Rage consumed Ulee as he shot six more men with his 44. Then Ulee was out of ammo. He was shot in the left side and swarmed by enemy troops who wanted to take him alive. Out came his family bowie knife. That and martial arts were used in a bloody fight for survival. He thrust the huge knife into the chest of a large enemy combatant and twisted the blade only to have a bayonet stuck in his side while he was clubbed over the head with an AK-47. That was the last he remembered in that nightmare.

Δ Δ Δ

The next morning, Ulee awoke to the sound of the NVA shooting the wounded. He was physically pulled along with them as they retreated to the jungle. He surveyed the dead friends over the battlefield as he felt himself dying. He watched as Red, Bull, and Leighton were executed, along with some women Montagnard that had been fighting by their side.

He screamed, "No!"

His last prayer to Jesus was, "I don't mind dying. All my friends are dead—I am a disgraced warrior. God please give me a warrior's death."

He was overwhelmed with grief that every human experiences sometime. The grief and shame felt like a horrible vacuum in his soul, as he desperately missed me, his family, friends, his dog, and life. A brutal NVA soldier came over to fulfill his prayer. Ulee's last sensation was horrible pain.

Chapter Seven

Odyssey of Ulysses

AS I COMPLETED the story all the kids had gone to sleep. Much of the story had been told to me by some of Ulee's friends who witnessed those final moments and survived the war. Some of the story, now folklore, were pieces I conjured from what I know in my heart must have occurred. Ulee's and my spirits were linked. After a coffee break, everyone in the lodge insisted on hearing more.

Δ Δ Δ

In Kennewick, a Navy car drove up to the Sundown home. A chaplain and another officer got out. Not all families are notified by a chaplain, but this was respect for a third generation Marine whose father was a pastor. Ulee's father saw them coming and told his wife, Elizabeth, to take this with honor.

Elizabeth teared up. "There is no honor in losing one of my babies."

Pastor Caleb invited the Navy chaplain and the Marine into the living room. The chaplain introduced himself to Reverend Caleb Sundown.

Pastor Caleb said, "It was only a matter of time with Ulee. My brother John was KIA in Korea. We all know what happens to heroes."

They handed a letter and told them that they regretted to inform them that their son was killed in action. Caleb's large hands took the letter.

Elizabeth spoke. "Will I get my son's body back?"

"We have his dog tags but it is impossible to identify . . . I'm sorry ma'am, but the bodies were desecrated. The body is in transport here now."

They handed the precious dog tags to Reverend Sundown.

"I understand you were a Marine and fought in Korea, and your father fought in WWI with the Marines," the chaplain said. "Your family has brought much honor to our nation. On behalf of our grateful nation, we thank you. Your son was an exceptional Marine."

Reverend Sundown said nothing; tears rolled down his cheeks. Ulee's mom began to moan as Grandfather Ephraim came in from the back door and hugged her. The whole neighborhood could hear her cries of grief.

Ulee would only have been a senior in high school. I was in a special chemistry lab during the Christmas break when I looked outside my class window at Kennewick high school and saw three of Ulee's brothers walking past the alley where Argos had been shot defending us. They spoke to the teacher at the door, and the teacher called me out of the class.

Patty spoke. "Ulee is dead. He died defending an allied village."

I cried out, "No it's not true! I don't believe it is true."

All of his brothers surrounded me and hugged me. I just kept crying. "No, it doesn't feel right—I don't believe it. There is some mistake."

My life has been about ups and downs, great joys and great losses. Somehow this most horrible tragedy seemed inevitable after all that I had been through. My grief for Ulee joined in the cold pit in my heart where all the other trauma that I had been through hid far from human understanding. I was numb.

We had a beautiful funeral for him. We had a drum circle, smoke ceremony, taps, a twenty-one-gun salute, and a flag presented to Mrs. Sundown. The local Buddhist community showed up also as Ulee's friend Dawa, a Buddhist priest, had notified them from Vietnam. One of the local Buddhist priests spoke at the funeral, saying they appreciated how Ulee had saved children and helped an orphanage.

The football coach talked at the funeral and told us how great an athlete Ulee was and how good he could have been. The church was not big enough for the service, so it was held at the Kennewick High School gym. In attendance were all the teammates and competitors of Ulee from the Big Nine Conference, which extended from Wenatchee to Walla Walla, from Yakima to Moses Lake. Gang members from Pasco came to the funeral, as did police officers and every retired Marine in the Tri-Cities. A plaque was placed in the trophy case along with three others high school athletes who had died in Vietnam. It was the first of twelve soul-wrenching funerals for the Kennewick boys who had died defending the Montagnard village. Eleven plaques were set up at Kamiakin High School. Our community was in grief. When the plaques went up, much of the student body joined a sit-in protesting the Vietnam War. It was all a nightmare. Both the antiwar group and the patriotic youth fighting a bully they perceived as monolithic communism seemed like they had a righteous cause.

Δ Δ Δ

With the US participation in the war slowing down, the United States command began to reduce the Marine participation in combined action forces. On September 21, 1970, the Marines officially deactivated CAP as a separate command.

We tried to go on with our lives, and so after an appropriate time of shock and grief we had a family get together at the Sundown residence. Mama Elicia made her famous *arroz con pollo*. Everyone was trying to celebrate when the conversation turned to our grief over the death of Ulee. His brothers told stories about how brave he was as he watched after them.

"I have lost two boys," Grandmother Elizabeth said. "No mother should ever have to lose one of their babies." She couldn't speak Ulee's name.

Pastor Caleb told us, "That is just our grief. Grief is the most profound emotion human beings experience. C.S. Lewis, who lost his mom, his friends in World War I, and his wife whom he married on her deathbed, thought that grief is one of the most powerful arguments for eternal life."

As we were eating dessert around the fireplace, the phone rang. A lady told Patty, I have a call from the President of the United States."

Patty said, "Who is this? This is one of my girlfriends playing a joke."

Then the President came on. "Son, can I speak to your parents?"

Pastor Caleb took the phone. "Your son Ulee is a hero." He went on saying that there was some kind of mix up and that even though Ulee's dog tags had been found and the entire combined action group had died at the battle that they now had word that Ulee was a prisoner of war of North Vietnam.

"We don't know where he is being held, but we received a television broadcast of him and a few other missing in action men." Caleb was speechless.

The President said, "This must be heart-wrenching for you. But I want you to know we are doing everything we can to get our boys home." He went on to tell Ulee's dad, "I will be praying for Ulysses Looking Glass Sundown." Pastor Caleb said in a monotone. "Ulee is still alive."

Our family let out a cheer with tears that we would never forget. Then it set in that Ulee was a prisoner of war. This nightmare would never end. The worst part was when the mothers of the Ranger boys from Kamiakin High School in Kennewick came by to congratulate us on our good news. Our hearts just broke knowing that they had lost their sons saving Ulee's life.

△ △ △

The journey on the trail as a POW took place mostly at night. He could see from the North Star that they were heading north. He was treated with a mixture of brutality and disrespect. He was stripped naked. The NVA would urinate on him and kick him. And then a young lady would come and attend to his wounds. He was blessed to be in a semi-state of unconsciousness. He wondered why he was kept alive. One day, as they hid in the shade of the jungle, the young woman who was operating as a corpsman spoke to him in English.

She said, "You are a Native American?"

"Yes," he said, "and you speak English?" He asked, "Why did they let me live when they massacred everyone else?"

She whispered, "We know you and hate you. You have killed many of us as a sniper. You use a bow and move through the jungle like a tiger. We call you the savage, but we also know that you do not kill women, kids, and the elderly, even when they are soldiers."

Later, when Ulee woke up in a Viet Cong prison camp, he saw a world that he had never imagined. The prison camp—or camps, for it was a moveable horror—was not easily imagined by a generation that had grown up watching World War II movies. There were no guard towers, no searchlights, and no barbed wire. Instead, the camp consisted of a muddy clearing hacked out of the jungle where sunlight barely penetrated the interlocking layers of branches and vines. A thatched hut served as the prisoners' shelter. It was encased in a bamboo cage called a tiger cage. A bamboo platform was their communal bed.

The young Americans, barefoot, in tatters, and on the verge of starvation, were given a little rice and forced by the Viet Cong to gather *manioc*, their potato-like food, which was sometimes poisoned with Agent Orange by US spray planes. They lived under constant danger of being bombed by their own forces. An American turncoat armed with a rifle—Marine Thomas Slater—helped the Viet Cong keep them in line.

Sixteen of the fifty-two prisoners of war who entered the camp died. Five were freed for propaganda purposes. One defected. The remaining twelve American survivors, plus two French nurses, were saved only by the North Vietnamese decision to send them on a forced march up the Ho Chi Minh Trail to Hanoi in 1971, where they remained until they were freed in 1973.

The men were all captured in 1970. The prisoner in command was Navy Captain John McCleary. His father was a famous admiral. Captain McCleary was a graduate of the Naval Academy. He was offered the opportunity to be released and refused preferential treatment. He was a real hero. He was a pilot and twenty-seven years old. He had been there for three years. He was shot down in 1967 and had been shuffled from VC camps hidden in the jungle.

McCleary told Ulee not to tell him anything—because the VC would beat it out of him. If he had any escape plans, he shouldn't let anyone know. "Don't trust anyone." McCleary said. "We all break—tell them everything you know and stay alive. Just keep your sanity and don't defect to their side.

As soon as Ulee arrived, a Russian team was allowed to shoot film of them exercising in formation for physical training. They were given one good meal of rice and a chicken—the only chicken the men had seen in three years. Slater was the only one interviewed and spoke as though all of the prisoners had become Marxist. This was the film that made its way back to the US and confirmed that Ulee was alive.

The first month, Ulee thought he was going to die. The depression and isolation were more than he could take. He was starving to death, and the torture was something for which he was trained. Escape seemed impossible until he heard one night a familiar howl in the jungle. It was Cerberus. God had not forgotten him even in a Viet Cong prison.

The prisoners were taken on runs to gather manioc. On one of the runs, they spotted Cerberus, and the guards shot at him, missing. They cursed the wild dog as if they were superstitious and afraid of him. Of course the POWs were under heavy guard during these runs. For Ulee the physical training and runs gave him hope and energy.

△ △ △

Every night Ulee would look into the jungle to catch a glimpse of his loyal friend Cerberus. He had somehow followed and found him and was waiting wisely in the jungle. One night they even found a dead chicken near their cage. Cerberus had killed and brought it to them. Cerberus licked Ulee's tears through the bamboo bars. The other prisoners could not believe their eyes. Then the loyal war dog disappeared into the jungle again.

The interrogations were indescribable. Ulee was hung from the ceiling of the interrogation hut. He was beaten with a bamboo rod. He was cut all over his chest and back. They cut off his ring finger a quarter of the way down. All of this took place with his fellow prisoners never hearing a sound except the shouting of the rat-faced commander of the prisoner of war camp. He spoke English and he yelled profanities, trying to get Ulee to break. Slater was a part of it, as he was at all of the torture sessions of each prisoner. Slater cried like a baby during the torture of Ulee, but there was no sound from this young warrior. Ulee was running in his mind in the high Wallowa Mountains. Sometimes as Ulee was being tortured they could hear Cerberus barking from the jungle. He could tell what was going on, and he was trying to encourage Ulee as well as warn the Viet Cong. Ulee finally broke down and let out long groans of pain. It broke the hearts of each of his fellow POWs. It was so sorrowful to see this strong man broken. Cerberus howled from the jungle as he heard his owner cry. It was eerie to the VC to experience the bond between this savage and his beast.

All of this torture was spaced so that Ulee could gather his strength again for more torture. They were trying to break his spirit. When he was brought back to the bamboo tiger box with McCleary, the captain begged him to break and tell them everything. They wanted to know passwords, strategy for recon teams, and how snipers were equipped and trained. Ulee gave them nothing. They told him what he already knew—how the Native Americans had been lied to, how their treaties had been broken, and how they suffered in poverty.

Ulee told them, "Every society had injustice, and in a democracy we overcome our difficulties."

One time after a very vicious torture session in which the jungle resonated with Ulee's broken moans and cries Ulee returned a completely broken man. It was a Vietnamese holiday and several of the prisoners were together in the tiger hootch made out of bamboo. Ulee was brought in and dropped in the middle of the floor. One of African-American prisoners said, come on, white man don't give up. You are going to live through this. Don't lose hope. Ulee yelled, "I am not a white man—I am a Nez Perce warrior." Captain McCleary said, "Let's do something Nez Perce." Ulee said, gather around and pretend it is cold and we have a crackling fire. I am going to tell you a story. One Marine POW started to pound on the bamboo like it was a drum. And

Ulee began, "it was a day like any other day. I was a kid in the Tri-Cities where the sun almost always seems to shine. It was a place where the most we worried about were sports. I was trying to pole vault for the first time and I saw the most beautiful woman in the history of the world, Penelope Morales Santos. Her eyes were so beautiful that I could get lost in her eyes for eternity." Everyone smiled as they started to hear the legend and then the guards came and separated us. But Ulee had found new courage in the telling of the story.

When the horrible torture continued, Ulee just kept saying, "The Lord is my shepherd," and thought how God had miraculously sent him his Beauceron to help him escape. When he passed out, they took him back to the cage. Two guards carried him, and one followed carrying the AK-47s. When they threw him on the floor, one of the guards kicked him in the ribs. On the second kick, Ulee grabbed his foot, surprising everyone. He did a kip-up and was on his feet. It was just as he had trained his whole life. He did a spinning kick and broke the neck of one of the guards. As he fell to the ground, it was obvious he was dead. He kicked the groin of a second guard and broke his neck with a side kick. He was too close to the guard with the AK to shoot. So, he hit him in the Adam's apple so he could not breathe. He broke his nose with his open hand and blinded him with the other hand, inserting fingers in his eyes. The two battled until Ulee thrust his hand through his solar plexus, killing his enemy. This all happened in less than two minutes. A guard with another AK came running, and Ulee dove at his legs and did a hard bodyslam takedown with him. As they scrambled, Ulee broke his wrist, then did a reversal and came around behind him and broke his neck with a full nelson.

Captain McCleary sat horrified, fearing that guards would certainly kill everyone in the hut. Ulee punched the captain with an upper cut and knocked him out; he fell over Ulee, who hoisted him in a fireman's carry. He picked up both AKs, and with them blazing, he ran for the jungle feeling like the captain who had been a prisoner of war for years weighed nothing.

Cerberus emerged from the jungle running at full speed. He jumped two fences, both higher than five feet, and then he landed on some of the pursuing guards. Their shots were ineffective against the speed of the war dog. He leapt at the throat of the first enemy, tearing it and killing him immediately. He grabbed another by groin as these dogs instinctively do. All the commotion caused the enemy to turn their attention to the dog as Ulee dropped the AKs and ran as fast as he could to the relative safety of the jungle wall. Ulee led the enemy for a chase in the dark for ten miles. That was his training range, and it was amazing how fresh he felt as he ran carrying the skinny captain on his back. Finally, he felt exhausted and dropped the captain. He buried him in the jungle floor and then buried himself. The VC guards ran right by them. The dogs that they had with them were on the scent of Cerberus who outran those dogs and turned back to kill each one—one at a time—grabbing by the neck and shaking them like they were rag dolls. The death howls by the guards' German shepherds echoed through the jungle. By the time the guards found that their Russian-imported guard dogs all were gone, it was too late. The sight of these dead dogs added to their superstition as to Cerberus and his master, "The Savage." The guards kept mumbling. *"Một cái gì đó về con chó đen này và tổng man rợ của mình không phải con người họ là quỷ."* Or in English, "Something about that black dog and his savage master is not human—they are ghosts."

△ △ △

Ulee and his captain were headed northeast towards Laos—the opposite way that the guards would expect them to go. Ulee left no tracks. He made a stone knife and then made a bow with three arrows with a stone arrowhead. He felt safe and confident. Thirty miles out, he left the captain buried in the jungle floor; again, his only companionship was Cerberus, who lay near the captain to guard him. Now McCleary was full from the meal that the jungle provided for them. But he reached out and put his arm around Cerberus like a boy with his puppy, scared at night. Cerberus licked him and comforted this heroic POW. Ulee circled back and set booby traps and ambushed those who were trying to follow them. He killed five with his bow, reusing the arrows. He left their bodies hanging naked from the trees upside down, (the same position they had tortured him) tied with vines to warn those who were following. They believed him to be an Indian warrior returned from the dead to punish them.

Ulee picked up McCleary and carried him once again for miles. The pursuing VC squad was nothing to underestimate. They tracked well in the jungle. When Ulee arrived at the Ho Chi Min trail, he encountered another squad. As fate would have it, the VC Ulee and Luau had faced—the enemy tracker Ulee had nicknamed Pinkerton—was hot on their trail. Ulee was outwitted; he did not know what to do. So he prayed. "Lord Jesus I wish I were home in the Wallowa mountains to escape my enemy." Just then he heard the territorial roar of a tiger.

It was just as when he was a boy encountering the grizzly.

He smiled as Captain McCleary trembled, saying, "That is all we need."

Ulee said, "Yes it is. Don't be afraid; that cat can smell fear. You have nothing to be afraid of."

Ulee used every trick he had learned as a child to hide their scent and let the tiger know that they were not the prey to be hunted. The Viet Cong were terrified, and the tiger could smell it. Ulee watched from the top of a tree as the tiger hunted the pursuing Viet Cong and North Vietnamese regulars. Their belief in reincarnation added to the fear that forces of demons were working under Ulee's control. This was the room the two escaped prisoners and their dog needed. The breeze was working with them and against the VC, so they moved towards the border to Laos.

Ulee knew of a Green Beret encampment there. As they approached the camp, they were both wearing Vietnamese clothing, and they took off their *"Nan La,"* or Vietnamese sun hats and both yelled, "We are Americans," as loud as they could. Bullets snapped by them from the M-16s. They yelled their names—Ulee had worked with this A-team before. They collapsed, wondering if they had been shot by friendly fire.

Ulee woke up in the Green Beret barracks with a sergeant telling him, "You were lucky you were not killed by friendly fire. God must have had a plan for your lives because very few escaped prisoner of war camps in this war."

Seeing that McCleary was safe, Ulee was quickly outfitted with sniper gear from the Green Berets, and as he walked out of camp in came Cerberus. The dog had been providing a distraction as they made the last leg of their journey to the American encampment. Cerberus was limping, missing one eye, and severely wounded, but what a reunion. Cerberus licked Ulee, and Ulee spoke to him in Nez Perce, petting him. Then Ulee left, after putting Cerberus on a leash and giving him to the captain.

Ulee picked up the trail of his enemies. He tracked them all the way back to the prisoner of war camp, taking the enemy out one at a time. The last one to die was Pinkerton who realized that all his friends had been killed and now he was the one being tracked and chased. Finally, Ulee stood before him, blocking the trail to North Vietnam. They both had AKs pointed at one another. Ulee threw his down, pulling out his Marine Kbar knife. Pinkerton laughed and aimed at Ulee and pulled the trigger.

Ulee dived into the jungle. As Pinkerton approached the spot where Ulee had once stood, Ulee jumped from a tree and covered his enemy in a chokehold, making him drop his weapon. Ulee ended his hated enemy's life with the knife. "I am sorry. We both knew it would end this way," he said.

Ulee returned to the POW camp where he had been held, but it was empty. The prisoners had been transferred to Hanoi. He reluctantly went back to the Green Beret camp and was flown to Da Nang in a helicopter. He recovered, lifting weights when he could; then it was off to a hospital in Hawaii for evaluation. I met him in Hawaii with Ulee's parents.

Δ Δ Δ

It was May, 1971. Ulee had joined the Marines in November 1968, so he had done three tours of Vietnam and been in the heart of the worst action. He was not alone. A few warriors always see most of the action and many see no action when it comes to war. For me this was unthinkable; I was emotionally worn out from loving someone who continued to sign up again and again for war.

In times of tragedy, of war, of necessity, women can do amazing things. The human capacity for survival and renewal is awesome. While we hugged and kissed when we met and I enjoyed his parents so much—we had a lot to talk about. We walked the white sandy beach at Walmanalo Park hand in hand. The ocean was turquoise blue and the water warm when we swam together and kissed underwater. The rocks coming down to the water in the distance and the shade of the trees gave us the feeling that we were in paradise. We were.

Ulee had injuries, but he recovered quickly. I asked him how he looked so good after being a POW. He said that he was serving in special operations; they were given weights, hard workouts, and shots that the training sergeant called juice.

"What is in the juice I asked?"

"No one asks—there are so many questions that no one asks when it comes to special operations."

We were too good of friends for me to beat around the bush. "Ulee, I am not comfortable with all the killing you are doing. And you keep signing up for more. You could have come home two years ago."

"Do you think I am comfortable with it? I never wanted to kill a human being. These are my people, villagers for the most part. They come from tribes of primitives. Their faces look a lot like the faces of my family." Ulee began to cry "Aheeeeeeee. What have I done, Jesus?"

I didn't say anything. I just hugged him. He seemed like a child in my arms. He sobbed so hard. I felt like this strong warrior somehow felt safe with me, that I could see a part of his heart that no one would ever see. I prayed for all those traumatized by war that did not have someone that loved them as much as I loved Ulysees Looking Glass Sundown.

After an hour of walking he spoke again. "I am good at war. It was like God made me to be a warrior. And so many of these soft hippies are nice people, but they can't shoot a gun under pressure even if they are called marksmen. They are courageous and have saved my life plenty of times, but they are not as gifted at war as I am. They are my friends and they die. Every time I see one die it is like watching a little boy die a horrible death. I believe I owe it to my brothers in combat to do the fighting for those that should be home watching TV or sitting at a desk job. For the most part, these city boys are just being sent off to be slaughtered. I can't come home as long as I know I have one friend serving. You have no idea, Penny, the heroic friends I have lost in this fight, the horrible pictures I have in my head. These friends saved my life. I need to be the last man out."

"There is such injustice on both sides. Penny, I care for the people of Vietnam. They feel like Native Americans. They are tribesmen with a war being fought over two philosophical powers that are both spotted with hypocritical elements. There is the good and bad on both sides, and I still believe that totalitarian communism must be stopped. Their dreams are our nightmares."

"So why does it have to be you?" I yelled. "Is it going to help if you get yourself killed? Haven't you made us suffer enough? Can't some other mountain boy come and be a star of the Special Forces?"

"I am not the star. There are country boys that have done far more than I have, and they never got any medals for it." There is one sniper named Carlos Hathcock with the First Marine division. He has a record ninety-three confirmed North Vietamese and Viet Cong kills. He even shot a general one time. He made a shot almost a mile long and won a dual against the North Vietnamese greatest sniper by shooting through his scope and hitting them in the eye. The Viet Cong nicknamed him White Feather and he is much more of a hero than I would ever be."

"It sounds like you have made up your mind that you are going to stay until the war ends."

Ulee looked into my eyes. "Your eyes are beautiful when you get angry. Listen, Penny, I love you more than I could ever put into words. I just want to be with you for eternity."

We were both crying when we came back. Ulee's mom was a strong woman of noble character. I talked to her for over an hour after we came back.

The beautiful Elizabeth Sundown never pulled punches when she talked. "Penny, maybe you should pray about asking Ulee to marry you. Ulee makes his decisions by his heart. He has a tender heart and he follows his heart."

"Maybe you need to give a young man a good reason to come home," Mrs. Sundown concluded.

Ulee and I were both eighteen. So I went out to look for him, and his dad told me that he had gone for his ten mile run.

"What is the juice that they are giving him?" he asked me.

"I don't know, Reverend Sundown," I replied. Caleb Sundown had fought in war and was well read. But he was even better at reading people.

He spoke with the wisdom of a chief. "You are a very smart girl who lives to study in the medical field someday—I think you have an idea."

"I know some East Germans and Russians are injecting anabolic steroids and human growth hormone to make them bigger, stronger, and faster," I said. "It is going to become a huge issue in the sports competition someday. My guess is that it is some kind of hormone. I am afraid because it is experimental and has to be dangerous."

"Well—walking through the jungle with Viet Cong after you is even more dangerous. We need him to come home. Did my wife talk to you about proposing to our son?" the wise older pastor asked.

"Isn't he supposed to propose to me?"

"Yes," laughed Caleb. "But if you haven't noticed, he is stubborn. He showed you he loved you when he fought that gangster for you. He is just lost in the quicksand of war, and maybe you are the one to rescue him."

"You know, Pastor Sundown? You are right. I am well read in the medical field, and this whole conversation isn't healthy. I don't want to be manipulated by my pastor. I love Ulee, but we need to have a healthy relationship—not one where we are trying to save each other."

Caleb patted me on my head like I was a little girl. "I can see why Ulee loves you, Penelope. You are a noble Christian woman—and beautiful."

I asked. "What does that mean?"

"It means you are right. We are sorry—it is not in our position to ask you to propose to our son. Please forgive us." He spoke with such sincerity.

"Yes, Pastor. Healthy Christianity is knowing that even pastors are imperfect people."

Δ Δ Δ

That night I couldn't get their idea out of my mind. The next morning, I ran with Ulee along the beach. We stopped.

"Penny, I want to marry you, but I don't want to leave you as a widow." He wrapped me in his strong arms and kissed me so gently.

"Then don't—don't go back." I cried. I got on my knees. "Ulee, will you marry me? I promise to protect you as long as I live."

He laughed. "Protect me from what?"

"From yourself—you are your worst enemy," I said as I smiled.

That afternoon we got a marriage license, and a Hawaiian pastor wedded us on the beach. Ulee's dad was his best man, and his mom was my maid of honor.

Right after the wedding, Ulee's folks flew back to the Tri-Cities. They explained that we didn't need a chaperone anymore. Our wedding pictures are one of the precious treasures that I have. We both look so young. Ulee could never have been more handsome. And I did not look so bad myself. And that night, when we returned to our room, we both had tears as he reached out for me. I grabbed his hand and felt where his ring finger had been cut off. I ran my hand down the knife scar on his cheek that he received fighting Raul for my freedom. Ulee was so handsome. We said nothing. I took off his shirt; he was scarred from the torture. I kissed each scar as I cried. We loved each other more than time or eternity. It felt so right to sleep with my husband that night; even though memories of abuse as a child ran through my mind, our Godly love and his gentle touch brought healing to me. The next three weeks were heaven on earth. We were together for only three weeks when he received a call to report to the airport for transport back to Vietnam.

I told him that he had to quit. He said he couldn't leave those orphans there; he needed to see this thing through and get them out, at least. We fought, and I even slapped him.

"I will always love you more than life itself. But I have to go back to war to see this thing through and at least try to bring some of these kids home. I know we are going to lose this war, and I know I am going to die. But I could never live with myself unless I do what I think is right. And it is wrong for me to survive and live out my life in bliss when so many are suffering."

Ulee looked so rugged and strong of body and heart. I told him he was suffering survivor's guilt and asked him how he could expect me to wait for such a fatal outcome.

"You are right. I love you and I need to set you free." He left and went to the courthouse to get our marriage annulled. As he did this, I did not mention that marrying him was my one shot at becoming a US citizen. I would not marry anyone else to become a citizen. I cried all the way home.

Later that month I found out that I was pregnant with our child. I did not write him. In our church, I was treated with grace as an unmarried mother. My family treated me with respect also, and both Ulee's family and mine told me they would help with the child. In February, 1972, I gave birth to a little brown-skinned boy that I named Telemachus Cruz Morales Sundown. He was a legal citizen of the United States.

Chapter Eight

Trapped with Calypso

AT THE LODGE the days were full of fishing, hiking, canoeing, reading, and long talks; most of them were about the series of stories that I was telling. Sometimes we would take a break from these oral history lessons about our family, allowing everyone time to absorb these stories and discuss them. These stories were not new, as I have said. But the way I tell them and what I emphasized sometimes changed. I have found that if you change the way you tell a story, you can create new meaning. After a few days of rest, I continued, speaking about my beloved.

△ △ △

Ulee was attached to the 3rd Division South Vietnamese Marines, based in Quang Ngai. The division was initially raised in October, 1971, in Quảng Trị. They collapsed in the 1972 Easter Offensive and were reconstituted and destroyed at Da Nang in 1975. This was not something that Ulee wanted to talk about because he was now serving in black ops. Black, or covert, operations take place in any war. It is heroism with secrecy—no more medals, no recognition, only plausible deniability. He would become a ghost because of his special skills. For Ulee, the benefit was that he was in range to look after the Buddhist orphanage that he had grown to love. He wrote a rare letter to me saying that he did not understand himself. He spoke about my beauty. He would never get it out of his mind how I looked on the beach in Hawaii: my brown skin, long hair, young figure—and he always talked about my eyes. He told his brother Patty in a phone call that he did love me with all of his heart, but he could not leave this war at this time. He honestly believed that if he did not fight the NVA that thousands of tribal people would be killed, massacred, and tortured. He was dumb enough at eighteen to believe that he could make a difference. I felt guilty for manipulating him into marrying me in Hawaii. Even though I would not trade that time or our child, Telemachus, for anything. At the same time, Ulee was being emotionally manipulated by his superior officers to join the black ops. He worked with Rangers, Green Beret, Marine Recon, and Navy Seals. He always played the role of sniper or hunter—a menacing threat as a diversion to instill fear in the hearts of the enemy.

After one mission, when it seemed like the whole nation was being silently overrun by Viet Cong, Ulee ran into the moral dilemma. He came upon a familiar village close to the orphanage. He could hear the terrible sounds of women and children crying. He took a position from where he could hit almost any target in the village. There was a US platoon of "advisors." They had found VC in the village and were burning it. Many of the men from the village lay dead, where a brief battle had taken place. The lieutenant colonel leading this group had just executed an old man; at the same time, a group of American and ARVN were abusing a young woman. Ulee spotted through the scope that the woman was Ahn, his friend from the orphanage.

Ulee walked in and yelled the name of the lieutenant colonel that he knew. "Wright, what are you doing?"

All the men looked like they had swallowed a frog. They knew what they were doing was wrong.

The lieutenant colonel said, "Savage, you have no room to talk or judge. This is a VC village. We found seven men with hidden AK-47s."

While Lieutenant Colonel Wright spoke defensively to Ulee, it was obvious that he was afraid of this native known as The Savage. Five American servicemen were abusing Ahn and they did not stop. The other men watched.

Ulee yelled, "You know before God this is wrong."

The lieutenant colonel said, "This is war and Aristotle said there is no morality in war because the Government becomes the parent—we are not responsible for this act of war."

"You know this is wrong. Regardless of your position, Immanuel Kant said that there are Categorical Imperatives that are binding upon all reasonable men. There is justice that transcends the fog of war and you are about to meet that justice."

Colonel Wright said, "I don't know Immanuel Kant. Is he some Mexican folk singer?"

The lieutenant colonel pulled out his 45 and pulled back the hammer as he stuck the barrel up against Ulee's forehead. The tall and muscular lieutenant colonel was a redneck in his forties. He snarled. "This is not the way you want to die." Ulee dropped his Remington 700 and raised his hands.

Wright smiled because he felt in control. "Don't make me do this; this stuff happens in every war. You don't have to be part of abusing this girl, you just have to watch."

Ulee spoke quietly as he had to Raul. "You are not going to get a warning—no bravado. But I can't stand for a bully."

"What? One kid who thinks he is an Indian is telling us we are not going to get a warning?"

The whole platoon began to laugh at Ulee. Then they stopped laughing because it began to dawn on them that he was serious. There was a long pause—everyone knew someone was going to die. Ulee turned his head just as Wright fired, taking the tip of Ulee's ear off. With a smooth, lighting-fast draw, Ulee pulled his 44 magnum from his vest holster, cocked back the hammer, and shot Lieutenant Colonel Wright between the eyes, practically blowing off the back of his head.

The four men who were abusing Ahn reached for their weapons. Ulee shot each one in the head. It all took place in the blink of an eye.

A fifth man abusing Ahn started to cry as he stopped. "I'm

sorry—you are right; I know this is wrong. I was just going along
with the others."

His platoon watched with frozen guilt. Ulee executed him
and his weapon was empty now.

Ulee turned and ordered the platoon. "Now get out of
here and tell your commanding officer the truth—exactly what
happened. You need to repent and maybe God will forgive you.
But be afraid—be very terrified—because I doubt if I can ever
forgive you."

Ulee picked up a poncho and put it over the naked body of
Ahn. She was broken and looked like—well something that no
man wants to ever have in his mind. Ulee picked her up and
carried her out of the camp, all the way to the orphanage, and
gave her to Dawa.

"I am sorry—this doesn't not represent the United States;
this represents the evil inside men."

Δ Δ Δ

In March, 1972, Ahn gave birth to a baby girl. She looked
Vietnamese but she had blue eyes. She named her baby, Nhung,
which means energetic and extremely likeable, after the kind
hero who had saved her life. Ulee would visit this little girl every
time he came to the orphanage, he told her that God had a plan
for this little girl even though a terrible hurt had brought her into
the world. Ulee treated the baby like a daughter even though he
never treated Ahn as a wife—more as a sister.

All US Marines and troops were pulled out of Vietnam. Ulee,
like others in the black ops, continued doing missions in Laos,
Cambodia, even North Vietnam looking for MIA prisoners. Like
others in black operations he assisted the South Vietnamese
in conflict when they were over their heads. It was an advisory
role, but for Ulee his advice was keep your head down while I go
hunting. Ulee kept visiting and helping out the orphanage and
continued dialogue with Dawa. The baby was told by her mother
that Ulee was her daddy. Ulee wasn't comfortable with that, but
he also didn't want to explain the real story to a two-year-old.
His brother wrote to him and told him about Penelope and
his son Telemachus, but being in black ops he never received
correspondence from home. He and his superiors thought of

him as a man who was yet to die. He did not plan on coming back from Vietnam.

Captain McCleary was becoming a lifetime friend. Ulee heard the captain was on his way to becoming an admiral. Ulee had been awarded the Navy Cross for saving the captain, and the captain was given the Congressional Medal of Honor for being one of the few to ever escape. Ulee's Navy Cross was awarded in secret, just as everything in Ulee's life in the black ops was a secret. Ulee and Captain McCleary met and Ulee told the soon to be admiral McCleary about his adopted daughter named after Nhung. A friendship had formed between the two that could never be separated.

Very few Americans escaped prison during the Vietnam. One of the most famous escapes happened on December 31, 1968. James N. Rowe, a Special Forces second lieutenant, was captured five years earlier. He overpowered a guard after five years of captivity and was picked up by a US helicopter. No other US military escaped successfully who were being held in North Vietnam, only Bud Day, who was recaptured in sight of a South Vietnamese base. There were thirty-three successful escapes of Viet Cong prisoner of war camps in South Vietnam. Of those escapes, thirty took place within the first year and only three were successful after one year.

△ △ △

The Yom Kippur War, also known as the 1973 Arab–Israeli War, was a war fought by the coalition of Arab states led by Egypt and Syria against Israel from October 6 to 25, 1973. The war began when the Arab coalition launched a joint surprise attack on Israeli positions in the Israeli-occupied territories on Yom Kippur, the holiest day in Judaism, which also occurred that year during the Muslim holy month of Ramadan. Egyptian and Syrian forces crossed ceasefire lines to enter the Sinai Peninsula and Golan Heights respectively, which had been captured by Israel in the 1967 Six-Day War. Both the United States and the Soviet Union initiated massive resupply efforts to their respective allies during the war, and this led to a near confrontation between the two nuclear superpowers. The war began with a massive and successful Egyptian crossing of the

Suez Canal. After crossing the cease-fire lines, Egyptian forces advanced virtually unopposed into the Sinai Peninsula.

Ulee had not made a promise to Luau to fight for Israel. This conservative Christian and their Jewish friend somehow knew that someday Israel would need Ulee's skills. Ulee never promised, but when the war broke out, he asked his commanding officers about it and Israel. It was a reasonable black ops assignment. So Ulee left for Tel Aviv officially as a private contractor or soldier of fortune. He was offered fifty thousand dollars—a fortune to him in 1973—to go and use his skills to carry out ambushes, as he had since he was fifteen years old. He was also given a battlefield commission and promoted to Marine captain. This would make him a far better consultant to the Israeli army.

For seventeen days, he fought to defend a kibbutz full of Marxist Jews from Muslim Egyptians who allied with the Soviet Union. It was almost like reliving the battle for the Montagnard village, only this time he could not get the kids out. He organized the defense of the walled kibbutz. The Israelis could fight just like the brave Viet Cong. Men, women, old, and young all took up arms. Even the children helped in the fight. Ulee disappeared into the night and again spent half his time ambushing the Egyptian army. The Egyptians in the desert of Sinai learned to fear the night just as the Viet Cong had when Ulee hunted. And during the day, his Remington 700 knew how to find his targets. There was so much killing that Ulee wondered if this was the battle of Armageddon described in the Bible.

The mayor of the little kibbutz, Abraham Schwarz, had seven children. His wife's name was Miriam, and they treated Ulee like a son. They were Hasidic Jews and very pious. Ulee did not understand all their mysticism, but he improved in his Hebrew even though the Schwartz family all spoke broken English. He admired the Jewish people and saw their ability to celebrate even in the face of difficulty as something that primitive people in Vietnam and Natives in the US and Central America had come to appreciate and to know their families and traditions.

It was a war of immigration again. The Jews had immigrated to Palestine after the Holocaust trying to gain safety and a homeland. There were moderate Muslims fighting on their side and radicals who had been deprived of their land fighting against them. In Vietnam, it was a battle between moving people groups. The Japanese, the French, and the Americans were trying to either colonize or defend the South Vietnamese democracy in the face of Communist aggression.

There was one widow named Bathsheba who would fight like a man but was one of the most beautiful women Ulee had ever seen. She was obviously infatuated with Ulee, as he proved his skills in saving the kibbutz from the enemy attacks. Ulee was drawn to Bathsheba, but he prayed to resist temptation, and the devout Hasidic Jewish girl did the same thing. After one battle, she put a bandage on a knife wound on his chest. She saw the many scars from his torture and she spoke in Hebrew about how he was a young man to have seen so much war.

"הברה דכ לכ סייוניעו המחלמ תא הארש ריעצ שיא התא." (You are a young man to have seen so much war and been tortured like this) Ulee answered her kindly but honestly. "You are a beautiful girl, very brave, and I respect you. I am sorry that your husband died in this terrible war. Yes, I am young and have seen a lot of war. But I have given my heart to the love of my life in my hometown. I pray that God has a wonderful husband and family for you in the future. But for today we are just fellow soldiers fighting for peace."

While Ulee's help was embraced by the community, there was a lot of work to do to survive this short, bloody war. He taught members of this Hasidic community how to shoot. Some of the older people showed him their concentration camp tattoos. He heard stories that were nightmares, but then he also had nothing against Islam that the Egyptians were following. They all believed in one God. Ulee respected the devout Muslims who abstained from many vices. It was all very confusing for a young man trying to make sense of senseless war.

Ulee had no idea how many men he killed in this war. The Egyptian tanks were destroyed by the Israeli air force. Even though the kibbutz was fighting against great odds, Ulee would not let them fail. He had tasted massacre before in Vietnam and would not stand for it again.

The fighting was fierce—night and day. Both sides were resupplied with artillery and tanks. It was its own kind of hell.

One moment after the kibbutz he was protecting was shelled, he saw half the village die. He watched beautiful and heroic Bathsheba blown apart by a mortar round while trying to save a child. When the walls were breached, it was bloody hand-to-hand combat. Ulee took out his bone-handled knife after his weapons were empty. It was horrible killing these honorable people. After the enemy retreated, he stood there covered in blood—his shirt torn off and he just yelled, "God, where are you in a war?" He was a broken man. Suddenly it was just over. The war ended after two weeks of hell for Ulee, but even worse for his enemy. On October 22, a United Nations-brokered ceasefire quickly unraveled, with each side blaming the other for the breach. A second ceasefire was imposed cooperatively on October 25 to end the war.

Ulee was given two medals, a medal of defense for fighting in the Yom Kippur War, and Golda Meir awarded him the medal of valor. Neither of these were mentioned to the press because of the nature of his black ops position

Ulee was designated as *Ger Toshev*, or righteous among the nations. He had a tree planted in Israel in his honor and was made an honorary citizen of Israel. He was also invited to visit Israel any time at the expense of Israel. While he was there, he spent a few nights in the King David Hotel in Jerusalem and ran around the walled old city of Jerusalem. He could smell Palestinian mothers baking their bread as he ran. He stopped on the Mount of Olives to look at the breathtaking view and prayed as the sun came up in the east, shining on the city. Jesus felt so close to him, but he again did not feel like a Christian. He was a mass murderer and carried the weight in his eyes.

△ △ △

In a moment's notice, he was on his way back to Vietnam. He had a layover in New York. He called one of his brothers and heard the news that he was a father and I was getting straight A's at Columbia Community College and working as a model at the Bon Marche. He called me, and when I answered, he could not talk. He could hear his son crying in the background. I finally said, "Ulee is that you? Are you alive? Where are you?"

Ulee couldn't talk—I could hear him crying softly. He finally said, "No, Ulee is dead." And he hung up. He was so full of shame. He stopped praying. But he kept reading his Bible and other compendiums of philosophy, history, and theology. None of it helped. Running helped, doing pull-ups and parallel dips helped, as did pushups and sit-ups.

Before he returned to Vietnam, he stopped by the Tri-Cities. It was a beautiful desert day in Pasco as he walked up the campus at Columbia Basin College. As he walked, wearing his captain uniform, one of his friends yelled out. It was a friend nicknamed Tank.

"Is that you Sundown?" He turned, and one of the CBC football players came walking to him, with the coach following close behind. His friend gave him a hug and introduced him to the coach.

The coach told Ulee how he was always hearing stories about him when he was in high school. He said, "If you want to join our team, we would love to have you. It looks like you have put on a lot of muscle."

I walked up to them, not believing my eyes. When he lifted his eyes and we looked into each other's faces for the first time since Hawaii, we both just started to cry and ran into an embrace. His friend and coach left respectfully. As we kissed in front of the student body, I believed that Ulee was my other half—my soulmate that I could not live without. We didn't talk; we just cried.

After a few moments some college students came up and started chanting, "Baby killer, baby killer. Ulee was wearing his Marine service C uniform with a piss cutter hat. Get out of Vietnam."

"I thought all that was winding down now that we are supposed to be out of Vietnam," Ulee said.

My sister pulled up in a car with Telemachus in a car seat. Belén got him out, and as she brought him over, Ulee smiled. "His skin is brown—his hair is brown. He is everything I wanted to be. He is manly for a little baby." The baby seemed to hold his daddy rather than the other way around. The way Telemachus gripped his dad, I was pouring tears seeing them together. It was as if baby Telemachus somehow knew this was his daddy.

Ulee only had a short time: one night. His family and the Santos family all had a barbecue in Columbia Park, close to where they found the Kennewick man. It was a salmon barbecue. His mom made fried bread and huckleberry pie. Mama Elicia made fajitas on the grill. As it grew dark and the stars came out, everyone left us there. We sat and kissed and held each other. He told me that he would not sleep with me because he was so stupid to have divorced me. I begged him to stay. He held my face with his big hand gently when he spoke to me. I could not believe how strong and handsome he had become as a man. His face had the knife scar from Raul. I loved him with all my soul.

He said, "Penny, I know you can't understand this because I don't understand it. But I am going back to Vietnam."

"But we are out of the war."

"This is top secret, but some of us have never been out of the war. There is a massacre coming when South Vietnam collapses. Nice people like the people from your village in Honduras and my tribe will be massacred and live as slaves. I have been watching after an orphanage, and I don't think I could live with myself if I didn't return and fight to the death trying to protect them and get the kids of that orphanage out." He told me the names of each child in his orphanage and what the kids were like.

I cried, "What about us? Telemachus, your son, and me. We have loved each other since we were children. Do you love the children of Vietnam more than your own son?"

"No," he said. "I love you both more than anything else in the world. It is just that I can't stand a bully. It's like the communists are the bear and I am Joey. I could not look Telemachus in the face when he grows up to be a warrior if I didn't do everything to try and save those kids."

I told him, "I am going too." He laughed. "This is no place for a woman."

I punched him in the face as hard as I could. I could tell he did not feel the pain. Then I kicked him. "I have been taking kickboxing—I am no longer dependent on any man to defend me."

He laughed as he groaned. "That is not the reception my groin had in mind from you."

"So your groin has a mind of its own. Such a typical man."

"If this world is going to be a better place for our grandchildren and great-grandchildren, it will be women who make it so," I lectured him.

"I forget how feisty you are Penelope."

"My life has been a war too. Do you know what it is like to be a slave, an illegal, or to compete to get into medical school? You men and your machismo forget who is the stronger sex."

We kissed, he got his family Nez Perce blanket from the car, and we sat talking on the park bench looking at the stars until we fell asleep sometime around dawn. Ulee left me there with his parent's car covered in his family blanket. He ran the ten miles to the Pasco airport, and I woke up crying. I guess he couldn't say goodbye. Vietnam was an addiction, just as the Trojan War was for his namesake, Ulysses, around 1180 BC.

When I think of the word hero, I think of a confused person. As I took psychology, I became more developed in my theory. Then I remembered how confused I am about childhood and life itself. Judge not lest you be judged. The veracity of the words of Jesus were becoming as much of a reason for me, being a Christ follower, as any religious experience I had ever experienced.

Black ops were closed down when a new US president took over. Ulee was stationed as a Marine guard at the US embassy in Saigon. He still forayed out to visit Ahn and Dawa and, in 1975, the two-year-old Nhung—the girl named after him who called him daddy. Every time he hugged her, his heart was torn for the warrior son he may never see again. The orphanage was doing a great job of teaching all its children English. He had left his grandfather Ephraim's bone-handled knife and bow for Telemachus. His gift to me was the years of faithfulness. The Buddhist thought of him almost as a monk. His brother let him know that I graduated with honors from CBC and had moved to Seattle University to get my undergraduate degree and work on getting into the University's medical school. I lived on campus, his son was in child care, and, yes, I started to date.

When Ulee heard, he screamed in anger, and his brother Crazy Horse told him over the phone, "Quiet down warrior; you left her pregnant and divorced her. Why don't you come home if you love her as much as I think you do?"

Ulee had no reply. He had the orphanage to take care of, a foster daughter, and he feared the slaughter that would take place when South Vietnam fell. But he was just as afraid to look his stupidity in the face by coming back to me and to beg my forgiveness. "Pray for me," was all he could say.

Ulee sent the $50,000 he had earned in Israel to his brother to give to me. The note said, *"I will always love you. And I will somehow make it home to help with our son. I don't expect you to wait for me. But I am your friend for eternity. Ulysses Looking Glass Sundown.*

△ △ △

When Ulee returned to Vietnam, he was recognized for his battlefield promotion to captain. As a black ops sniper, they needed the South Vietnamese to respect him.

His colonel told him that if he wanted, at any time he could return to the Naval Academy and earn the promotion to make a career out of the Marines. "With your record, son, you could be a general someday."

Ulee enjoyed the respect. He also enjoyed the first time he walked into the officers' club in Saigon. They all knew him and had heard of him, and none of them could believe the jump in pay grade that he had taken. But he was a Marine's Marine. And the other officers got used to the idea in no time. He sent most of his pay to me—no notes, no promises, just the support a man should have for his son.

Ulee had mastered the Vietnamese language and culture. But he missed the winters in the Wallowa Mountains. And he came to love living in the Vietnamese highlands with his faithful dog Cerberus. He continued to battle the Viet Cong, ambushing them, but now following his own code. No women, no children, and no elder combatants were targets. In fact, the Viet Cong learned that if they laid their guns down and ran, he would spare their lives.

He knew he was in enemy territory even when he was back at the orphanage. The people seemed to leave him alone whether it was fear or respect. But he never went anywhere unarmed. He slept with his 44 magnum under his pillow. He and Ahn were growing closer; he had to find some way to get her out to the United States if his adopted daughter Nhung was going to have a chance to make it. It was only a matter of time before everything collapsed. He was told that if he married Ahn that she could have a chance to go home with him.

The Vietnamese wedding ceremony is one of the most important in their culture, with influences from Buddhism, Taoism, and Catholicism. It involves the whole village and is very expensive. It starts with fireworks. There is an extravagant meal, prayers in front of the altar of ancestors in the Buddhist temple, a tea ceremony, gifts for family members, and the bride wears three different dresses for different parts of the ceremony.

Ahn was beautiful; Ulee had seen a lot of beautiful women in Vietnam, but Ahn was by far the most striking. In the vows, he told her in English that he loved me whom he was betrothed to but that he would take care of her and her daughter to get them to the US. Ahn cried when she heard those words because she loved Ulee. The ceremony was completed with the final seven-course traditional dinner.

Ulee never consummated the marriage, keeping his vow to me. Ahn was grateful for Ulee's attempt to bring her and her daughter to the United States. She determined that she would not leave Vietnam when Ulee refused to consummate their marriage. But she would get her daughter named after Ulee to the United States. Even though Ulee was trying to do the right thing, the story would still be spread that he had married. Ulee was trying his hardest to be honorable, but he never felt so far from God. He was a murderer and had married a beautiful woman that he did not love. He was twenty years old and never dreamed that his life could be so screwed up.

△ △ △

The speed at which the South Vietnamese position collapsed in 1975 was surprising to most American and South Vietnamese observers and probably to the North Vietnamese and their allies as well. Ulee, too, was surprised. The South Vietnamese forces began a disorderly and costly retreat, hoping to redeploy its forces and hold the southern part of South Vietnam, perhaps an enclave south of the 13th parallel.

Ulee moved Ahn and her child to Saigon and secured a passport for each. When he picked up Ahn, he could not find Dawa. Another old man and woman were caring for the orphans. It was then that Ahn told Ulee that Dawa was VC. Ulee could not believe it.

"I knew he was a sympathizer, but I never dreamed that clergy would be VC." Ahn said, "It was the only way he could protect the children from the orphanage." The horrible war was so full of lies and confused goals and immorality. He hated war, and he felt betrayed, misled, and beguiled. Now he just wanted to go home to the Wallowa Mountains to hear the voice of the creator in the high mountain meadows.

When Ulee returned to the airport, he found Ahn had sold her passport for a fortune. She also had abandoned her daughter, leaving her with refugees escaping on a boat. Ahn knew her daughter would be better off if she could somehow connect with her father and go with him to America. It was a risk leaving the girl, but it was a bigger risk and hardship leaving her in Vietnam.

During the turmoil Ulee was summoned to the US Embassy to help defend it. It was being overrun by Viet Cong and civilians as helicopters airlifted out troops and refugees. Ulee would be one of the last to flee the compound as Viet Cong sacked the embassy. He wanted to look for his daughter and wife—it was complete chaos. You cannot imagine the day that Vietnam fell. It was the end of an era, the collapse of a broken civilization and the surprise humbling of the United States.

Δ Δ Δ

In command of the fleet and in charge of the evacuation was Rear Admiral John McCleary. He kept looking for his friend, Captain Ulee, hoping he was among the Marines and civilians to have escaped the embassy. Ulee had refused to leave Vietnam without getting the kids out of the orphanage. He thought with his heart again jumping from the last helicopter to try the impossible rescue. When Admiral McCleary learned Ulee was not among those airlifted to his ship, he ordered sailors to call out Ulee's name to the hordes of refugee boats in the harbor."

"Has anyone seen a Marine named Ulysses Looking Glass Sundown?" sailors called out. Finally, a three-year-old girl answered. "My Daddy's name is Ulysses Looking Glass Sundown," she spoke with her tiny voice.

The girl was brought to Admiral McCleary.

"I know Ulysses Looking Glass Sundown." The admiral cried, "Do you know the Marine Ulee?"

"Yes, he is my daddy."

"Then you are coming with me young lady."

△ △ △

A Navy car stopped in front of the Sundown home. Two men got out with a little girl. Ulee's dad saluted Admiral McCleary who said, "Your son saved my life. I regret to inform you that your son stayed behind to try and rescue some children with the collapse of Vietnam. He is listed as MIA." Ulee's mom said.

"Well, he has been listed as KIA, POW, and now MIA. I still think my son will find a way home." She picked up the girl. "And who is this?"

The cute little girl said, "My name is Nhung, my Daddy's name is Ulysses Looking Glass Sundown and you are my grandma."

Grandma Elizabeth did not care if this was the biological child of her son. The fact that her son had named her after himself was enough. She broke out in tears, giving little Ulee the tightest hug. She was family—she was Nez Perce—she was home.

Chapter Nine

Return to Attica

ANOTHER NIGHT AND another chapter in our story. This was the heart of our vacation in the Wallowa Mountains. I hardly felt sixty when telling this dream of mine. It made me young. It was my vision my dream. My way of coping while preserving history. I wanted to have an epic life. I wanted to tell my life with big adjectives. I wanted to forget all the grays in between, legend and harsh realities become mixed with could have been and hopes that I cannot live without. I am not looking for sympathy, just shared understanding. I want these lessons to benefit my family.

Δ Δ Δ

Ulee was found by Special Forces wandering from Cambodia into Thailand a month later. He was injured and carrying Ahn (Nhung's mother) who was dead from a bullet wound. Walking with him were two orphan boys. They were half US and half Vietnamese. He introduced the kids as Plato Ho Chi Min Sundown and Aristotle Luau Sundown. Plato was twelve and

Aristotle was eleven. Ulee was fond of these football-loving boys in the orphanage. They had escaped the Montagnard village together and now as the only survivors of the orphanage, they became family.

As the two boys flew back to Eastern Washington with their newly adopted dad, people in the Sea-Tac Airport came up to them and made comments about the war and how Ulee, who was in Marine uniform, was a baby killer and a kidnapper by bringing these kids back. One long-haired young man came up and spat on Ulee. He was tall and lanky; Ulee never once thought about retaliating—not in front of his boys.

"I'm trusting God to turn me into a pacifist," Ulee would say under his breath.

As they boarded the prop jet for Horizon Airlines to commute from Seattle to the Tri-Cities, the boys seemed excited to see their new homes. They flew over Mount Rainier, which is majestic and the most glaciated peak in the lower States, then over the rich farmland in the high desert of Eastern Washington. They landed in Yakima and unloaded passages. A few service men stopped here—Ulee wished them good luck. There was a bond between all Vietnam vets. On came men and women cut out of a different mold, wearing cowboy hats and looking one another in the eye. Around these parts, Eastern Washington almost seemed like it belonged to Texas or Montana rather than to the liberal city of Seattle.

Ulee trembled a little on the inside as he spotted the Pasco airport. How in the world could his life become so messed up? He had a son out of wedlock and had adopted three Vietnamese kids. He had divorced his one true love (me) and had married a beautiful Vietnamese woman who was now dead, or at least missing. He had no idea how to face a future.

He missed the simplicity of a being a warrior. As they landed, he looked out the window to see the winding Columbia River flowing from Canada, meeting the Snake River coming from the Wallowa Mountains and Hells Canyon. Standing on the landing strip was his grandfather Ephraim and his grandmother Quanah, looking a century old. By them stood his aging father Joseph Caleb and his beautiful mother Elizabeth. There was his next younger brother, Petrocolas Crazy Horse Sundown; he was not tall but strong. His cousin, Jackson John Sundown, was there—you could see his smile as the prop jet passed over. Next to Jacky was "Stick" Donny Pielstick Sundown, who was tall and skinny as a rail. Next to them was Whitey, now a tall Hector Whitebird Sundown; he was taller than Ulee. At his side, as always, was Dunk "Heath Duncan Sundown"—he was much shorter but was very muscular in his build. And then there I stood, feeling as uncomfortable as I had ever in all my life.

Telemachus Cruz Morales Sundown was standing next to me, wearing Nez Perce regalia. He was four years old. And as he held my hand, he was sweating with nerves at meeting his dad.

Nhung was dressed in Nez Perce regalia also. She was holding onto her grandma's hand. As Ulee and his two adopted boys walked down the stairs of the prop jet, we were all a bit surprised. How many kids did Ulee have? They all walked across the tarmac, and it was a wonderful, terrible moment for all of us. The top of his left ear was missing, and his light brown eyes were filled with sorrows too deep to explore. His hair looked like a white man—one of the first times I had seen him like this. He wasn't wearing his dress blues, but he wore the captain insignia on his green Marine service uniform with a hard framed service cap called a barracks cover.

Nhung ran into her daddy's arms. "Where is Mama and my puppy Cerberus?" Ulee spoke, choking on his tears.

"They didn't make it, Hun. Your mama loved you very much but she died in Vietnam with all the chaos of its collapse. Mama Elizabeth gave her eldest son a hug and wept openly—so many grandchildren—she couldn't be happier. Nhung introduced her to Plato and Aristotle, her friends from the orphanage.

I stood my distance. "Ulee, this is your son, Telemachus Cruz Morales Sundown." Telemachus was a cute brown-skinned four-year-old wearing elaborate Nez Perce regalia. The colorful feathers and his proud bearing just melted the heart.

Telemachus saluted his dad—then he said in his rehearsed speech. "I am glad to meet you father. I have heard many stories about you." Ulee picked him up and kissed him, giving him a big hug. And then he turned to me, and I stepped back, saying, "Hello Ulee."

I could not hide the hurt I felt, the hesitation or the wanting to move on with my life after being rejected by this handsome warrior so many times. I wanted Ulee to be a part of Telemachus' life but not mine. I needed to find out who I was without this mythical hero in my life. And now he had four kids. I guess the wall of ice was pretty visible to his family. And my family—Telemachus. Ulee walked to get his bags, carrying Telemachus and Nhung, as his mom had Plato and Aristotle in tow, holding their hands and presenting them with gifts.

Ulee was mobbed by his brothers telling him all about their athletic accomplishments. Whitey said, "Did you kill anyone in Vietnam?" There was a long, uncomfortable pause. Ulee changed the subject.

"Family, I want to introduce you to my two new adopted sons. Aristotle Ho Chi Min is twelve years and Plato Luau is eleven years old. Both these boys love football, and we have been through so much together."

They looked like their father might have been dark skinned and their mother was Vietnamese. They were both really bright boys and spoke English surprisingly well. They bowed to meet their new daddy's family.

Ulee said, "These boys have seen more than any kids should see, so let's not talk about the war. Let's just say I was an administrator."

"Then how did you win all those medals?" Patty asked.

"They give those out to almost everyone as a publicity stunt. Listen family, I don't want to talk about the war ever. I have prayed and asked God that it would be as if it never happened in my life. Please, if you love me, don't ask any questions about the war. Remember how Chief Joseph said, 'From where the sun stands now I will never fight again?' That is me—right now. Where the sun stands now, I will never fight anymore."

As they walked back to the terminal Ulee asked to talk to me.

I said no. "We must be cordial because we share Telemachus together, but I am studying at the University. I graduated with highest honors in pre-medicine. I am in medical school, and I am a citizen of the United States on my own merits. I have become an American citizen, and I love this country. I think that this country has incredible potential for goodness, and incredible possibility for doing the wrong thing, too."

I continued. "I am dating someone else, and I have moved on from you. You divorced me and left me; you married and have three other children. Ulee, don't expect to pick up in our relationship where we left off."

Ulee looked confused as he replied, "I understand, Penny, but know this—I have always and always will love you." I could not process all of this emotionally or spiritually, so I turned around, picked up Telemachus, and started to run to the car. Ulee followed me, and I didn't know he was behind me.

When we got to my car, he said with a smile, as if everything were alright with us, "Congratulations on medical school and your citizenship. You are an amazing person. I am really happy for you."

Ulee's grandfather Ephraim turned to his son, Caleb. "We always knew Ulee was one stubborn boy—I wonder how Jesus is going to help him out of this quagmire."

△ △ △

Breaking up with Ulee was not easy because his family had become my family. When Telemachus was born, the Sundown family did all the rituals that were customary for Nez Perce at the birth of a baby. Nez Perce was the name given to them by Lewis and Clark's French translator but they called themselves Nimi'ippu, which means authentic people. We all went to LaGrande to the pow wow, and I enjoyed watching all of the Sundown family dance to the drumbeat, wearing their ancient feathered regalia.

During the time that Ulee was away, I had nothing to do but study. I graduated from high school a semester early, December, 1971. I enrolled in Columbia Basin College winter quarter, and I graduated with my two-year credentials in 1973. Then I was accepted on scholarship at Seattle University in the pre-med program. By the spring of 1975, I had graduated with degrees in biology and psychology and was accepted into medical school at Stanford, UCLA, and Seattle University. I chose Seattle because I needed to keep Telemachus close to the Sundown family. Our son, Telemachus, needed his father's heritage just as much as he needed my Spanish heritage. So Mama Elicia moved to Seattle just to help me with him.

I attended Seattle's University Presbyterian Church. There I met a young man who was younger than me. He was tall, clean-cut and very handsome. His name was Alexander Messe. His nickname was Ace, as he was the starting quarterback for the university football team. Why did I have a crush on football players–I didn't even care for the sport? Ace was a real Christian and I needed that in my life. Most of our dates were going to church, as we became members together at the University Presbyterian Church. He was an honest man. He was kind to Telemachus, and he seemed to appreciate my Spanish heritage.

I did not tell Ace much about Ulee except to say that Telemachus' dad was a Vietnam vet who had become a POW and had divorced me and remarried a Vietnamese lady. The last I had heard he was missing in action and still in Vietnam. I told him this before I heard that Ulee had made it out with three adopted children. I just felt like I needed to move on with my life. My trust in men was destroyed. I didn't know if Ulee would go to war again. Something inside of me expected him to either stay in Special Forces or join the FBI or CIA. So I just moved on, telling my boyfriend that he was MIA. I know a half-truth is a lie, but life was such a mess. Ace and I progressed in our relationship slowly, and there was romance between us. I was very lonely and emotionally fragile. He began to influence me. Ace talked me into being a cheerleader. Even though I was in medical school, I agreed to try out for the cheer squad, and I made the team. It was one way that I could share in his life. I struggled with our blossoming romance because deep in my heart I still loved Ulee. I just didn't know who Ulee was anymore.

Ulee wasted no time and climbed Eagle Cap, the highest peak in the Wallowa Mountains. Standing near 10,000 feet in a thunderstorm, Ulee read the eighth chapter of *Romans*. It was like a symphony for his soul.

Now because of Jesus Christ there is now no condemnation. The spirit of God intercedes with our spirit when our groans cannot express our hearts' deepest thoughts. If God be for us who can be against us. All things work together for the good of those who love him. Nothing can separate us from the Love of God.

All the people he had killed flashed by his mind. Now Jesus

was there crying with him, knowing more than he knew about how wrong war can be. Ulee was filled with the Holy Spirit of God, and he was made new. He had peace about me and knew that he would be able to win me and Telemachus back. And he would never, never give up. Inside his heart, he wanted to be a peaceful pastor like his father and grandfather. He wanted to pray for the dying, help those who mourned, seek lost teenagers, reach out, and break up gangs and prostitution rings with the gospel of Jesus Christ. He had dreams and visions about building a great caring network for every nation to be friends in Christ through one country church in the city. He imagined worship in Spanish, Native languages, Vietnamese, English, Korean, Portuguese, Russian, Chinese, Tangalle, German, Arabic, and Hebrew. This kind of peace would be a light shining on the hill for all humanity to see. The church would be like the church in *Acts*.

Ulee came back and told his dad that he had been called to be a pastor, and his dad said, "Well, you are going to have to go to four years of college and three years of seminary."

"What!" cried Ulee. "Dad, you know I hate school."

His dad calmly replied, "You said you want to be a pastor; it is a professional job—you have a lot to learn. Most of all humility. You can't do this job without humility."

"Dad, you know I am humble after all those years of war."

Pastor Caleb said, "You are shame-filled; that is a long way from being teachable, humble in the Lord. You have so much healing to take place in your heart; and hurt people end up hurting people. You can't help people until you make a lot of pilgrim's progress in your journey of spiritual and emotional healing."

Later, Ulee was out in the backyard playing basketball with his little brother Whitey, and they began to play one on one. Ulee could barely dribble; his kid brother was a dribbling wizard. Whitey jumped up and slam-dunked: two nothing. He did that four times before Ulee finally got the ball; this time he took it in and jumped.

"Wow," Whitey said, "You can still jump." Whitey stole the ball and started to hit long jump shots against his big brother until Ulee swatted back one of Whiteys jump shots. When Ulee got the ball, each drive was a power drive with a willful slam-dunk. He was still quick, even if he could barely dribble. Whitey toyed with him, letting him catch up before swishing a long jump shot. Ulee was mad. His brother was only a senior in high school and had beaten him in basketball.

His baby brother ran after him. "Don't take it so personally. I am going to be pro basketball player. I bet you are still a better shot with the Remington than I am—for at least a year more." Then he said, seriously, "Ulee go play football. Try out for the Seattle Division One Wolf Pack. You are the fastest of us of all. And you still have your athleticism."

Whitey had their high school coach call Coach Don James from Seattle Division One powerhouse football team. Coach James was in town and came by to meet Ulee. Coach James was a class coach—one of the best college coaches of all time. He and his wife Carol were fine Christians. He was a standout in fighting against racism.

Coach James said, "We have our quarterbacks, but if you are willing to switch positions and are the athlete your coach claims you to be, I'll give you a walk on chance."

"No, I want to play quarterback."

Coach James left.

Whitey's basketball coach had played at State College at LaGrande Oregon, where Ulee was born. LaGrande bordered the Wallowa Mountains and the Blue Mountains.

"I got you a tryout as a quarterback," said the basketball coach. "They said they need a quarterback."

LaGrande was a tiny school in the mountains. They were currently playing in the NAIA small college division.

Ulee's dad called Sunny Sixkiller, the famous Cherokee quarterback for the Seattle College football powerhouse team and a pro backup. Sunny traveled at his own expense to the Tri-Cities, stayed with the Sundown family, and worked out Ulee to train him as a quarterback. He did this all for Native brotherhood.

Sunny had been an assistant coach at his alma mater and was looking for a head coaching position. He had heard there might be a job opening at LaGrande, which motivated him even more to work with Ulee.

Ulee, Patty, Stick, and Jackey all went to try out for the football team at LaGrande. They brought along with them twenty-two

atheletes that any Division I school would covet. Rod Halvorson
had been playing basketball with his brother Randy and working
for their dad in construction. Rod was probably the best wide
receiver in college football. Marquis Lincoln had been the fastest
man in the country in high school but had gotten in trouble
with his life. Richard Johnson (Pastor Joshua Johnson's son)
came as a running back. But he and Ulee were childhood friends
who could practically read each other's minds. Rich King never
had bothered to go to college. But he was a pro-style tight end.
Together, with every kid Ulee and his brothers had met in their
high school days—black, Chicano, Native, white, and veterans
—made up a treasure of talent for a little school like LaGrande.

But the best news was that Sunny Sixkiller became the head
coach at their school. The first year they won the NAIA small
college national championship, going undefeated. It was like a
group of men, some with criminal records, who were regaining
their childhood again. They had a great recruiting class after
the national championship, bringing in five-star recruits from
around the country. They came because they sensed there was
something special about this team of misfits. They were best
friends and on a mission while having a lot of fun together in
the process.

△ △ △

Ulee and I hardly spoke when he was at LaGrande studying
and playing football. There was too much hurt between us, and we
were both busy. But he did visit with Telemachus once a month. I
was happy for Ulee. I can't tell you how healing it was for him to
be a part of a team and the excitement of college football.

Their sophomore year, LaGrande moved up to NCAA
Division II. Their offensive and defensive line was made up of
junior college five-star recruits that just loved hanging out with
the guys in the Wallowa Mountains. They could have played for
any team in the nation and they had professional written all over
them. The team was powerful and went undefeated and won the
national championship twice again. Whitey turned down major
basketball scholarships to join them as backup quarterback.
Heath could have played football at Notre Dame, but he went
with Whitey.

△ △ △

Although we were not geographically far apart, the distance between Ulee and me had grown. We were living separate lives at different schools.

When Ulee's senior year began, LaGrande football team appeared in *a half dozen sports magazines*. His coach and school were getting national press. And they were playing a preseason game against Seattle.

Telemachus let everyone know that Ulee was his dad, and he wore a little LaGrande jersey with his daddy's number on it. Before the big game Ulee came unannounced. He came to see Telemachus and me. My boyfriend was at a team meeting listening to his coach go on and on about how they needed to take this team seriously. I felt very uncomfortable when Ulee came over. He kept staring at me—I knew he loved me. I avoided eye contact with him.

In Seattle, Ulee tried to visit me before the game, but my boyfriend showed up. He was visibly mad. Telemachus sided with his father.

"Why don't you leave so my mom can fall back in love with my dad and we can become a family."

I yelled at Telemachus. My boyfriend looked like he wanted to fight Ulee. My boyfriend moved toward him. I stepped in between the two and asked my boyfriend to walk away.

"You don't want to fight Ulee—believe me, I know him."

My boyfriend lost it—shouting at me that I needed to choose. Telemachus started to rush my boyfriend, and I picked him up as he was swinging at my fiancé.

"Leave my mommy and daddy alone." My boyfriend ran out. I handed Telemachus to Ulee and ran after him.

I told Ulee, "I have chosen my new boyfriend." Ulee asked, "Really?" as if he knew me better than I knew myself. I left with my boyfriend. I called an hour later and asked Ulee to leave Telemachus with my roommate. I just wanted him to leave.

Ulee said, "Okay. But I have a surprise for you tomorrow night after the game." I said, "Ulee, the last thing I need is a surprise from you. We have been friends since we were kids and you don't know me at all."

∆ ∆ ∆

Even though it was just a preseason scrimmage, the game between LaGrande and Seattle garnered a lot of attention. It was a David versus Goliath battle. Seattle was a Division I powerhouse with more than ten times the number of students. The school would be embarrassed even if the game was close. Losing was unconscionable,

"We all know this is the biggest game we have all ever played in," Coach Sixkiller said. "We are ready for this game. We can't beat them with size, but we can with speed. The bigger they are, the harder they fall."

Ulee always dressed in a private restroom before practice and games. The coach did not want the team to see the embarrassment of his scars. I was worried about Ulee's statement to me on the phone: that he was going to surprise me in the game. I was especially worried about a fight between Ulee and Ace—as I had witnessed those many years ago when he lost his temper and killed the M-13 gang leader with his bare hands. So I slipped down from the field to find Ulee to talk to him before the game. A manager showed me to the coach's locker room, where Ulee was dressing. When I came in, he was just starting to get dressed. He looked up and saw me, and it seemed like he stopped breathing. His brown eyes were full of so much hurt and hope.

I said, "Ulee, you scared me when you said you were going to surprise me today. You might not like Ace, but he really is a nice guy and a Christian. He is good to me and to Telemachus—you divorced me and left me pregnant to choose a war over me. And then you married some girl and got her pregnant."

"Penelope. It is not like that. I married a pregnant girl to try give them a shot at getting to the United States. I have never kissed another woman beside you. I have been faithful. I have so many scars. I was sure I wasn't going to come back alive, and I wanted you to move on." Then he took off his shirt. He was covered with burns, napalm spots, and scars.

I said, "Ulee, I saw your scars on our wedding night."

Ulee said, "I know, but I wanted to remind you who I am—and with your help I believe we can heal. Nhung is not my daughter—I saved her mom as she was getting abused by US troops. She worked at the orphanage that I helped out, and I married her to take away her shame. She was beautiful but I treated her as a sister. And I was faithful to you. I broke a lot of God's commandments, but that one by the grace of God and my love for you I stayed true. I lived through hell and I am willing to work hard to experience a little heaven with our family. There isn't a night that I don't have nightmares. The scars you see on the outside are just the tip of the iceberg of what is in my soul. I hate that I killed so many, even in combat. I hate that I would turn over the bodies of those trying to kill me and my men and find kids and women and old men. I hate that I killed Americans because they were abusing Ahn and threatened to kill me. It is all a bad dream. The only thing I don't regret is killing Raul to save you. And that set it all in motion. Every night for five years I just dreamed of coming home to you and Telemachus. When I was in Israel or Laos . . . "

"I said, "You were in Israel and Laos?"

"There is so much I haven't told anyone. I served in black ops, and many times I was surrounded by the enemy knowing that I was going to die and praying that there was some way out of hell to come back home. And when I came back home with Aristotle and Plato, they spit on me and you were gone from my life."

He was crying, tears running down his face. I didn't know what to say.

I said, "This is too much for me to process. Just don't do anything dumb during the game."

"Me do something rash and stupid?" We both laughed. And I cried when I turned and left the room to the field to cheer against him.

Δ Δ Δ

Back in the locker room, with Ulee gone. Patty stood up. "My big brother Ulee is someone I always tease, but he is not only my big brother, he is light-skinned Nez Perce warrior. When we were kids, we had an older big brother named Joey. He was bigger and stronger than all of us. We were pursued by a grizzly bear in the high Wallowas, and it was quite an adventure for us to try and elude this big bear. He grabbed one of my younger brothers from a cave we were hiding in, and our brother Joey took on this

ten-foot, thousand-pound bear all by himself. He took him off a
10,000-foot ridge, saving all our lives. Today that bear rug is on
our lodge wall, and the elders tell stories to the children about
it. There isn't a day that we don't all miss our big brother Joey.
Ulee has tried hard to be that big brother to all of us. He fought
for his country and came into football late. He doesn't talk about
his service for five tours in Vietnam. But somehow his childhood
sweetheart and he got separated in all of this. They have a little
boy that most of us have met, Telemachus, and his dream is that
somehow in today's game that something will make his daddy
win his mommy's heart. I know that everybody thinks we are
overmatched in this game. Shoot, we probably all think that
too. But could we go out and beat this team for Telemachus?
I don't know if it will do any good. They may never get back
together, but if there is any chance that having the game of our
lives will in anyway help—then let's do it. Let's win this game
not for Ulee—but for Telemachus and his dream that his daddy,
Ulysses, and his mommy, Penelope, will somehow have a shot at
being together. Ulee wasn't in the room when this talk came—he
was following his tradition of dressing in another room so the
team did not see his scars. He walked into the room just as Patty
completed his talk.

Δ Δ Δ

When they ran out on the field, there were very few cheers
from the few hundred La Grande fans who were spotted among
the thousands for the Wolf Pack. Wolf Pack Stadium was an
imposing sight with tens of thousands of screaming fans booing
the Mountaineers as they took the field. You could see Lake
Washington in the distance and the fleet of wealthy yachts
anchored there for the game.

Ulee watched my boyfriend Ace, take the field. It was hard
not to like this guy. He was a Christian and visited a children's
hospital every week. He had been good to me and to Telemachus.
Ulee watched him rifle the ball; he had a pro arm. Ulee walked
over to midfield and called Ace over.

He extended his hand. "I want you to know that I appreciate
the way you have treated Penelope and Telemachus—you are a
true Christian, so that makes us brothers. Good luck in the game."

Ace smiled, shaking hands and saying, "My my, you are as cocky as they say you are—you are the one that is going to need the luck. But peace, brother."

Patty came up to Ulee and said, "Seen enough yet big brother? Stop admiring the enemy. That enemy stands in between you and your family."

Ulee slapped and punched his brother hard on the shoulder pads. "Patty, don't ever compare football to war. Now let's go beat these guys."

The LaGrande kickoff team blasted the ball against the swirling wind into the end zone. Kicker Randy Halvorson was fast becoming a prospect for the pros with his kicking game. But as a basketball player he also had the attention of pro basketball. At the back of the end zone was a Wolf Pack safety who was a world-class sprinter. He took the ball and ran right towards the middle. He was the fastest man that the LaGrande team had played against in three years, and even though the teams matched up in team speed and size, the LaGrande Mountaineers just were not ready to play. The speedy safety took the length of the field for a touchdown to begin the game, and he was untouched as the wedge in the middle of the Seattle return team came out with a vengeance, blocking as if they expected to take it all the way back. With the extra point it was 0-7 Seattle on top.

Ulee took the field, called the play in the huddle, but forgot to take his mouth guard out.

His big center patted him on the back. "One more time so we can understand." Don't make this game too big in your mind, warrior, even though you are fighting for your wife and child. It's just football."

Ulee slowly called the play, "Johnson carries the ball—let's show them we came to play football."

LaGrande tackle Mike Hernandez was never intimidated by anyone, and as they lined up he heard, the right defensive end yell at Ulee, "I—watched you in game films, Indian, and if we take you out then you don't have a team. I am going to break your freakin' arm."

Mike sent him flying, and when he landed, the loud-mouth defensive end had a compound fracture. Mike walked up to him and said, "Hey Essay, he's a Native American, not an Indian, and nobody is going to break my Native American's arm."

The two teams battled to a tie at the half—each scored twice. Rod Halvorson was just unstoppable. Ace and his teammates were rattled and their coach furious. The Mountaineers went into the locker room feeling brazen and invincible.

The third quarter went quickly. Ulee was such a scrambler the Seattle players couldn't contain him. He ran for a touchdown.

Ace stepped up his game, passing for two touchdowns with his rocket arm.

With the score tied in the fourth quarter, Ulee scrambled, put on his afterburners and slid into the end zone for the winning touchdown. Then he jumped up in the air and slam-dunked the ball on the goal post. The crowd was stunned, and they looked for a flag. I was embarrassed because I was cheering, forgetting my position until one of the other cheerleaders reminded me. There was silence on the field—no one had expected that LaGrande could compete with Seattle's national powerhouse in its prime. During this silence—when everyone was just stunned, Ulee ran to the Wolf Pack sideline and kneeled down in front of me and pulled from his waistband a ring. My heart was pounding and I started crying.

"Penelope you are flesh of my flesh, my soul mate, the mother of my child. Neither of us can be happy unless we spend eternity together. Will you marry me?"

I protested, Ace was standing right there. "Ulee, I am already engaged."

Ulee picked me up and kissed me, and as I kissed him back, Ulee said, "You are engaged, not married, so it's not too late for a happy ending to this fairy tale."

Ace turned his back and walked to the tunnel. He didn't want someone who was in love with another person. A Wolf Pack lineman, insulted by it all, ran up to floor Ulee, and Coach James stopped his team. He never allowed team fights.

When we finished kissing, I said, "Yes," and it was all caught on national television. Telemachus ran up and gave both of us a hug.

Coach James said, "Get back to your side of the field, son."

Δ Δ Δ

Our wedding was held in June at Joseph Methodist Church. Ulee's dad Joseph Caleb and his grandfather Ephraim performed the ceremony together. It was a small wedding. Belén was my maid of honor, and Ulee's best man was his friend Rod Halvorson. Nhung was eight years old and a beautiful flower girl. And our son Telemachus, the ring bearer, was also eight years old and seemed to enjoy it more than anyone. Telemachus escorted Nhung and they were followed by their honor guard, Plato Ho Chi Min Sundown and Aristotle Luau Sundown. We were wrapped in a family-made blanket at the close of the ceremony. It is a native tradition.

Ulee cried all the way through the service. I just smiled. It was the most beautiful wedding I could have possibly ever imagined. We walked out the front stairs of Joseph's Methodist church, where two Appaloosa waited for us with a string of pack mules. Ulee put me on my horse, and we made our way for our honeymoon—we backpacked in the Wallowas to Mirror Lake underneath Eagle Cap. This is one of the most beautiful places in the world. Ulee had already set up a teepee for us to spend two weeks in the high mountains that looked like heaven.

Chapter Ten

Game of Heroes

THE NEXT PART of the story was told over breakfast as Grandmother Elizabeth fried trout on the wood stove with corn bread. The girls in the family started questioning me to get me going again. As I drank coffee my mind started waking up with memories.

△ △ △

There were 2,500 people in attendance during my graduation from the University Medical School. It was hot in the old University Pavilion. Ulee, Telemachus, Nhung, Plato, and Aristotle were all there. I felt their joy and pride in what God had done in my life. Mama Elicia, Pedro, Belén, Grandma Elizabeth, and Pastor Caleb were also there. And then all of Ulee's brothers—Patty, Jacky, Stick, Whitey, and Heath—were there screaming war cries as they announced my name to receive the Ellen Griep Award, which comes with only 250 dollars but it goes to the graduating MD who was voted by their fellow students to be the most inspirational medical student. It was such an honor to receive this reward from my fellow students. I never have been very good at controlling my tears.

When they announced my name as one of twelve students awarded an M.D. and a simultaneous Ph.D., I burst into tears. It was a long way from the dump in Tegus. Once a little girl who struggled with English, damaged goods without any personal control of her future, it was a journey from tragedy to triumph. The more I cried, the more my fellow students and family cheered. As the president of the medical school put my hood on my robe in recognition of the degrees, he stopped and gave me a hug. "Your life represents the very best in humanity, Penelope."

After the ceremony, my fellow students and professors came over to congratulate me. I was given many offers because of my accomplishments. I even received an offer from NASA to become an astronaut. But I had my heart set on helping children; therefore, I was assigned to the UCLA School of Medicine to specialize as a pediatric neurological surgeon. It was a very prestigious appointment. But almost every person that came to give me a hug asked if they could get Ulee's autograph. The president of the school even brought a football with him.

He told Ulee it was for his son, and his wife said, "We don't have a son." Ulee laughed.

Ulee's four years of college football at LaGrande would not be forgotten, even though he had refused offers to put his name in the draft. Three of his fellow teammates went in the first round of the draft. And two offensive linemen from LaGrande were chosen in the second round. We were very proud of them, but Ulee made it clear—no pro football for him. He was called to be a pastor.

We were planning on moving to LA, where I would do my internship as a neurological surgeon and he would begin seminary at Fuller Theological Seminary in Pasadena. Now we could finally reach for our dreams together. We felt like such a family—it was just an extra blessing heaped on my fortunate life. The first chance I had after putting the kids to bed that night, I ran to my prayer place (the kitchen) and fell on my knees, letting loose a torrent of silent tears and whispers of thank you to Jesus. There wasn't a day in my life that I was not cursed by the nightmare of my childhood trauma. Now I would spend my life helping children facing the trauma of medical conditions that could be combated by the skill of a trained surgeon.

We moved to LA in the heat of the summer in Ulee's Volkswagen van. He called it Woodstock, or the hippie mobile. He had bought it from a hippie who had taken it to Woodstock. And Pedro, who was an amazing mechanic, helped him keep it running. It was the right size for our family. At rest areas, someone came over and actually thought it was a museum. They were embarrassed when we told them it was our family car.

Δ Δ Δ

While we were getting settled in LA into our apartment over a church in which Ulee's job was to be the janitor, the kids and Ulee spent as much time running, playing basketball, and going to the beach as possible.

When Ulee started seminary, he was very excited. Most people in the school did not recognize him as a football player. He just looked more like an Indian. In those days, most of the students were older white men. They were very conservative in their dress. Ulee stood out like a sore thumb. There were a few other Vietnam War vets attending seminary, and they could usually spot one another by the scars or the spots of skin discoloration that came with exposure to Agent Orange. Telemachus and his brothers and sister spent every school break back in the Wallowas, being raised in the old ways by Ulee's parents.

They made them run the daily runs with his cousins. And they lived to hunt and fish. Ulee took several trips into the mountains that first year with his kids, even climbing Mount Rainier in the winter together. It was a failure in that they never reached the summit. A huge blizzard came in, and they were snowed in for three days, unlike when Ulee was young, now they had the right equipment and they held out in a snow shelter. It was cold—they laughed together a lot—Ulee rubbed the kids' feet and legs to keep them from frostbite. They had to ration their food and fuel. There were nights where they just listened to the howling wind, praying that they had picked their spot away from any avalanche danger. Ulee explained to the kids that in life you don't always get your way. When you are a mountain climber, you work hard to prepare, but the mountain may not let you win this time, so patience is not only a virtue—it keeps you alive.

When they finally descended the mountain, they were roped together using crampons and ice picks to safely retreat from the peak. At one point, by Camp Muir, an avalanche came down, and a daring run was made to get out of its way. Ulee had the kids glissade or slide down a slope almost out of control using their ice picks to keep some semblance of control. They stopped at the bottom, when Ulee fell into a crevice and the kids had to dig in with their crampons to save their dad. The rope held. It was a lesson in teamwork. It all turned into just another adventure to tell around the campfire at Sundown Lodge. When they told me about it later, their eyes sparkled with confidence and meekness, and I was thankful that Ulee was there to raise them in the way he had been raised—the old way.

This was a happy life for our family, and Ulee was ahead in credits after his first year of his three-year masters of divinity degree.

Ulee played pickup basketball at UCLA with his high school friend, split-end Rod Halvorson, who was a first-round draft pick by the LA team. It was during this time that Ulee was discovered by the receivers' coach after a slam-dunk contest. Everyone was impressed by Ulee's basketball skills. So one of the coaches talked Ulee into not only accepting a job as the LA team's maintenance man but to go to the open tryouts.

When tryouts came, they started with the 40-yard dash. When Ulee ran, the head coach said, I must have miss-timed it. Teams time the forty with three other clocks, and they all read 4.3 seconds. This was the fastest on the team and one of the fastest in the league. It looked like Ulee was gliding. The coach called Ulee's friend over. Rod was a celebrity not only as a first round draft pick but his twin brother Randy had made the Seattle Space Needles as rookie in the pro league. He would go on to a long career becoming the sixth man of the year and then a very distinguished coaching career in the NCAA and the pros.

"Who is this guy?"

"He is from the neighborhood and he is going to surprise you." Ulee bench-pressed 225—thirty times. His strength put him in the linebacker class. He set the team record on the shuttle run, the three-cone drill, and the standing broad jump. He also had the team's best vertical jump and threw the ball seventy-five yards with a really tight spiral.

He was the find of the open tryouts. The team had three great quarterbacks. They were all highly sought after in the league, so it was decided that he would play defense, and he was listed as a free safety backup wide receiver and running back as well as a special team's man.

You can imagine our families' surprise when Ulee came home and said he had a job playing for the Los Angeles team. The kids were so excited; I was concerned. "What about seminary and becoming a pastor?" Ulee responded, I will probably just make the practice squad and won't travel." Well, one thing was for sure; it paid the league minimum, which was a heck of a lot more than the janitor job.

When our kids bragged about their dad, their friends were skeptical. So Ulee showed up at school with a very recognizable muscular 6'5" Rod Halvorson wearing an LA Jersey. The kids went crazy, asking for autographs of this number-one draft choice of LA. I was there on that day, and I loved the way Telemachus admired his dad. It was really crazy. All the things that people should be admiring such as a moral man and a responsible father really do not hold a candle compared to being a professional football player. But that misperception went both ways. It had been Ulee's boyish dream to play professional football and he was getting as big of a kick out of it all as the fans were.

What a surprise it was when in the second pre-season game, I was working at the hospital and everyone started to cheer a player called Ulysses who had just run back a punt for a touchdown. No one in LA seemed to really know who he was, but he became the fan favorite to make the team. I wish you could have been there when we got the phone call from his brother Whitey and every other brother was in the room cheering, teasing, and laughing that he had become a pro football player. He was even interviewed on a local television sports program.

We took a walk on Newport Beach and played in the waves with the kids. As Ulee and I held hands and watched the sunset, Ulee leaned over and gave me a kiss on the cheek. I asked, "What is going through that white Indian mind of yours?"

He said with a smile, "Maybe God can wipe away all my past sins. This is kind of a dream we are living."

△ △ △

When Ulee got his playbook he memorized it and knew what every position was doing. When they scrimmaged, he learned the audibles and the intricacies of the quarterback play—not because he had designs on taking someone's job but because he loved football.

The first game of the year was going to be at Philadelphia— always a tough place for the Los Angeles football team to play. Ulee wasn't supposed to travel, but a player was fined for a DUI and was sent home for breaking team rules and Ulee took his place on the special teams. So before classes ever started at Fuller, Ulee was a pro football player. When Ulee came to Philadelphia, he was assigned to kickoff and punt teams—and of course the return teams.

On Saturday night before the game, all the quarterbacks went out with their coach for seafood. Before the last course, it was apparent that the clams were not right, and the starting quarterback started to get sick. It wasn't long before the backup quarterback became overwhelmingly sick, too. That night the two quarterbacks and the quarterbacks' coach became violently ill. By four in the morning they were sent to the hospital, and the head coach of the LA team, needed an emergency plan. Ulee got a knock at the door at six that morning and was told to be in the meeting room in fifteen minutes. There he was told about the situation and informed that he would be the starting quarterback. Ulee looked dumbfounded.

"Is this part of rookie hazing?" The look on the coach's face let him know this was no joke.

"You played in college. This is going to feel like a bowl game only you don't get to prepare and you have never played with your offense before. Are you nervous?"

"Well, it's not like Vietnam. At least no one will be shooting at me."

"No, I don't think anyone is going to try and shoot you," the coach said. But some very angry men are going to try and injure you. Listen, we are going to give you five plays. The offensive

coordinator coach is going to talk them through with you. Then
we are going to have a walk through in the hotel ball room with
the offense, and your job is simple: don't make a mistake; let our
defense and running game win it for you."

"Yes, sir," said Ulee, and he saluted out of habit.

Δ Δ Δ

Philadelphia drove it the length of the field and scored first.
When LA had the ball, it was three and out and they punted. The
Philadelphia offense took it on a drive the length of the field and
scored again.

Ulee had been nervous during the first two sets of downs and
his timing was off. His teammates could sense it. But when he
took the field a third time he calmed himself, rehearsing in his
mind the plays he had so rigorously studied.

You can do this, he thought. *You've done it before.*

Ulee called shotgun formation and called all the receivers to
run their routes to the right. This wasn't one of the five plays, but
it was in the playbook he had memorized.

Ulee took a shotgun and took a three-yard drop back. The
defensive end took an inside route, and Ulee did a spin and came
out of the pocket on the left side. It was wide open, and no one
knew how fast he was. He blazed down the sideline and scored.
No defender was within ten yards of him. Philadelphia scored
again, but when LA got the ball back again, there was a new
confidence in him as the team leader. When they got to the line
of scrimmage, there were eight defenders within seven yards
of the line of scrimmage, so Ulee changed the play at the line
of scrimmage with a special audible and completed a pass for
fifteen yards. A defensive player smashed Ulee from the back
seconds after be completed the pass. It was a "welcome to the
big time" hit. Ulee couldn't believe how much harder they hit
than they did in college.

In the huddle several team members were shocked.

"How did you know our audibles or our plays?" one of the
wide receivers asked.

"I read the playbook and what I read and understand I
remember."

The coach sent in a play for Ulee to run. But Ulee said, "I am changing the play pro right. Halfback motion right set up as trips—tight end split wide out."

The team responded, and the halfback followed the fullback and ran for thirty-five yards. The coaches were livid that this rookie disregarded their instructions, but they couldn't argue with the results. They sat back to see what else the kid could do.

Ulee threw a twenty-yard touchdown pass on the next play to his best friend Rod Halvorson. LA's defense held and Ulee had the ball again with less than two minutes to go. Ulee led the team down the field with and called time out with forty-five seconds left in the first half. The coach told Ulee to run a play to the right, but Ulee said he wanted to do another shotgun-style play "We ran it before and we scored," he told the coach.

Ulee took the ball and dropped deep. The tight end was open on the right for the screen. He gave it a hard pump fake, tricking the defenders into believing he was going to pass the ball. Instead, Ulee took off running, blazing down the middle of the field. No one came close to catching him.

Ulee scored and then leaped in the air, slamming the ball over the goal post, just as he had done in the big game against Seattle.

I cried as I watched Ulee celebrate. I had seen him as a football hero before, but never on this kind of stage. I thought of him missing high school because he killed a man defending me. I remembered what it was like when we heard he was KIA, POW, and MIA. He deserved this. Telemachus and Nhung kept asking, "Is that my daddy?"

"Yes," I cried, "that is your daddy."

At half time, the LA coach, called Ulee to the side and asked him how he knew their playbook so well.

"Coach, I read the playbook. What I read and understand I remember."

"Really?" asked the coach incredulously.

"Give me a try," said Ulee. "I know every play for every player. And I learned the audibles listening in practice."

"I am glad you are on my team," replied the coach.

In the second half, Ulee took control of the game, running for 160 yards and passing for another 250. He threw just one

interception on a miscommunication play. The final score was
LA 42, Philadelphia 38. The first week in the NFL, rookie Ulysses
Looking Glass Sundown had the highest quarterback rating in
the league.

△ △ △

Around the seminary, they never put two and two together
to understand that Ulee Sundown was the war veteran who
set NCAA Division II college records at tiny State College of
LaGrande Oregon. The word spread slowly through the school
until it hit the LA newspaper sports page headline with the
headline *"Seminary student shocks pro-football world!"*

We met Ulee at the airport. To his family he was a hero. His
grandparents flew down, his parents and his children were all
there to greet the plane. He was our hero.

I kissed him when I saw him and said, "You are really doing
well for just being part of the practice squad."

The executive vice president of the Rams and general
manager Tom Brently, was there to greet Ulee. He reached out
his hand and said, "I don't think we have met."

"Nice to meet you, sir. This is my wife, Dr. Penelope
Sundown, and this is my son, Telemachus Sundown, and my
daughter, Nhung Sundown. Over there getting autographs are
my two other boys, Plato and Aristotle."

Mr. Brentley said, "Sundown . . . is that Spanish?"

"No sir," said Ulee. "We are proud Nez Perce Native
Americans."

Mr. Brentley said, "I don't think I have seen a quarterback
come in with zero repetitions in practice and play the way you
did. I look forward to seeing what the future holds for you and
your family."

Ulee said, "If I never play again I am thankful to God for
this game and this moment. Thank you for the opportunity, sir.
I hope they told you that I had it written in my contract that I
would not play before noon on Sunday. I have strong beliefs and
the fact that our society is pulling the local church out of our
priorities will contribute to the downfall of our society. So I am
good as long as I am not competing with God."

This pretty much sealed Ulee's football fate. LA would accommodate its new star: no practice or games before noon Sunday. Ulee and the team went to the playoff that season, losing only two games. The team lost in the conference final, but had a spectacular year.

I can't tell you how much the kids and Sundown family enjoyed watching Ulee play and reading stories about him.

The greatest aspect of sports is that it is truly a melting pot built on ability. Ulee was star, and no one asked me if I was his housekeeper because I was Hispanic and his skin was light. The Sundown family, itself, was a melting pot of races and cultures. But first and foremost, we were all Nez Perce—even our Vietnamese kids.

Δ Δ Δ

The family loved my Spanish heritage and cooking. And we learned as much about the Vietnamese heritage of our children. Ulee and I learned to cook traditional Vietnamese and Ulee kept us all using all the languages. Spanish, Nez Perce, Vietnamese, and English. We attended a Vietnamese missionary alliance church when we could as well as a large Latino church, this was another way we could save our cultural identities and treat one another with Godly respect. And you can imagine there was no one with more American patriotism than our family. Often in the pregame the TV camera would pan to Ulee, then to me and our kids all crying our eyes out as we sang proudly our nation's national anthem.

Ulee had become a national celebrity but was fined by the league for not making himself available to the press. He had his reasons; Ulee did not want our lives scrutinized or judged. And he did not want to discuss Vietnam.

Chapter Eleven

The Past Invades the Present

THE CHILDREN SMILED as I told about Ulee's heroic accomplishments on the football field. And then next day they were all out playing catch with the football, which is not easy in the woods. Living along the Wallowa River is an experience close to heaven. The sound of the roaring river colors everything. The deer around our house come up and eat out of our hands. The chipmunks are always begging for food and the raccoons even enjoy playing with our Beauceron. The blue jay watches as we wash our dishes over the open fire pit outside. The Eagles cry always makes us look up to the granite mountains towering over our lodge. A lot of family members sleep out under the stars they are so majestic from this altitude. All of this leads back to our legend-telling time around the fire each evening as the darkness changes the Wallowa Mountains and our imaginations begin to see in technicolor—again.

△ △ △

The second season Ulee became much better. The coaches had confidence in him and he passed practically every down and they seldom punted because he could pick up fourth downs so frequently. Together, LA was setting every record in the book. It was unheard of to string so many 300-yard passing games together, but Ulee and his receivers were averaging above that number.

They came up with a two-quarterback system to accommodate Ulee. Quarterback Jack Kirk started on days when Ulee couldn't because of church. The Rams only lost two games and won Pro Championship, crushing its opposition with their air blitz attack

We were invited to the White House to meet the new Democratic President and were meeting influential people all over the country. Ulee used his celebrity to advocate for Native American causes, and he often did football camps at Native reservations.

I spent time working with the impoverished and marginalized immigrant population, practicing medicine there on Saturdays. And our children helped out at Asian community centers with their volunteer efforts. One day we were in a favorite bagel shop and some young men came in and started giving the Vietnamese owner a bad time.

"I thought we fought you guys in Nam, and now you come over and buy up everything here," one man said.

The Vietnamese owner named Peter tried to be kind. I grabbed on to Ulee's hand. He did not like a bully. But Telemachus, who was nine years old, stood up and walked right up to the guy giving the proprietor a bad time.

"You should be ashamed," Telemachus said, staring down the man. "This is a hardworking man and heroic."

The man felt ashamed and walked off with his friends. Ulee beamed with pride.

△ △ △

On the third season of Ulee playing for LA we had our own home in Malibu on the beach. We also built our own large cabin and ranch up near Hurricane Creek. We had a heard of Appaloosa ponies, a Nez Perce caretaker with his own cabin and a herd of buffalo running our range land. We had a large guest lodge for visiting tribesman. It was a little bit of heaven for us. At the same time, we certainly were not accustomed to the celebrity life.

Ulee still would not cooperate with interviews, adding to the mystery of his life. The team had improved through the draft every year and was being called one of the greatest in pro football history. They really focused on a balanced attack with both running and passing.

It was during this amazing undefeated season that I came to work and the nurses asked me if I had read the paper, heard the news on the radio, or seen the news on television. My hands started to shake and I sat down.

"What?" I said.

One of the nurses said, "It is not so bad. They didn't catch your husband with another woman or drugs or something typical."

"What?" I said. One of them handed me the Los Angeles newspaper. It was front page: *"Star Quarterback Accused of Being Mass Murderer."* It had the team publicity photo of Ulee on it.

The article went something like this.

> *"According to eye witness sources, Ulee Sundown, professional quarterback and most valuable player in the league has been accused of being a mass murderer. The source said he has killed women, children, and men by the hundreds. On further investigation, this paper found that Ulee had a checkered past with gang activity in the Tri-Cities of Eastern Washington and was kicked out of high school after killing another student. The majority of the US public is still ashamed of the war in Vietnam, but Ulysses Looking Glass Sundown (Nez Perce) took it to a level never imagined in US history. He was, according to sources, better at war than he is at football and became a merciless murderer with the nickname of Savage. He even scalped his victims and hung them naked from trees."*

They showed a picture of him in uniform and covered with blood, and at least twenty dead Vietnamese piled behind him.

The article continued:

"At one point, he pulled the heart out of a living man in a fistfight with him. Maybe the most concerning part of the information is that he killed a United States lieutenant colonel by shooting him in the head along with five other American Marines serving in Vietnam. He was never prosecuted for this because he was deeded a very valuable asset as a sniper who could live in the field and produce record body counts. Evidently, Sundown fought as a mercenary for Israel in the Yom Kippur War and killed hundreds there also. His military records were sealed, but he was given an honorable discharge after the fall of Vietnam in 1975. The question we have to ask is not only, "Do we want a murderer from the most unpopular war in US history to get away with these actions, but also, should we permit someone of this kind of character to be a role model for the youth of America by playing for a professional sports team?"

I was devastated, but I had to complete my shift. People's lives depended on it. I did call Ulee when I got the chance. He was almost catatonic with depression and said he did not want to talk about it. He said he had called in to miss practice. When I got home, the kids let me know that he had left in our fishing boat and that they did not know where he was headed. There was nothing I could do but pray. I guess that is a lot. And it helped me, but I knew how sensitive Ulee was about his past. We did not see him till Friday. I told him that he at least owed his team a call.

The coach made the decision to start Ulee on Sunday. That was a tough decision, since Ulee would not explain to any of us his side of the story. When Ulee took the field, he was booed by both home and away fans. His fellow players even scorned him, except those who had played college with or against him.

Ulee played flawless football using the running game effectively, but even when he ran for a touchdown himself, his own fans booed. They won and Ulee came home without showering and hardly spoke to anyone. His friend Rod tried to talk to him but Uleee was just silent. Even Telemachus could not get him to speak. Now the press was really wound up. They tried to interview him, but he refused. Letters to the editor were horrible. Our house was egged. Telemachus got into a fight at school and came home with a black eye.

Nhung got a split lip trying to defend him, and all three of them ended up going to the emergency room. Telemachus was livid and looking for revenge. He tried to wear war paint to school the next day, so I kept all the kids home. The press met us every time we left the house and came home. They were at my work, and my fellow workers left me peace symbols on my office door.

Ulee played the next game against their Western Division rivals San Francisco. Ulee played like the savage, as he seemed to play with a vengeance. The fans of this antiwar city threw garbage at Ulee when he took the field. This time he never handed off. He just threw long passes to his wide receivers until the crowd became silent. Finally, the coach took him out when they were ahead by thirty-five points. After the game, some of the LA players did interviews saying they had heard nothing from Ulee and would refuse to play if they didn't hear an explanation. That night Mike Wallace on *60 Minutes* interviewed a Marine who had been a POW with Ulee and who had served with Ulee. Marine Slater would not allow his face to be shown or his name to be used.

"Ulee had fought illegally until 1975 and fought in Cambodia, Laos, North Vietnam, and Israel. I had heard that Ulee abused a girl at the massacre of a village," one of the anonymous sources said. The next day the owner announced that the commissioner of pro football had demanded to have Ulee suspended until further notice.

I came home to find the kids at a friend's house. Ulee was sitting in our bedroom with a loaded 44.

"Are you okay?" I asked, trying not to look at the gun. "Can we talk?"

"I don't want any of the psychiatric psychobabble that you learned in school! You know what honor and dishonor means to a warrior."

"I love you—and cherish you, as do all our family."

Ulee repeated, this time in monotone. "We both know what honor and dishonor means to a warrior."

"Ulee, have you noticed how I have never asked you to

explain anything about the war after hearing these reports?" He said nothing.

I asked again. "Have you noticed that none of your family or friends have asked you to explain?"

Ulee said, "I guess I have been so self-occupied that I didn't notice."

Ulee could hardly speak the words. "I can't talk about it. It just hurts too much. If they want to take me out and shoot me that is all right with me. I know this sounds crazy, but I feel guilty for even surviving. And I did kill hundreds of people. I see their faces all the time."

We hugged, and I kissed him. "We will get through this together. Remember—we have both been through hell, and we deserve a little heaven."

Ulee said, "You do—I deserve hell."

"You are the preacher. For by grace are we saved, not of works lest any man should boast?"

"We all need forgiveness from the cross of Christ, and we all need to live in that grace."

"Ulee, let's live in that grace. Any other path is going to cause so much hurt to everyone you love." Ulee moaned hard while I held him, and we both kneeled at our bed and prayed together.

News reporters mobbed us everywhere. Ulee didn't trust any. Mike Wallace had tried calling Ulee several times before he aired his report. He left numbers where he could be reached. I decided to call him, since Ulee would not. There was another side to this story.

"Mr. Wallace. You're one of the best investigative journalists in the country. But the story you did on Ulee was filled with half-truths and lies. Ulee was a distinguished war hero. He will never speak with you, but there are others who can."

I suggested that Wallace start with now retired admiral McCleary.

△ △ △

Ulee was ordered by the league and the team to take a leave of absence. And we just could not take the pressure of staying in LA, so we headed out for the Sundown Lodge at Wallowa Lake and we took the kids out of school.

One morning Joseph returned from the general store down the road, excitedly waving a newspaper. I grabbed the Portland paper. It had a picture of now US Senator John McCleary and a Buddhist monk.

Ulee said, "That is Dawa; I thought he was dead." There was also a picture of the President saying that he had ordered Ulee's black ops military file be opened to the public. The President was committed to bringing healing to the US after the scars of Vietnam. *President Clears Native American Quarterback of All Accusations!* the headline read.

The story told of Ulee's heroism and how he had become integral to US Marines and special operations. It told of the several medals Ulee had won for valor, but were awarded in secrecy. It explained how he enlisted as a teenage boy and how he had risen to the rank of captain because of his skill and service.

The President called him a "hero." Senator McCleary said Ulee was the most dedicated Marine he had ever served with. The reason Ulee shunned the press, McCleary explained, is because he was sworn to secrecy. And as for allegations that he was abusive, McCleary called them "absurd fabrications." He said Ulee had saved orphans and even adopted two. The senator called the anonymous Marine who spoke to *60 Minutes,* "a coward."

△ △ △

Ulee and I walked to our pickup with silence. The mountains looked so beautiful. I spoke first.

"Have I ever told you how much I love you?"

Ulee said," Don't say it; cook me up one of your famous Latino dinners and show it. I am starved."

The next day, Ulee was on a plane flying back to LA to get ready for a game. The whole world was watching.

People cried when Ulee took the field. They cried not for Ulee but for themselves and how lost our nation was during the Vietnam conflict. The President was working hard to bring peace to this torn part of US history.

LA won the game. It was a sweet win. And it was a moment that impacted imagination of every Native boy.

△ △ △

After the game, our family loaded up everything and went to our personal cabin on Wallowa Lake, which was just a few miles from the Sundown Lodge on the Wallowa River.

Ulee and I went for a walk up to the falls at the Sundown lodge. We held hands as we worked our way through the forest. Ulee pointed out a hummingbird and picked me some huckleberries—some to snack on and others for his mom to make her famous huckleberry pie. With the roar of the Wallowa River behind us, Ulee apologized to me for his depression and desperate thoughts in the whole disgrace over his military record. He pointed out that bringing out a gun was unacceptable and that he would go to counseling to a Christian psychiatrist to work out his issues with pride and honor and handle all the post-traumatic stress in his life. I will always remember that kiss in front of the rainbow that is almost always there at the Wallowa River falls at that time of the day. We prayed together that night, letting go of all our angst about the nation's anger and misconception about Ulee in Vietnam—in fact, about Vietnam all together—and we prayed for all the other vets and what they were going through. And we both knew that Ulee needed to get back to being a pastor.

Ulee met with the owner of the football team and said, "I quit. I graduate with my master's degree this year, and I am off to start a church in Seattle, Washington."

The owner said, "We can renegotiate your contract."

Ulee said, with a smile, "It's not you. It's me."

They both laughed. "It's just time for me to get down to my life's calling. It's time to stop being a warrior and come home."

I came up and hugged him. And with his arm around me, he said, "And my beautiful smart wife has a job at a children's hospital in Seattle."

Many people believe that the undefeated season and the National Championship win by Los Angeles under Ulee's leadership is the reason the team was able to build a stadium in Los Angeles and stay there as a team and a positive force in the community. If that had not happened, they may have ended up moving to some place like St. Louis, Missouri. Instead St. Louis got an expansion team that prospered there.

"So we're out to build a new kind of church. One for non-church people from all nations and backgrounds. We are going to try and build the greatest caring network that the world has ever seen."

Chapter Twelve

Courageous Path of Love

I TOLD THIS part of the story after a hike up to Horseshoe Lake. We built a fire, most of the kids were in their sleeping bags and the story continued under the spectacular star-filled sky.

△ △ △

Ulee decided to build a church in the inner city of Seattle that was for all nations, ethnic groups, and religions. It was a church for "unchurched people." We did not want to take anyone out of another church—we would not wish that upon them or upon us. This was going to be very different. After Ulee's troubles with the press, we got a lot of donations and we built a small country church in the city.

The steeple was glass because Ulee wanted to worship in the mountains as the Natives did, so we had to let the light in. And there was a waterfall behind a glass wall at the altar. Hummingbirds would come down and milk the roses. Even a bald eagle from Lake Washington or the sound would swoop in to catch one of the trout that Ulee planted in the massive waterfall.

We put everything we had into building this church. The church seated 400, but that was filled once the people visited and found out what a different kind of church we were. We served a meal after every service and invited the homeless and poor to church so they could enjoy the meal. People would visit church and find a homeless person cleaning their underwear in the bathroom sink and not come back. One lady spread newspapers out to sit on before she took her seat, and she usually wet her seat. There were gang members, goth kids, and lots of people who did not speak English.

At the first worship service, Ulee took the pulpit dressed in a robe as his grandfather had worn as a Methodist pastor. He started to cry when he began the service with the words, "This is the day that the Lord has made; we will rejoice and be glad in it." Nhung went up and took his hand. He picked her up and said the words again. He tried to describe his dream using *Isaiah 61*, the opening words of Jesus when he began his ministry. But it was a tear-fest. The crowd of prostitutes, gang members, and homeless chased away the Christians who were church shopping. It wasn't too long before we opened a second service in Spanish, which was mainly attended by illegal immigrants. This really riled the Christian population. Immigration is such a controversial issue.

One kind Christian took Ulee to the side and said, "I don't mind other races coming to church, but they need to speak English or go home."

"They don't speak English and they don't have a home. Shouldn't we as Christ followers speak the good news into their lives in a language they understand?"

The kindly Christian man said, "Well, this is not a safe Christian church for me then."

We poured every cent we had into buying the property and building this little chapel. It cost us three million dollars. We sold our boat and our cabin in the Wallowas. Then we incorporated as a legal church and business with the state of Washington. We filed for nonprofit status with the IRS and set up a constitution that was governed by a democracy made up of a senate (our board) and a house of representatives (lay pastors in the church) as well as a supreme court (highly esteemed pastors from the community who could vote out the senior pastor for moral or theological heresy.) We were not getting enough from offerings to pay for electricity or the meals we served. I had a great job at Seattle Children's Hospital, and surgeons are paid extremely well. But Ulee just gave all our money away. Every con person who came up and asked for money he gave it to them. We also always had a family living with us:

Church growth was slow. And a lot of people joined saying they would be our friends for the rest of their lives only to leave over the slightest complaint. The chairs were not soft enough, we didn't have a youth pastor, and the Sunday school wasn't nice enough. Ulee's sermons were always talking to those with doubts, and they wanted something deeper. They said they wanted more meat in the teaching. But Ulee always preached an expository sermon laced with quotes from Jesus Christ. But he also quoted atheists like Bertrand Russell. Others did not like our music. I have to admit our music was pretty bad.

The Natives didn't like Christianity. They had been burned by it, but they still invited us to the pow wows because we used the old ways such as drum circles, group dancing, smudging, vision quests, and sweat lodges. It was a hard population to reach.

Our singing at church was so bad that sometimes we would sing a song and they all sounded like the hymn "Holy, Holy, Holy." We would not be able to finish the song; there were so many giggles that Ulee would say, "Just forget it." Ulee's first wedding was for a celebrity athlete, which brought in a huge crowd. They had a string quartet, candlelight, and flowers all over the sanctuary. There were eight formal bridesmaids and groomsmen in tuxedos. Ulee had been ordained by his dad.

Ulee started the ceremony by saying, "*Dirty* beloved" instead of "Dearly beloved."

When he was handed the ring, he reached over to pick it up the same time as the groom, and they smacked heads really hard. A couple of minutes later, the groom passed out from the concussion. So when they revived him, they put him in a chair while the bride stood. Ulee skipped a page of the wedding as his marriage manual was so new that the pages stuck together. He lost his place and instead of saying you may kiss the bride he said, we may kiss the bride. Everyone got a good laugh out of that one.

And then to top it all off, he pronounced the couple Mr. and Mrs. Marvin *Hog*. Their real names were Mr. and Mrs. Melvin Haug. People laughed so hard they were just shaking—all at the expense of a very embarrassed new pastor.

One night, Ulee was called to pray for an old grandmother who was dying at home in the mountains of the east side. It was a foggy night when Ulee finally found the house at three in the morning. He knocked, hoping that it was the right house, as he was feeling a bit lost. A lady from his church who had been an accomplished college basketball player finally answered the door. She had no make-up on, and he hardly recognized her. He introduced himself even though she knew him well from church.

She said, "My grandmother is near death and looks horrible, so don't be shocked or scared when you see her."

Ulee said, "Don't worry about it—I have seen so much in my lifetime."

When Ulee walked back to the second bedroom on the left, he quietly opened the door, and in the poor lighting in the room he saw a very old lady laying on a blow-up bed on the floor. He knelt beside her, and she looked so old, with no makeup, a pale greyish look on her face and long grey hair. It was a spooky night near Halloween, so Ulee took her hand, kneeling and praying for this lady.

He prayed something like this. "Lord, I know this lady is dying; help her not to be afraid." The lady sat up almost like a vampire would.

"I am not dying, and who are you?"

"I am your granddaughter's pastor."

The lady said, "My granddaughter lives in Romania."

Now they were both confused. At about that time, the granddaughter stuck her head in the room and said, "Pastor Ulee, that is not my grandmother—that is her nurse." The grandmother didn't look nearly as scary.

All of this pastoring was the hardest challenge of Ulee's life. One time there was a baby girl who had experienced a head trauma and was not going to recover.

The family asked for a pastor and said, "Isn't your husband a pastor?"

I said, "Yes, he would be glad to come and help."

When Ulee arrived, the family was devastated; the uncle was someone that Ulee had played football with—he was a huge lineman.

When we told them that it was only a matter of time before the little girl died, the mom left, saying, "I can't witness this."

The dad said, "I can't stay either."

The uncle said, "Pastor, would you hold our little girl while she dies?"

The dad handed him a tape saying, "Here are some oldies that I used to dance with her. Could you dance with her while she dies?"

So, Ulee gently took the little girl in his arms as they unhooked her from the oxygen, the probes for the EKG, and IV lines. Ulee anointed the little girl with olive oil he had brought back with him when he served in Israel.

Pastor Ulee said, "The Bible tells us to anoint because the oil is the sign of the invisible. Kings, prophets, and prophetesses were anointed to show the Holy Spirit's presence in their lives. In the New Testament, we are told to anoint the sick when we pray for them." He anointed the sweet little girl in the name of the father, the son, and the Holy Spirit, making the sign of the cross on her forehead and then touching her chin in a signal to look up with faith. Ulee quoted Jesus: "Let the little children come unto me for such is the kingdom of heaven."

All of the nurses were sobbing at this gentle moment. Ulee began to sing in the little girls ears his songs of faith, telling her about the love of God. "Jesus gentle shepherd lead us, much we need thy gentle care, precious Jesus, precious Jesus much we need they gentle care," Ulee said as he danced with the little girl. It was a very emotional scene.

Ulee kissed her forehead as he usually did when someone died. He prayed, a very touching prayer. He laid the little girl down and gently closed her eyes. He turned and gave the dad and then the uncle a hug. He walked out of the hospital to find the mom and to give her a hug and a prayer.

As a doctor, I was never more proud of my husband. It was like this all the time. Ulee was at the hospital all night almost once a week. He would help someone who was scared and lonely that was dying. He met with those who were mentally ill and could not afford care—people that others were afraid to see: schizophrenics, felons, pedophiles, depressed people with chronic illnesses, homeless, criminals, prostitutes, homosexuals, transsexuals, students no one loved, people in broken marriages, suicidal people, domestic violence participants, bankrupt broken people, people who were bipolar, people with borderline personality disorder, lonely widows, and widowers. I wish critics of religion could just sit in his waiting room as he spent a day in counseling. All of this did not bring in any money for the church to operate. In fact, our twelve-step ministries used our building for free seven days a week, building hundreds of anonymous small groups.

The leader of the small group's ministry came to see Ulee one time and said he was really upset because the treasurer, who was addicted to gambling, had taken all their money and lost it gambling. Ulee asked how much they had in their account. It was 142 dollars. Ulee wrote them a check to replace the lost money. And told me that he thought it was going to be some large sum of money the way everyone was acting.

It was third-generation work for him. It seemed to come to him more naturally than athletics. Ulee was really good at building ministries that lost money. He refused to charge for coffee or even for the meals that so many needy people joined it. It was all by donation only. And the meals now were every night of the week. The working homeless began to sleep in their cars in the parking lot. They showered at the church, and when it got cold they would sleep inside the church. We had to call the police quite often as the church sound system disappeared more than once. And people on meth would sometimes flip out.

Ulee's cousin Jackson was wrestling, like many natives, with a drinking problem. He went through a treatment program and did some time in prison for resisting arrest and aggravated assault. But sober, he was the nicest man in the world. He lived with us and ran the program for the working poor. He could relate to anyone.

Δ Δ Δ

Hector Whitebird Sundown had gone on to play in the pro football league, following in his brother's footsteps. LaGrande had by then become a powerhouse, maintaining its dominance as a Division II school and drawing great recruits from throughout the West Coast. Hector, a quarterback like Ulee, was drafted by New York and led the team to a championship his rookie year. He was the first rookie to accomplish this, but New York was a team ready to win.

At half time during the championship game, the new Republican President awarded Ulee the Congressional Medal of Honor for his sacrifice in defending the Montagnard village. Ulee accepted it on national TV, which cemented his legacy as a war hero. Ulee stood before the president in his dress blues Marine captain uniform with his chest covered in medals. He seemed emotionless, but I cried. His brother, Hector, came out of the locker room at half time to watch. He held his helmet high over his head as the crowd applauded his brother. No wonder his second half was inspired. He truly was a better quarterback than Ulee, and now he was on the cover of all the magazines and the guest of all the talk shows. He had no problem communicating to international press. He was entertaining and cute. And he knew it.

While we were at the game, Nhung asked if she could stay home. She had seemed kind of melancholy lately and had had a bad case of influenza, followed by a cold that would not leave. I had her tested for allergies, but nothing showed up, so we left her with Grandmother Sundown who had been an outstanding nurse most of her life. When we came home from the mountain peak experience of watching Hector play so well and win the most valuable player and Ulee awarded the Congressional Medal of Honor, Grandmother Sundown did not seem to be too excited about her boys' achievements.

When we were alone, she told me. "I know I am not a doctor, but I think you need to test Nhung's blood cell count."

I asked, "Why, would you think that?"

Grandmother gave me a hug. "Because I think she has leukemia."

I tried to quiet my fears until we could get her back to Seattle for a blood test. I told myself that my mother-in-law was probably just overly cautious because Joey had it when he was a boy. But Ulee immediately began to grieve in private. He told me that Agent Orange must have done damage to everyone who was exposed to it. When the hematologist called us in for an appointment, I knew there was something wrong. He would have told me over the phone if it was a false alarm. It was like living through a nightmare. *I am a fine doctor; why didn't I see this earlier?* I thought.

Fortunately, we were in one of the best spots in the world to battle leukemia. Fred Hutchinson Cancer Research Center was world famous for their Nobel Prize winning treatment.

Leukemia used to mean almost a zero chance of recovery until one innovative doctor did what no one thought could be done. He labored in the basement of a rented facility, leading a team of dedicated scientists to kill the diseased bone marrow through near lethal doses of radiation and chemical therapy and then replace it with a bone marrow transplant to establish a healthy bone marrow and blood cancer free system.

Going through the treatment was brutal, and for a while we all practically lived at Fred Hutchinson. Ulee really fell to pieces and was losing his faith.

He kept asking, "How could God allow children to suffer in this world."

I would say, "You are the pastor—you are supposed to tell us."

Ulee would scream, "I don't have an answer." He spent most of his time on his knees asking for a miracle. He had seen God do amazing things before through prayer. *Why not now?* But nothing.

Nhung asked him, "Daddy, why doesn't God make me and all the other children in this hospital well?"

Ulee would just say, "I don't know baby. I don't know." Nhung said, "Well, you are a pastor. Tell God to heal me." Ulee got on his knees and prayed with all his heart. Others that he had prayed for through the years had seemed to miraculously experience healing. Why did this only happen sometimes. When Ulee prayed, there were no lightning bolts. Just love flowing into his heart.

One day when Nhung was going through a torturous dose of radiation and chemotherapy, Ulee couldn't look her in the eye. He talked about her but not to her. He prayed about her but not with her. She was a patient, not one of the loves of his life. I followed him out in the hall and grabbed him by the neck.

"Everyone who visits Nhung treats her like a science project; you are her father and her pastor. How dare you treat her that way?"

Ulee cried. "I am sorry; I just don't understand how I can believe in God when there is so much terrible unjust tragedy in the world."

"Well, quit crying like a baby—you have a man's job to do: deal with the world the way it is not just the way we hoped it would be. Faith doesn't cause us to avoid all tragedies; it's how we navigate the very worst in life by being surprised by the love and joy in the midst of it. Now get back in there and love my daughter and make her laugh. Then you can say a prayer. Because if you don't, no one is going to."

Ulee walked back in. Now he touched the plastic cover over her bed protecting her from infection.

"Daddy, I'm scared."

Ulee said, "I know, but I love you." Ulee told her about heaven—about Jesus and how much he loved her since she was born. He told her that she looked like Winston Churchill when she was born. She laughed. Then Ulee prayed. I could feel heaven in the room when he prayed. Then he kissed the plastic where she put her cheek up to it.

Δ Δ Δ

One day as we rode down the elevator, I nudged Ulee and whispered, "That is her oncologist."

Ulee reached out his hand. "I would like to shake your hand, doctor. You saved my sweet daughter Nhung Sundown's life."

The doctor said, "Can I buy you and your beautiful wife lunch in the cafeteria?"

We both said, "Let us buy."

At the end of lunch, the doctor saluted Ulee. "Winning the Congressional Medal of Honor is a big deal."

Ulee saluted him back. "Someday you will win the Nobel Prize for medicine, but it's not the prizes, it's the thousands of lives you saved. You are the hero."

Nhung just kept getting better after the bone marrow transplant . . . thanks to God and our oncologist, and all the nurses and staff that did God's work at Fred Hutchinson Cancer Center.

It wasn't too much later that a single mom came to our church. She had escaped with her son by climbing out the bathroom window in Wyoming to keep them safe from domestic violence. She came to meet with Ulee, telling him she was always afraid and her boy was growing up with anxiety as a constant part of their lives. Ulee promised them that they were a part of a community now—a church fellowship.

"You are safe. We will call the police. You know we have a lot of police officers in our church. We will call the FBI. One of the assistant directors goes to our church. We'll call the Marines, the Navy, the Army, the Air Force, and the Coast Guard if we need to." He even said, "We even have boy scouts in our church and we promise to protect you."

It wasn't more than three months later that Ulee got a call from her seven-year-old son at home. He said, "Pastor Ulee, how are you doing?"

Ulee said, "Fine—a bit tired. How are you doing, Nick."

The boy spoke casually, "Not too well. I think my mom just died."

Ulee said, "Nick, what do you mean?"

He said, "I was talking to her in the kitchen and she just fell hard on the ground and isn't moving."

Ulee said, "I am going to be there in five minutes Nick, and I'm calling 911. They will probably call you. Follow their instructions carefully. I'll be there as fast as I can." I called 911 and gave them Nick's phone number and address. Ulee jumped in his old Volkswagen bug and sped off. When he got there the fire department and police had already arrived. The police captain was talking to Nick. When Nick saw Ulee, he yelled, "That is my pastor!" and tried to break free to run to Ulee.

The police captain (same as the one at the suicide incident) said, "Let him go." Nick ran into Ulee's arms, crying. Nick said, "I don't have a family now."

Ulee said, "Our church is your family. That is the reason God made churches."

∆ ∆ ∆

As good as Ulee was at being a pro quarterback, he was better at being a pastor.

But the church was struggling financially. Ulee just was not the best financial manager. His heart was too big and the church gave so much to the poor. After one business meeting, Ulee decided to go back and play football one more season to make some money to pay off our church building that would always be a real sanctuary of refuge.

Ulee contacted the Seattle Sharks who immediately signed him. There were soon calls from around the league of players who wanted to play for Ulee's team. Patty came down from Canada and made the team as a backup fullback. That season was the most fun Ulee ever had playing football.

The Sharks made it to the conference playoffs but had sustained so many injuries that their defense was overwhelmed. Ulee volunteered to play the final quarter going both ways. Playing quarterback and free safety. It was a brutal game and Ulee broke two ribs, both thumbs, and a big toe. Seattle was fortunate to win.

Ulee's first and last Championship was against his brother's team, the powerful New York Lumberjacks. Everyone knew Ulee was injured and they were not sure if he would start. But when the game started the stadium was full of Marines from around the world. New York won the coin flip and elected to play offense. When the announcer announced the starting defense for Seattle was named Ulysses Looking Glass as starting at free safety the crowd went wild. Even the New York fans cheered, and Ulee's little brother Hector smiled from ear to ear. It was an historic game down to the last moment.

Ulee intercepted his brother on the last drive and ran it back for the game-winning touchdown. He was awarded the most valuable player on defense and offense. If you have never been to a Championship Game then it is hard to imagine when they play the song from Queen, "We Are the Champions," and grown men cry like little boys. The Sundown family had a group hug. And Ulee lifted me up on is shoulders saying I was his hero. It was a moment we would all never forget.

Chapter Thirteen

The Hero as Archetype

AS WE HIKED down the trail back to the Sundown lodge, I was peppered by questions about churches and organized religion. I tried to answer truthfully and biblically. Always defending the fact that churches are not perfect but Christianity was meant to be lived as a team. The church as imperfect as it was is still the bride of Christ and the family of God. That night back at Sundown lodge the story continued.

△ △ △

Ulee was through with football, and it was time to move on, but he turned his attention to the World Athletic Games in Seoul Korea and the US track team. Since he had donated his salary to his church he was technically still an amateur qualifying for this team. A Canadian sprinter and long-time friend of Ulee's encouraged him to compete in distance-running. He was convinced that Ulee could be one of the fastest men in the US if he were trained properly. So, Ulee began to train with his Canadian friend to prepare for the World Athletic trials.

I thought, *here we go again—what is it with this man? There is always one more mountain to conquer.* For Ulee there had always been this comparison to Jim Thorpe, the world-class athlete who had won in the Olympics to bring fame to Natives for generations.

Ulee made the team as the third runner in the 10k, 6.2 mile run. It was a huge honor just to make the team. Ulee would have the honor of competing in the 1988 Seoul World Athletic Games.

Ulee had run ten miles practically every day of his life, so the grueling training schedule seemed almost effortless for Ulee. In fact, he breezed through the preliminary races.

Ulee explained to me one night that competing in these games felt like his destiny. He thought his competitive turmoil had ended with his retirement from pro football—but he was wrong. His fire still raged.

Ulee was not expected to finish better than last place in the 10k event. He had never run a world-class time, and he had no experience in world-class races. It was an accident that there were only two remaining hopes of the United States to medal in this event. But Ulee wanted to make a great noise for all Native people, like Jim Thorpe before him.

Ulee went out fast and took the lead. "Find your pace quarterback! Find your pace!" his coach called. Ulee stretched out his stride as he had so many times in his mountain runs. He held the lead at a pace he could not maintain for one mile before being challenged and pushed by a Kenyan runner and another from Great Britain. They took the lead, and Ulee pushed them for the next two miles. The pace was too fast, and the three led all others by 75 yards. At three miles, the Kenyan and Brit dropped back into the pack and then fell behind. They were spent. The pace Ulee set was too grueling. Ulee also fell back into the pack, catching his breath, running through the pain, trying to stay with these world-class runners.

The pain was grueling for Ulee—he regretted the hubris that had made him think he could run with world-class runners. But that pride would not let him quit. The two miles of pain he had left was nothing compared to the pain he endured in Vietnam and that of his POW brothers.

Ulee smiled as he looked in the stands and saw his son

Telemachus and his daughter and the two boys, Plato and Aristotle, all cheering,

Ulee thought of Achilles Joseph Sundown. He thought of his parents and his grandparents—of Jackson Sundown winning the world championship rodeo. He thought of Chief Joseph and the Wallowa Mountains. And he thought of the kids and me and of Vietnam and Israel—fighting hopeless battles. He thought of Columbia Park and sitting on the front hood looking at the stars with me that night in between wars.

As I watched him, I thought of Hawaii and how I wished we could have stayed there together. But Ulee was a Nez Perce warrior, and that was not his place. I thought of how I beat him in grade school, and I wondered if I kept running competitively if I could have made it to the Games. I think I could have—I think that could have been me. But then I remembered my work as a pediatric neurologist and how fulfilling that was: I was helping kids going through their own torture—kids who were running their own impossible race.

At 200 meters left in the race, he had accomplished the impossible; he was still in the middle of the pack, shoulder to shoulder with the premier distance runners in the world.

But he was exhausted with nothing left. The pace of the pack picked up. Ulee knew this was his last chance. He remembered carrying the Navy captain and running as Viet Cong shot at him. He thought, *This is nothing—no one is shooting at me.* He went into a full sprint just as he had done there in Vietnam, exhausted but needing to run hard.

Δ Δ Δ

The crowd roared as Ulee emerged in the front of the group, neck and neck with two other runners. Ulee leaned into the finish-line tape, winning the gold medal. Telemachus, Nhung, Plato, and Aristotle came down on the field and took the victory lap with their dad, taking turns carrying the US flag. We all cried as they played the national anthem. Ulee had tears gushing down his cheeks. Sitting by us were football coaches and Ulee's parents, not to mention all his brothers and their families.

As the national anthem played, he flashed back to Luau's death, Bruce's death on their first mission, and all those who died in the last stand for the firebase that was overrun. They were like apocalyptic scenes no one should have fixed in their mind. And you can imagine the emotion Ulee felt—it took everything he had not to sob.

Ulee became a worldwide celebrity with his fame from the World Athletics Games. Now, he was more than just a football player who could scramble and throw. He was an inspiration.

Ulee believed that every nation should be patriotic and that patriotism was only dangerous when people defined it by comparing and degrading other cultures and people groups. He believed that nothing could ever be accomplished if we hated ourselves or others. And the lack of loving one's nation does not bring more peace and respect to this world; it robs us of a platform to live at a higher level of expectation for improvement and freedom.

We started receiving lots of invitations for Ulee to speak or make appearances, including North Africa. We had heard my sister Maria Jose was there and hired a detective to find her. The detective found her working in a house of prostitution. We traveled to the city, sending word that we were coming to get her. As Ulee and I walked up, we were met by a man who told us that my sister did not want to come home after all. Ulee forced his way into the brothel with the private detective and myself following. He made his way to the back where there was screaming. There lay my beautiful Marie Jose, dead in her vomit from an overdose of heroin. The spoon and the needle were right there. The man with her told us that he had tried to stop her— that he knew that was too much heroine. I rolled her over and wiped off her face with my dress, and I let out a scream.

Ulee tried to comfort me. I slapped him and said, "Men abuse so many women." I must have stayed there for thirty minutes crying before Ulee could bring me back to sanity.

After Ulee and I returned from North Africa, one morning, I had a call from one of my colleagues, and they asked if I had seen the Seattle papers. I rushed out to get ours on the steps before Ulee woke up. There was the headline: *"Multiple Sports Star Accused of Steroids."*

Sprinter Husain Knight had been stripped of his gold medal in the 100 meters because of performance-enhancing drugs. The story said there were rumors of widespread steroid use on the team and accounts that Ulee had taken steroids while serving in Special Forces. He was probably using them again, one source told the newspaper, which would explain why he performed so well in the World Games.

"That explains how someone who never ran on the national collegiate or amateur circuit came out of nowhere to win gold," the source said. "And it probably explains why he was so good."

My mind flashed back to Hawaii; I had guessed back then that Ulee might be taking a growth hormone when in the Marines because his muscles were extremely developed even though he was so young. I knew that there was no science to determine with certainty that use of a steroid as a teenager could have lasting impact. But there it was—our nightmare coming true while we were awake. It was the Jim Thorpe Story repeated.

The front yard was full of paparazzi again.

Δ Δ Δ

Ulee was called to testify in the inquiry with the Athletic Games Committee about his performance-enhancing drugs. He honestly said that he did not know what he was being injected with, and in Vietnam he did not really care. He had asked if it was a drug, and they had told him that it was medicine to help him recover from injury. A pulled muscle could mean death on a mission in the jungle. Others testified that these were anabolic steroids and human growth hormone that were used by East Germans in the Games and that had been brought to the Marines through sources that were impossible to trace. Most of the men did not know what they were taking—they just knew that it allowed them to come back from injury quicker and to break through the plateau that every weight-lifter or runner would come up against in their workouts.

The Committee came to a conclusion quickly. Even though Ulee had been young when possibly taking steroids it could have had a lifetime impact on him being the world-record breaking athlete that he had become. Therefore, like Jim Thorpe before him, he was forced into the emasculating position of having to return his gold medal.

Chapter Fourteen

The Vengeance of Telemachus

EVERYONE AROUND THE fire at the Sundown cabin seemed saddened by the injustice Ulee faced. He was their hero, too, and was now seen as a victim. I hoped that they would see that strength overcomes setbacks. I would now tell them about how good character prevails over misfortune.

△ △ △

While Ulee had become a hero to so many he felt an emptiness. Celebrity was a roller coaster ride and it wasn't worth debasing your life pursuing the admiration of others. Ulee began to focus once more almost entirely on his church and trying to bring together all kinds of people into one respectful kind family. It was a huge endeavor. We had a lot of missionary projects. I was determined that I would go back to the city dump of Tegucigalpa to turn that Dante's Inferno into a better place. Ulee raised the money for us to build a medical center, housing, a church, and a school there. I found a Honduran family that had started a

project there that was working miracles and we decided to bring
our full strength as a church to bear on this endeavor.

Nhung moved to Honduras to help with this project. She
was now so beautiful and noble. It worried me sick to see our
kids grow up. After the 2001 attack on the World Trade Center,
Telemachus, Plato, and Aristotle all joined the Marines. Our
beautiful kids were growing up.

One day I went for a walk with Ulee along the Wallowa River.
I told him that I loved him and thanked him for his heroism in
my life. But Nhung had told me that MS-13 was demanding a war
tax or protection money for the Honduran school and medical
clinic to continue. I told him that I needed to go and confront
this problem. Ulee said, I am trained for this. Let me organize
a team. I laughed and said, you are getting old; he laughed and
gave me the same compliment. I explained that someday I had
to confront my own demons and see if I could do something
lasting to help my countrymen. I did something I almost never
do. I quoted his own sermon back to him.

"Everyone has a Goliath that they need to step out in faith and
face trusting God to do what only he can do; this is my Goliath."

"Ulee, you have been my hero and tried to be everyone's
hero. But there comes a time when the best thing a hero can do
is realize that he or she has woken the hero that hides in even
the most common human beings." There was silence. I said, "I
need you to be the one who stays this time while I go off on my
crusade."

Then an amazing transformation in Ulee's life took place
and he promised me that he would not interfere and that he
would be the one waiting at home and praying.

Honestly, I worried about Ulee. Former professional football
players often die in their late fifties from all the pounding and
concussive syndrome. Ulee certainly had his share of war
wounds and even though he always surprised everyone someday
he would have more brash machismo than he could deliver on.
He had fought his wars–I was actually in better shape than he
now. He had trouble walking, let alone running.

Δ Δ Δ

My adopted daughter, Nhung, looked like a supermodel, but she had the soul of Mother Theresa. Of course, Ulee made sure she knew the old ways and could survive in the mountains, but she refused to go hunting and didn't like fishing—she was a vegan. Still, she enjoyed the hiking and mountain climbing trips that she would take with her Nez Perce cousins.

Nhung excelled at kickboxing, and it seemed to come natural to her. After she graduated from Seattle Pacific University, she went on to Princeton Seminary on scholarship. She took classes in Arabic to learn about Islam. She prayed for peace, and she studied the Quran so that she could be a Christ follower and dialogue with those who seemed so far from her Christian roots.

My mother Elicia had moved to Honduras to live with the pastor's family who lived in the community bordering the dump. We felt the best thing we could do was back this Godly family with all our strength as they developed this holistic ministry to the people of the dump.

In Honduras we built something as a congregation that churches should strive to accomplish. Under the courage and skill of Elicia, we were able to build a school that had 180 children from the dump attending as students. It was a nursery and pre-school through high school. They had a computer lab that any school in Seattle would be proud of. We established a medical clinic and a locker room so they could shower and practice hygiene. We built hundreds of homes for families in the dump. And we fed all the dump people, a hot meal once a day. I could see myself in the little fresh-faced kids being dropped off at this Dante's Inferno. I can't tell you enough about the great local Pastor Juan Carlos and his wife Carmen who God had raised up to courageously pioneer this ministry. They were really the genius behind the whole project, and we trusted him and his family. Christians from all over the world began to help. Together as supporters of this great pastor, we provided for any graduate of the high school with a college scholarship. Twice a year, we sent mission teams down to work with the people. They would build homes or do some project in a neighborhood. Quite a few young couples from our church moved down to live around the dump to give their community a degree of safety.

At this moment, Honduras was the most dangerous nation

in the world that was not at war. Gangs ran Honduras. The US had a treaty with them for years, since the Cold War, and would deport prisoners to Honduras. The gangs had made a Supreme Court justice disappear, and a powerful politician who was the head of the presidential task force to fight gangs had disappeared. The gangs charged a war tax (protection money) on almost everyone.

I went to the downtown cathedral in Tegus and spread the word that I wanted to speak to the head of MS-13. By the time I had returned to Juan and Carmen Carlos School I found that my daughter Nhung had been kidnapped. I returned downtown where I had once walked as a slave in front of the international hotel. I walked up to the prostitutes and asked them where I could find the head of MS-13. I told them that I too had once been enslaved as they had and Jesus had set me free. The pimp came out and I told him with confidence as my mother Elicia held my hand that I demanded to speak to the head of MS-13. The pimp smiled and said, "Okay senoritas, come with me." We both rode in his pickup truck as he traveled out of the city toward the cloud rain forest to wealthy compound surrounding a mansion. We walked up the stairs to see my nemesis, an old, evil-looking Hernando Cortez.

Δ Δ Δ

There, holding Nhung, was the same old man that had killed my family, took the life of my little brother, and tortured me as a little innocent girl. His name was Hernando Cortez, and I will never forget his tattoos; they are the material of my nightmares.

I walked up to this very evil man and prayed under my breath just before I slapped him. I counted coup on this enemy just as a Nez Perce warrior would do to demonstrate his complete lack of fear for his enemy. The large old man just laughed.

"What was that and who are you? I will have you all tortured and killed or I will turn you out on the streets again." He looked over at the younger stronger right hand man that pretty much ran the gang now. He was covered with tattoos over his face as his leader Cortez was also. Mama Elicia took my hand and said, "We are under the protection of almighty God so I would be careful if I were you."

Cortez laughed, "You were under his protection when I abused you before. Who are you anyway?"

I spoke quietly as Ulee had to Raul that day when we were kids. My name is Penelope Morales Santos Sundown. You killed my parents, you sold my little brother Homer into slavery and you robbed me of my childhood. I am the terror every criminal should tremble about—a victim who is no longer afraid of you—I am a warrior ready to avenge all the children you have hurt."

Cortez began to laugh as he totally lost control to his crazy laughter.

Nhung took the cue; she stomped on his foot, head butted him, and kicked him in the groin with a powerful forward thrust kick. Just then shots were fired coming through the window as a sniper prevented any of the gangsters from helping. The evil gang leader turned and dove out the window and landed in the pool. Several of his young thugs ran to protect him. He ran for the jungle, and I was in full pursuit, diving into the pool right after him. Catching up to me was my son Telemachus.

"You really didn't think Dad was going to let you try this without backup. He called and had me flown back from the Middle East, and I have been following you the whole time." Telemachus looked strong and handsome. He was the best of his dad and myself.

Telemachus asked, "What are you going to do, Mom, to an armed gang lord?"

Telemachus was fast like his father and determined and had learned well the tracking skills from his Nez Perce heritage. The old gangster godfather had a shootout with my boy. Three of the four thugs were wounded by Telemachus' Marine shooting skills. After Telemachus was out of shells, he still pursued heroically. I picked up a rock, determined that these evil men would not hurt my son.

I threw a rock and hit Cortez in the head. He pointed his gun at me and walked up to me, punching me in the gut and grabbing my hair, holding me hostage once again.

Cortez said, "You were always too pretty to kill." I felt all the pain of my childhood as the man slapped me and told me how sexual I was. My son ambushed them, jumping down from a tree. Cortez had to let me go during the fight. I kicked him with a strong roundhouse kick slamming his head and punched my fist into his Adam's apple.

I heard a shot from Cortez's last bodyguard, and I disappeared into the jungle to find my son wounded. I took his belt off and tied off a tourniquet. It was getting dark, so we used our Nez Perce knowledge to prepare a well-hidden shelter just as the buzz of the bugs signaled the rise in humidity and it began to rain a torrential downpour. I found the right herbs and made him a compress and then found plants for a medicinal tea to work as an antibiotic. The rain was so thick our tiny fire could not be seen or smelled very far at all. As Telemachus slept after I took his bullet out, I sanitized the wound, stitched him up with one of my hairs, and I began to look for Neolithic tools—the kind the Kennewick man would have used. Ulee's father, Caleb, and his brothers had taught me the art of making weapons. I could not create a recurve bow in the time the short time I had. And I had no time or tools for the bow string. My mind went back in time to the time Ulee showed me how to make an *atalei* like the Kennewick man may have used. An *atalei* was a spear thrower and would increase the speed and distance of light Clovis pointed spears. It was once the revolutionary weapon that allowed humanity to prevail.

I found some soft rock and used Telemachus' k bar knife to make the spears and chip the Clovis spear points. I slipped out of camp and hunted Cortez and his right hand man. They were both armed, so I decided to wait until morning when Telemachus could help. But now I knew the lay of the land. I looked forward to the coming battle tomorrow; I wanted my enemy to know that my husband wasn't the only savage he needed to fear. When I returned to Telemachus, he woke up to hear the roar of a jaguar. I wasn't the only one feeling predatory instinct. He asked me where I was going. I said, "I am going hunting."

"Mom—you are no longer a little defenseless girl; you are a Nez Perce—you know how to be a warrior."

I felt Ulee speaking to my heart when Telemachus called me a warrior. I looked over to Telemachus to see he was in no shape to fight anymore. There was no one else coming to chase this terrible criminal—only I and everything the difficulties of my life had taught me. And I was still fast. I had run all my life. One big gangster who smoked dope, snorted cocaine, and lived an epicurean life was going to be easy prey, even if he was armed. I stopped by a jungle bog and pushed my hand in the mud, then carefully making three stripes of war paint down each side of my face. I was his worst nightmare—a former victim who had strength that he never imagined.

I followed their trail as a Nez Perce. I was not going to let these men continue to impose their evil ways on little children any longer. I could hear war drums, but they were in my mind. I eliminated my scent with certain plants from the jungle. I saw how Cortez followed a jungle trail and noticed that a large jaguar was trailing him ahead of me. He moved, not knowing he was leaving a scent in the breeze for the jaguar and for me. I circled around to ambush them. I enjoyed seeing the terror in their panting bodies. They knew they were being hunted by the jaguar and by me. I camouflaged myself—it was evening and they could not see me. I could hear from the bugs, birds, and monkeys where they were. They stopped, and I listened to him talk to his lone bodyguard. I enjoyed sensing their fear. They wondered, "*Is it an American Special Forces soldier?*"

When his fear reached its peak, I let my first spear fly. It hit Cortez in the leg, right where I was aiming. I am not a killer—I am a doctor, and I had vowed to do no harm, but I was not going to let them get away to continue harm. The Neolithic spear's damage was a horrible sight. I didn't enjoy the bloody mess, but I enjoyed the fear in Cortez' eyes. I stepped into the open. He pointed his semi-automatic pistol at me.

He laughed, "You fool. You don't even have a gun." I had gone shooting many times with my Ulee, so I knew at forty yards in this light this was not an easy shot. I didn't have to be quick—I just had to be quicker than Cortez expected. His young second in command was gone; perhaps he had gone for help. Cortez' hand was shaking. I was calm with the confidence of justified vengeance.

He said, "Who are you?"

"You don't remember me, Cortez?"

"I know I kidnapped you and forced you into sexual slavery, but that includes so many children that I can't remember one from the other."

"You abused my brother, you killed my family, you tried to

turn me into a prostitute, but I was too strong for you. I am Dr. Penelope Morales Santos Sundown, and your evil did not ruin my life. Now it is going to end. No more children sold into slavery."

He laughed with the force of evil. "You don't know this world as I do, good intentions never win—you idealists are weak—evil is so much stronger."

I just said, "Not today. Women have always been courageous. They are always fearless when protecting their children."

"Now I remember you and your little brother. Wasn't his name Homer?" He started to laugh hard. He shot, but I saw it coming in his eyes before he pulled the trigger and ducked to the left behind a bush. The sweat in his eyes made it seem as though I disappeared in the dark—he shot into the jungle, emptying his gun, swearing and laughing in his evil laugh, which I remembered from a lifetime of nightmares. Then he was shooting with no bullets. He searched for more ammunition, fumbling to fill up his magazine. I smiled. A Neolithic spear is much more painful than a modern bullet. He was struggling in pain. He begged me to kill him.

I said, "That is not my way. I am a doctor and I am going to take you back to civilization to face justice"

He laughed again. "The gangs own Honduras; there will be no justice for me."

Our verbal battle was interrupted by the roar of an approaching, 250-pound jaguar, smelling the blood and the fear of Cortez. Before anything else could be said, the apex predator found its dinner. There was no more laughter, only swearing and screaming. I turned my head—not something a doctor wanted to see. I guess Honduras has its own vengeance. Evil had its day, but justice would eventually find its way—the souls of so many children demanded it.

As I returned, moving away from the Jaguar, I ran into his henchman, who also was covered with evil tattoos all over his face. He had his gun pointed at Telemachus.

The young man sneered with evil and said, "I am going to kill your boy in front of you and then kill you. After hearing the roar of the Jaguar and the scream of Cortez, the young man said, "Cortez will be avenged, and MS-13 will go on under my leadership."

I said, "No!"

"Why not?" laughed the evil tattoo-covered gangster."

Because that is your nephew, Homer Morales, and I am your sister, Penelope."

The gangster looked shocked. Telemachus made a Marine move and took the gun from him.

The table was now turned. Homer cried, "I thought you were dead."

I ran to hug him. "I thought you were dead also." We both sobbed.

Homer said, "Son, go ahead and shoot me. I am an evil man and deserve to die."

I stroked his head as I hugged him. "You are not an unredeemable person. Your life is more than just the sum of your past actions. God loves you and you can change your life just the way I was changed. That is why Jesus died on the cross. If all we have is vengeance than there is no hope for the world. We need a savior who can take the worst in us and love us as we discover the best for us."

Homer replied from the pain of his soul, "That is just a myth that has given people false hope."

I said, "Maybe, and maybe it is a truth so great that it can only be approached by exploring what seems like a myth that seems too good to be true. It is people on the sidelines who know all the answers and make perfect judgments of everyone else. Those on the battlefield of life who have been broken by unimaginable injustice know they have a limited understanding. Maybe our modernistic enlightened society hides behind what we believe are absolute paradigms and we are afraid to admit that we still have a lot to learn—especially when it comes to forgiveness and change. Surprisingly, it is our narratives, even our myths determine what we learn or are open to learn. What we believe makes us better or worse. I have chosen to follow the radical Jesus Christ as revealed in what I believe are inspired scriptures. What you choose to believe will determine the meaning of your life."

Homer said, "You have always been very intelligent, big sister, and you sound like a doctor. But this Biblical Christianity is not for me."

"Why?" I asked. "This could be a turning point for you."

Homer cried, "Because I am gay, sister. I have read the book of *Romans* and the warnings in the books of the law in the Old Testament, and there is no room in heaven for homosexuals."

I hugged my brother tighter. "I tell you that God does love you. I love you. The Bible said, for God so loved the world. We are all part of the world. It says that while we were yet sinners, Christ died for us. None of us is perfect; all of us need forgiveness. When Paul spoke about it in *Romans*, he was speaking to people who were accusing homosexuals, and he was telling them that gossip is just as bad. I think that God intended marriage for a man and a woman and he intended us not to divorce or to kill other people, or to falsely judge people. But all of those are part of this imperfect world that can only be healed by the mighty love of God shown through people. God loves us right where we are, but he loves us too much to leave us that way. We can spend the rest of our lives not judging others and trying ourselves to follow God's will as it is shown to us."

Homer said, "You mean I can become a Christ follower even though I am gay?"

"Yes," I said emphatically. Homer replied sobbing with guilt and hopelessness.

"But Christianity doesn't agree with you about this issue."

"That is the point that everyone misses," I replied with a hug. "You are not an issue; you are my little brother."

I was allowed to take Homer home to Wallowa. First he went through rehab to get off his addiction to drugs and alcohol. I visited him when they let me. And our family accepted him.

Grandpa Caleb and Grandma Elizabeth both gave him a hug. "Welcome to our family."

Δ Δ Δ

When we returned home to the Sundown lodge, which was surrounded by the individual Sundown family cabins, we had a great celebration. Ulee's wealthy brother Stick booked up the Wallowa Lake Lodge and showed great hospitality for all of our guests. Telemachus brought his new Arabic love interest, who it turned out was a shiite Muslim of Iranian descent. I knew in my heart she would someday be my daughter-in-law. Nhung stayed right by my side—I was so proud of the courage she had shown through the whole experience.

Our family and guests enjoyed long hikes to secret fishing spots; they played in beautiful Lake Wallowa, and we always rode our noble Appaloosas throughout the meadows and canyons of the mountains. There was a new generation of Sundown warriors: young men and women with more optimism and pride in the old ways than ever.

At night Grandpa Caleb Joseph Sundown told stories around the campfire, a position once reserved for his dad, Ephraim, who was in heaven with his wife. Grandma Elizabeth Sundown gave Nez Perce blankets to Homer and all of our guests. It was a great moment. As the story was told of our last adventure, I was proud. I had moved from being a victim in my early life to become a hero.

I sat down smelling the ponderosa pine smoke, seeing the smiling faces of my grandchildren, the wisdom of Ulee's parents both smiling, and the love of my life Ulysses Looking Glass Sundown. He was more handsome now as a 60-year-old man than ever in his life. His scar on his face showed his love for me and his rugged good looks. His hair was long and gray. My children and grandchildren listened with eager smiles. Grandpa Caleb started the drumbeat. Grandma Elizabeth harmonized with the flute. "And, I began, it was a day like any other day. Seven young brothers were running ten miles into the high Wallowa Mountains with their faithful dog Argos."

Epilogue

IT WAS A cinnamon grizzly bear being reintroduced to these Wallowa Mountains. The arctic wolf was also reintroduced much to the objection of ranchers. Telemachus stood face to face with the opponent. He drew his axe and bowie knife and stuck them in the log in front of him. There were many fallen logs in between the two making the twenty-five yards a much longer distance. Telemachus sighed as he pulled out his compound bow with carbon arrow and deadly sharp metallic arrowhead more deadly than a bullet. Telemachus felt guilt at the display of this modern weapon in this ancient place against the heir of his tribal nemesis. The bear could sense the danger in this brave. But there was an instinctive score to settle between these two alpha predators.

Telemachus felt fear, opportunity to prove his brave heritage, and the adrenalin of a coming battle that he had been prepared for by many generations. The strangest thing happened. The bear discovered a treasure covering the ground surrounding them. The forest fire that had swept through this swamp a couple years earlier had prepared the ground cover to become a solid mile of rich sweet huckleberries. This treat of the mountains usually came in small plants spread around taking almost as much energy to gather as to eat. But now it was the first and last time either of them had found such a gold mine of huckleberries. Then the massive grizzly sat down in front of his enemy—his prey. The warrior looked down to see what the bear was doing. Excitement and wonder filled the brave as he had never heard of so many huckleberries massed together. It was a perfect resolution to the conflict between man and beast; there was a bond between the two enemies and a truce before the fight. Telemachus sat to eat his fill of berries. *If I die here now,* the warrior thought, *I might as well enjoy this piece of heaven.* Maybe the bear was thinking the same thing.

The man made sounds of pleasure as he ate his fill. The bear seemed to moan his delight. They looked up at each other as if they shared their excitement. The rare pleasure was bonding. They felt their kindred spirits. These two rare wild beings were always on the edge of extinction. They lost their hunger for battle as they filled their stomachs. Telemachus looked up to see the bear quiet and resting. They sat and looked at each other closely admiring the fight in each other. Sensing their common bravery, the bear stood up as if to say, "I have killed your ancestors." Telemachus stood up with his axe and said, "You know that you will die fighting this warrior." The bear growled as if to say "We would both die." Then Telemachus smiled and spoke out loud in strong calm voice, "My friend, those huckleberries were good."

The bear's furry face was covered with the stain of huckleberries. He wandered away looking back over his shoulder, two endangered enemies who had evolved upon the miracle of mutual respect. Our family prays that heroes will emerge to bring an end to human trafficking, to foster treating indigenous people with respect, and most of all to embrace the freedom that comes with the idea of the United States of America. May future generations look around at the mountains and the people and believe in what might be for our world.

CPSIA information can be obtained
at www.ICGtesting.com
Printed in the USA
LVOW12s2111171216
517778LV00001B/188/P